The setting is Berlin. Into this divided city, wrenched between east and west, between past and present, comes twenty-five-year-old Leonard Marnham, assigned to a British-American surveillance team.

Though only a pawn in an international plot that is never fully revealed to him, Leonard uses his secret work to escape the bonds of his ordinary life—and to lose his unwanted innocence.

The promise of his new life begins to be fulfilled as Leonard becomes a crucial part of the surveillance team, while simultaneously being initiated into a new world of love and sex by Maria, a beautiful young German woman. It is a promise that turns to horror in the course of one terrible evening—a night when Leonard Marnham learns just how much of his innocence he's willing to shed.

THE INNOCENT

BY IAN McEWAN

THE INNOCENT

IAN McEWAN

A BANTAM TRADE PAPERBACK

BANTAM BOOKS

New York   *Toronto*   *London*   *Sydney*   *Auckland*

*All of the characters in this book are fictitious,
and any resemblance to actual persons,
living or dead, is purely coincidental.*

This edition contains the complete text
of the original hardcover edition.
Not one word has been omitted.

THE INNOCENT

A BANTAM BOOK / PUBLISHED IN ASSOCIATION WITH DOUBLEDAY

PRINTING HISTORY

Doubleday edition published June 1990

Bantam edition / October 1991

Library of Congress Cataloging-in-Publication Data

McEwan, Ian.
The innocent / Ian McEwan.
P.   cm.
ISBN 0-553-55000-4
I. Title.
[PR6063.C4I54   1991]
823'.914—dc20   91-839
CIP

PUBLISHED SIMULTANEOUSLY IN THE UNITED STATES AND CANADA

Bantam Books are published by Bantam Books, a division of Bantam Doubleday Dell
Publishing Group, Inc. Its trademark, consisting of the words "Bantam Books" and the
portrayal of a rooster, is Registered in U.S. Patent and Trademark Office and in other
countries. Marca Registrada. Bantam Books, 666 Fifth Avenue, New York, New York 10103.

PRINTED IN THE UNITED STATES OF AMERICA

OPM   0 9 8 7 6 5 4 3 2 1

TO
Penny

My labours on the Castle Keep were also made harder, and unnecessarily so (unnecessarily in that the burrow derived no real benefit from those labours), by the fact that just at the place where, according to my calculations, the Castle Keep should be, the soil was very loose and sandy and had literally to be hammered and pounded into a firm state to serve as a wall for the beautifully vaulted chamber. But for such tasks, the only tool I possess is my forehead. So I had to run with my forehead thousands and thousands of times, for whole days and nights, against the ground, and I was glad when the blood came, for that was a proof that the walls were beginning to harden; and in that way, as everybody must admit, I richly paid for my Castle Keep.

—FRANZ KAFKA, *The Burrow,*
translated by Willa and Edwin Muir

After dinner we saw an amusing film: Bob Hope in *The Princess and the Pirate.* Then we sat in the Great Hall and listened to *The Mikado* played, much too slowly, on the gramophone. The PM said it brought back "the Victorian era, eighty years which will rank in our island history with the Antonine age." Now, however, "the shadows of victory" were upon us. . . . After this war, continued the PM, we should be weak, we should have no money and no strength and we should lie between the two great powers of the USA and the USSR.

—JOHN COLVILLE, describing dinner with
Churchill at Chequers ten days after the
end of the Yalta Conference.
*The Fringes of Power:
Ten Downing Street Diaries, 1939–1955*

THE
INNOCENT

1

IT WAS LIEUTENANT LOFTING who dominated the meeting. "Look here, Marnham. You've only just arrived, so there's no reason why you should know the situation. It's not the Germans or the Russians who are the problem here. It isn't even the French. It's the Americans. They don't know a thing. What's worse, they won't learn, they won't be told. It's just how they are."

Leonard Marnham, an employee of the Post Office, had never actually met an American to talk to, but he had studied them in depth at his local Odeon. He smiled without parting his lips and nodded. He reached into his inside coat pocket for his silver case. Lofting held up his palm, Indian greeting style, to forestall the offer. Leonard crossed his legs, took out a cigarette and tapped its end several times against the case.

Lofting's arm shot out across the desk and offered his lighter at full stretch. He resumed as the young civilian lowered his head to the flame. "As you can imagine, there are a number of joint projects, pooled resources, know-how, that sort of thing. But do you think the Americans have the first notion of teamwork? They agree on one thing, and then they go their own way. They go behind our backs, they withhold information, they talk down to us like idiots." Lieutenant Lofting straightened the blotter, which was the only object on his tin desk. "You know, sooner or later HMG will be forced to get tough." Leonard went to speak, but Lofting waved him down. "Let me give you an example. I'm British liaison for the intersector swimming match next month. Now, no one can argue with the fact that we've got the best pool here at the stadium. It's the obvious place for the venue. The Americans agreed weeks ago. But where do you think it's going to be held now? Way down in the south, in their sector, in some greasy little puddle. And do you know why?"

Lofting talked on for another ten minutes.

When all the treacheries of the swimming match seemed to have been set out, Leonard said, "Major Sheldrake had some equipment for me, and some sealed instructions. Do you know anything about that?"

"I was coming to that," the lieutenant said sharply. He paused, and seemed to gather his strength. When he spoke again he could barely suppress a yodel of irritation. "You know, the only reason I was sent up here was to wait for you. When Major Sheldrake's posting came through, I was meant to get everything from him and pass it on. As it happened, and this had nothing to do with me, there was a forty-eight-hour gap between the major's departure and my arrival."

He paused again. It sounded like he had prepared this explanation with care. "Apparently the Yanks kicked up an almighty fuss, even though the rail shipment was locked in a guarded room, and your sealed envelope was in the safe in the CO's office. They insisted that someone had to be directly responsible for the stuff at all times. There were phone calls to the CO's office from the brigadier, which originated with General Staff. There was nothing anyone could do. They came over in a lorry and took the lot—envelope, shipment, the lot. Then I arrived. My new instructions were to wait for you, which I've been doing for five days, make sure you are who you say you are and explain the situation, and give you this contact address."

Lofting took a manila envelope from his pocket and passed it across the table. At the same time Leonard handed over his bona fides. Lofting hesitated. He had one remaining piece of bad news.

"The thing is this. Now that your stuff, whatever it is, has been signed over to them, you have to be too. You've been handed over. For the time being, you're their responsibility. You take your instructions from them."

"That's all right," Leonard said.

"I'd say it was jolly hard luck."

His duty done, Lofting stood and shook his hand.

The Army driver who had brought Leonard from Tempelhof airport earlier that afternoon was waiting in the Olympic Stadium car park. Leonard's quarters were a few minutes' drive away. The corporal opened the trunk of the tiny khaki car, but he did not seem to think it was his business to lift the cases out.

Platanenallee 26 was a modern building with a lift in the lobby. The apartment was on the third floor and had two bedrooms, a large living room, a kitchen-dining room and a bathroom. Leonard still lived at home with his parents in Tottenham, and commuted each day to Dollis Hill. He strode from room to room, turning on all the lights. There were various novelties. There was a big wireless with creamy push buttons, and a telephone standing on a nest of coffee tables. By it was a street plan of Berlin. There was Army issue furniture—a three-piece suite of smudgy floral design, a pouf with leather tassels, a standard lamp that was not quite perpendicular, and, against the far wall of the living room, a writing bureau with fat bowlegs. He luxuriated in the choice of bedroom, and unpacked with care. His own place. He had not thought it would give him so much pleasure. He hung his best, second-best and everyday gray suits in a wardrobe built into the wall whose door slid at the touch of the hand. On the bureau he placed the teak-lined, silver-plated cigarette box engraved with his initials, a going-away present from his parents. By its side he stood his heavy indoor lighter, shaped like a neoclassical urn. Would he ever have guests?

Only when everything had been arranged to his satisfaction did he allow himself to sit in the armchair under the standard lamp and open the envelope. He was disappointed. It was a scrap of paper torn from a memo pad. There was no address, only a name—Bob Glass—and a Berlin telephone number. He had wanted to spread out the street plan on the dining table, pinpoint the address, plan his route. Now he would have to take directions from a stranger, an American stranger, and he would have to use the phone, an instrument he was not easy with, despite his work. His parents did not have one, nor did any of his friends, and he rarely had to make calls at work. Balancing the square of paper on his knee, he dialed painstakingly. He knew how he wanted to sound. Relaxed, purposeful. *Leonard Marnham here. I think you've been expecting me.*

Straightaway a voice rapped out, "Glass!"

Leonard's manner collapsed into the English dither he had wanted to avoid in conversation with an American. "Oh yes, look, I'm terribly sorry I . . ."

"Is that Marnham?"

"Actually, yes. Leonard Marnham here. I think you've been—"

"Write down this address. Ten Nollendorfstrasse, off the Nollendorf Platz. Get here tomorrow morning at eight."

The line went dead while Leonard was repeating the address in his friendliest voice. He felt foolish. In solitude he blushed. He caught sight of himself in a wall mirror and approached helplessly. His glasses, stained yellowish by evaporated body fat—this, at least, was his theory—perched absurdly above his nose. When he removed them his face appeared insufficient. Along the sides of his nose were red pressure streaks, dents in the very bone structure. He should do without his glasses. The things he really wanted to see were up close. A circuit diagram, a valve filament, another face. A girl's face.

His domestic calm had vanished. He paced his new domain again, pursued by unmanageable longings. At last he disciplined himself by settling at the dining table to a letter to his parents. Composition of this kind cost him effort. He held his breath at the beginning of each sentence and let it go with a gasp at the end. *Dear Mum and Dad, The journey here was boring but at least nothing went wrong! I arrived today at four o'clock. I have a nice flat with two bedrooms and a telephone. I haven't met the people I am working with yet but I think Berlin will be all right. It's raining here and it's awfully windy. It looks pretty damaged, even in the dark. I haven't had a chance to try out my German yet . . .*

Soon hunger and curiosity drove him outdoors. He had memorized a route from the map and set off eastward toward Reichskanzlerplatz. Leonard had been fourteen on V-E Day, old enough to have a head full of the names and capabilities of combat planes, ships, tanks and guns. He had followed the Normandy landings and the advances eastward across Europe and, earlier, northward through Italy. Only now was he beginning to forget the names of every major battle. It was impossible for a young Englishman to be in Germany for the first time and not think of it above all as a defeated nation, or feel pride in the victory. He had spent the war with his granny in a Welsh village over which no enemy aircraft had ever flown. He had never touched a gun, or heard one go off outside a rifle range; despite this, and the fact that it had been the Russians who had liberated the city, he made his way through this pleasant residential district of Berlin that evening—the wind had dropped and it was warmer—with a certain proprietorial swagger, as though his feet beat out the rhythms of a speech by Mr. Churchill.

As far as he could see, the restoration work had been intense. The pavement had been newly laid, and spindly young plane trees had been planted out. Many of the sites had been cleared. The ground had been leveled off, and there were tidy stacks of old bricks chipped clear of their mortar. The new buildings, like his own, had a nineteenth-century solidity about them. At the end of the street he heard the voices of English children. An RAF officer and his family were arriving home—satisfying evidence of a conquered city.

He emerged onto Reichskanzlerplatz, which was huge and empty. By the ocher gleam of newly erected concrete lampposts he saw a grand public building that had been demolished down to a single wall of ground-floor windows. In its center, a short flight of steps led to a grand doorway with elaborate stonework and pediments. The door, which must have been massive, had been blasted clean away, allowing a view of the occasional car headlights in the next street. It was hard not to feel boyish pleasure in the thousand-pounders that had lifted roofs of buildings, blown their contents away to leave only facades with gaping windows. Twelve years before, he might have spread his arms, made his engine noise and become a bomber for a celebratory minute or two. He turned down a side street and found an *Eckkneipe*.

The place was loud with the sound of old men's voices. There was no one here under sixty, but he was ignored as he sat down. The yellowing parchment lampshades and a pea souper of cigar smoke guaranteed his privacy. He watched the barman prepare the beer he had ordered with his carefully rehearsed phrase. The glass was filled, the rising froth wiped clear with a spatula, then the glass was filled again and left to stand. Then the process was repeated. Almost ten minutes passed before his drink was considered fit to be served. From a short menu in Gothic script he recognized and ordered *Bratwurst mit Kartoffelsalat*. He tripped over the words. The waiter nodded and walked away at once, as though he could not bear to hear his language punished in another attempt.

Leonard was not yet ready to return to the silence of his apartment. He ordered a second beer after his dinner, and then a third. As he drank he became aware of the conversation of three men at a table behind him. It had been rising in volume. He had no choice but to attend to the boom of voices colliding, not in contradiction but, it seemed, in the effort of making the same point more forcefully. At first he heard only the seamless, enfolded intricacies of vowels and syllables, the compelling broken rhythms, the delayed fruition of German sentences. But by the time he had downed his third beer his German had begun to improve and he was discerning single words whose meanings were apparent after a moment's thought. On his fourth he started to hear random phrases that yielded to instant interpretation. Anticipating the delay in preparation, he ordered another half-liter. It was during this fifth that his comprehension of German accelerated. There was no doubt about the word *Tod,* death, and a little later *Zug,* train, and the verb *bringen.* He heard, spoken wearily into a lull, *manchmal,* sometimes. *Sometimes these things were necessary.*

The conversation gathered pace again. It was clear that it was driven by competitive boasting. To falter was to be swept aside. Interruptions were brutal; each voice was more violently insistent, swaggering with finer instances, than its predecessor. Their consciences set free by a beer twice as strong as English ale and served in something not much smaller than pint pots, these men were reveling when they should have been cringing in horror. They were shouting their bloody deeds all over the bar. *Mit meinen blossen Händen!* With my own hands! Each man bludgeoned his way into anecdote, until his companions were ready to cut him down. There were bullying asides, growls of venomous assent. Other drinkers in the *Kneipe,* hunched over their own conversations, were unimpressed. Only the barman glanced from time to time in the direction of the three, no doubt to check the state of their glasses. *Eines Tages werden mir alle dafür dankbar sein.* One day everyone'll thank me for it. When Leonard stood and the barman came across to reckon up the pencil marks on his beermat, he could not resist turning to look at the three men. They were older, frailer than he had imagined. One of them saw him, and the other two turned in their seats. The first, with all the stagy twinkle of an old drunk, raised his glass. *"Na, junger Mann, bist wohl nicht aus dieser Gegend, wie? Komm her und trink einen mit uns. Ober!"* Come and join us. Here, barman! But Leonard was counting deutsche marks into the barman's hand and pretended not to hear.

The following morning he was up at six for a bath. He took time choosing his clothes, lingering over shades of gray and textures of white. He put on his second-best suit and then took it off. He did not want to look the way he had sounded on the phone. The young man who stood in his Y-front underpants and the extra-thick undershirt his mother had packed, staring into the wardrobe at three suits and a tweed jacket, had an intimation of the power of American style. He had an idea there was something risible about his stiffness of manner. His Englishness was not quite the comfort it had been to a preceding generation. It made him feel vulnerable. Americans, on the other hand, seemed utterly at ease being themselves. He chose the sports jacket and a bright red knitted tie, which was more or less concealed by his homemade high-necked jumper.

Ten Nollendorfstrasse was a tall thin building undergoing renovation. Workmen who were decorating the hallway had to move their ladders to allow Leonard up the narrow stairs. The top floor was already completed and had carpets. Three doors faced onto the landing; one of them stood ajar. Through it Leonard could hear a buzzing. Above it a voice shouted, "Is that you, Marnham? Come in, for Chrissakes."

He entered what was partly an office, partly a bedroom. On one wall was a large map of the city, and under it was an unmade bed. Glass sat at a chaotic desk, trimming his beard with an electric razor. With a free hand he was stirring instant coffee into two mugs of hot water. An electric kettle was on the floor.

"Sit down," Glass said. "Throw that shirt on the bed. Sugar? Two?"

He spooned the sugar from a paper package and dried

milk from a jar, and stirred the cups so vigorously that coffee slopped onto nearby papers. The moment the drinks were ready he turned off the razor and handed Leonard his cup. As Glass buttoned his shirt, Leonard had a glimpse of a stocky body beneath wiry black hair that grew right across the shoulders. Glass buttoned his collar tightly round a thick neck. From the desk he picked up a ready-knotted tie attached to a hoop of elastic that he snapped on as he stood. He wasted no movements. He took his jacket from the back of a chair and walked to the wall map as he put it on. The suit was dark blue, creased and worn in places to a shine. Leonard was watching. There were ways of wearing clothes that made them quite irrelevant. You could get away with anything.

Glass struck the map with the back of his hand. "You been around it yet?"

Leonard, still not trusting himself to avoid more of his "Well, actually, no," shook his head.

"I've just been reading this report. One of the things it says, and this is just anyone's guess, but what they say is that between five and ten thousand individuals in this city are working in intelligence. That's not counting backup. That's guys on the ground. Spies." He tilted his head and pointed his beard at Leonard until he was satisfied with the response. "Most of them are free-lancers, part-timers, kids, *Hundert Mark Jungen* who hang around the bars. They'll sell you a story for the price of a few beers. They also buy. You been over to the Café Prag?"

"No, not yet."

Glass was striding back to his desk. He had had no real need of the map after all. "It's the Chicago futures market down there. You should take a look."

He was about five foot six, seven inches shorter than Leonard. He seemed bottled up in his suit. He was smiling, but he looked ready to wreck the room. As he sat down he slapped his knee hard and said, "So, welcome!" His head hair was also wiry and dark. It started well up on his forehead and flew backward, giving him the high-domed appearance of a cartoon scientist facing into a strong wind. His beard, in contrast, was inert, trapping light into its solidity. It protruded as a wedge, like the beard of a carved wooden Noah.

From across the landing, through the open door, came the urinous scent of burned toast smelled at a distance. Glass bounced up, kicked the door shut and returned to his chair. He took a long pull of the coffee that Leonard was finding almost too hot to sip. It tasted of boiled cabbage. The trick was to concentrate on the sugar.

Glass leaned forward in his chair. "Tell me what you know."

Leonard gave an account of his meeting with Lofting. His voice sounded prissy in his ears. In deference to Glass, he was softening his *t*'s and flattening his *a*'s.

"But you don't know what the equipment is or what the tests are that you have to carry out?"

"No."

Glass stretched back in his chair and clasped his hands behind his head. "That dumb Sheldrake. Couldn't keep his ass still when his promotion came through. He left no one accountable for your stuff." Glass looked pityingly at Leonard. "The British. It's hard to make those guys at the stadium take anything seriously. They're so busy being gentlemen. They don't do their jobs."

Leonard said nothing. He thought he should be loyal.

Glass raised his coffee cup at him and smiled. "But you technical people are different, right?"

"Perhaps we are."

The phone rang while he was saying this. Glass snatched the receiver and listened for half a minute and then said, "No. I'm on my way." He replaced the phone and stood. He guided Leonard toward the door. "So you know nothing about the warehouse? No one's mentioned Altglienicke to you?"

"I'm afraid not."

"We're going there now."

They were on the landing. Glass was using three keys to lock his door. He was shaking his head and smiling to himself as he murmured, "Those Brits, that Sheldrake, that dumb fuck."

2 THE CAR WAS A DISAPPOINTMENT. On his way to Nollendorfstrasse from the U-Bahn Leonard had seen a pastel American vehicle with tailfins and swags of chrome. This was a dun-colored Beetle, barely a year old, which seemed to have suffered an acid bath. The paintwork was rough to the touch. From the interior all comforts had been stripped away: the ashtrays, the carpets, the plastic moldings round the door handles, even the gearstick knob. The silencer was deficient, or had been tampered with to enhance the effect of a serious military machine.

A blur of road surface was visible through a perfectly round hole in the floor. In this cold and resonating shell of tin they were creeping under the bridges of the Anhalter Bahnhof at a roar. Glass's method was to put the car in fourth and drive it like an automatic. At nineteen miles an hour the frame was shuddering. The pace was not timid but proprietorial; Glass clenched the top of the wheel in both hands and fiercely surveyed pedestrians and other drivers. His beard was raised up. He was an American, and this was the American sector.

Once they were on the wider run of Gneisenau Strasse, Glass opened out to twenty-five miles an hour and moved his right hand off the steering wheel to grip the stem of the gearstick.

"Now," he called out, settling deeper into his seat like a jet pilot. "We're heading south to Altglienicke. We've built a radar station just across from the Russian sector. You've heard of the AN/APR9? No? It's an advanced receiver. The Soviets have an airbase nearby, at Schönefeld. We'll be picking up their emissions."

Leonard was uneasy. He knew nothing about radar. At the G.P.O. research laboratories his work had been in telephones.

"Your stuff is in a room there. You'll have testing facilities. Anything you want, you tell me, okay? You don't ask anyone else. Is that clear?"

Leonard nodded. He stared ahead, sensing a terrible mistake. But he knew from experience that it was poor policy to express doubts about a procedure until it was absolutely necessary. The reticent made, or appeared to make, fewer mistakes.

They were approaching a red light. Glass dropped his speed to fifteen before riding the clutch until they had stopped. Then he shifted to neutral. He turned right around in his seat to face his silent passenger. "Come on, Marnham. Leonard. For Chrissakes, loosen up. Speak to me. Say something." Leonard was about to say he knew nothing about radar, but Glass was embarked on a series of indignant questions. "Are you married or what? Where did you go to school? What do you like? What do you think?" It was the changing light and the search for first gear that interrupted him.

In his orderly fashion, Leonard dealt with the questions in reciprocal sequence. "No, I'm not married. Haven't even been close to it. I'm still living at home. I went to Birmingham University, where I did electronics. I found out last night that I like German beer. And what I think is that if you want someone to look at radar equipment—"

Glass raised his hand. "Don't tell me. It all comes back to that asshole Sheldrake. We're not going to a radar station, Leonard. You know that. I know that. The aerial on the roof connects to nothing. But you don't have level three clearance yet. So we are going to a radar station. The screwup, the real humiliation, is going to come at the gate. They're not going to let you through. But that's my problem. You like girls, Leonard?"

"Well, yes, actually, I do, as a matter of fact."

"Fine. We'll do something together tonight."

Within twenty minutes they were leaving the suburbs for flat, charmless countryside. There were large brown fields divided by ditches choked with sodden, matted grasses, and there were bare, solitary trees and telegraph poles. The farmhouses crouched low in their domains with their backs to the road. Up muddy tracks were half-built houses on reclaimed portions of fields—the new suburbs. There was even a half-built apartment building rising from the center of a field. Further on, right by the roadside, were shacks of recycled wood and corrugated tin which, Glass explained, belonged to refugees from the East.

They turned down a narrower road that tapered off into a track. Off to the left was a newly surfaced road. Glass tilted his head back and indicated with his beard. Two hundred yards ahead, obscured at first by the stark forms of an orchard that lay behind it, was their destination. It resolved itself into two principal buildings. One was two storeys high and had a gently pitched roof; the other, which ran off from the first at an angle, was low and gray, like a cell block. The windows, which formed a single line, appeared to be bricked in. On the roof of the second building was a cluster of four globes, two large, two small, arranged to suggest a fat man with fat hands extended. Close by were radio masts making a fine, geometric tracery against the dull white sky. There were temporary buildings, a circular service road, and a strip of rough ground before the double perimeter fence began. In front of the second building were three military trucks and men in fatigues milling around them, unloading perhaps.

Glass pulled to the side of the track and stopped. Up ahead was a barrier, and a sentry standing beside it, watching them. "Let me tell you about level one. The Army engineer who built this place is told he's putting up a warehouse, a regular Army warehouse. Now, his instructions specify a basement with a twelve-foot ceiling. That's deep. That means shifting a hell of a lot of earth, dump trucks to take it away, finding a site, and so on. And it isn't the way the Army builds a warehouse. So the commander refuses to do it till he has confirmation direct from Washington. He's taken aside, and at this point he discovers there are clearance levels, and he's being upgraded to level two. He's not really building a warehouse at all, he's told, it's a radar station, and the deep basement is for special equipment. So he gets to work, and he's happy. He's the only guy on site who knows what the building is really for. But he's wrong. If he had level three clearance, he'd know it wasn't a radar station at all. If Sheldrake had briefed you, you'd know too. I know, but I don't have authority to upgrade your clearance. But the point is this—everybody thinks his clearance is the highest there is, everyone thinks he has the final story. You only hear of a higher level at the moment you're being told about it. There could be a level four here. I don't see how, but I'd only hear about it if I was being initiated. But you . . ."

Glass hesitated. A second sentry had stepped out of his hut and was waving them forward. Glass spoke quickly. "You have level two, but you know there's a level three. That's a breach, an irregularity. So I might as well fill you in. But I'm not going to, not without covering my ass first."

Glass drove forward and wound down his window. He took a card from his wallet and passed it up to the sentry. The two men in the car stared at the midriff buttons on the soldier's greatcoat.

Then a friendly, big-boned face filled the window and spoke across Bob Glass's lap to Leonard. "You have something for me, sir."

Leonard was pulling out his letters of introduction from the Dollis Hill research unit. But Glass murmured "Christ, no" and pushed the letters out of the sentry's reach. Then he said, "Move your face, Howie. I'm getting out."

The two men walked toward the guard hut. The other sentry, who had taken up a position in front of the barrier, kept his rifle raised in front of him in almost ceremonial style. He nodded at Glass as he passed. Glass and the first sentry went into the hut. Through the open doorway it was possible to make out Glass talking on the phone. After five minutes he came back to the car and spoke through the window.

"I have to go in and explain." He was about to leave when he changed his mind, opened the door and sat down. "Another thing. These guys on the gate know nothing. They don't even know about a warehouse. They're told it's high security and they're going to guard it. They can know who you are, but not what you do. So don't go showing letters. In fact, give them here. I'll put them through the office shredder."

Glass slammed his door hard and strode away, folding Leonard's letters into his pocket as he went. He ducked under the barrier and headed toward the two-storey building.

Then a bored, Sunday silence settled on Altglienicke. The
sentry continued to stand in the center of the road. His colleague sat in the hut. Inside the perimeter wire there was no
movement. The trucks were lost to view, around the other
side of the low building. The only sound was the irregular
tick of contracting metal. The car's tin plate was drawing in
the cold. Leonard pulled his coat around him. He wanted to
get out and walk up and down, but the sentry made him
uneasy. So he banged his hands together, and tried to keep
his feet off the metal floor, and waited.

Presently a side door in the low building opened and two
men stepped out. One of them turned to lock the door behind
him. Both men were well over six feet tall. They wore crew
cuts, and gray T-shirts that were untucked from their loose
khaki trousers. They seemed immune to the cold. They had
an orange rugby ball which they lobbed back and forth as
they walked away from each other. They kept on walking
until the ball was arcing through an improbable distance,
spinning smoothly around its longer axis. It was not a two-
handed rugger throw-in but a single-handed pitch, a sinuous,
whiplike movement over the shoulder. Leonard had never
seen an American football game, never even heard one described. This routine, with the catches snapping high, right
up on the collarbone, seemed overdemonstrative, too self-
loving, to represent any serious form of game practice. This
was a blatant exhibition of physical prowess. These were
grown men, showing off. Their only audience, an Englishman in a freezing German car, watched with disgusted fascination. It really was not necessary to make such extravagant
play with the outstretched left hand just before the throw, or
to hoot like an idiot at the other man's pitch. But it was a

jubilant uncoiling power that made the orange ball soar; and the clarity of its flight through the white sky, the parabolic symmetry of its rise and fall, the certainty that the catch would not be fumbled, were almost beautiful, an unforced subversion of the surroundings—the concrete, the double fence and its functional Y-shaped posts, the cold.

That two adults should be so publicly playful—that was what held him, irritated him. Two British sergeants with a taste for cricket would wait for a team practice, properly announced, or at least get up a proper impromptu game. This was all swank, childishness. They played on. After fifteen minutes one of them looked at his watch. They strolled back to the side door, unlocked it and stepped inside. For a minute or so after they had gone their absence dominated the strip of last year's weeds between the fence and the low building. Then that faded.

The sentry walked the length of the striped barrier, glanced inside the hut at his companion, then returned to his position and stamped his feet on the concrete. After ten minutes Bob Glass came hurrying from the two-storey building. At his side was a U.S. Army captain. They ducked under the barrier, passing on both sides of the sentry. Leonard went to get out of the car, but Glass motioned to him to wind down the window. He introduced the man as Major Angell. Glass stepped back and the major leaned in and said, "Young man, welcome!" He had a long, sunken face to which his closely shaved stubble imparted a green hue. He wore black leather gloves and he was handing Leonard his papers. "I saved these from the shredder." He dropped his voice in mock confidentiality. "Bob was being kind of zealous. Don't carry them around with you in future. Keep them at home. We'll issue you a pass." The major's aftershave invaded the cold car. The smell was of lemon sherbet. "I've authorized Bob to show you around. I'm not authorized to make exceptional clearances over the phone, so I've come out to speak to these guys myself."

He moved away toward the sentry hut. Glass got in behind the wheel. The barrier lifted, and as they passed through the major saluted comically, with only one finger raised to his temple. Leonard started to wave, then, feeling foolish, let his hand drop and forced a smile.

They parked alongside an Army truck by the two-storey building. From somewhere around a corner came the sound of a diesel generator. Instead of leading Leonard to the entrance, Glass steered him by the elbow a few steps across the grass toward the fence and pointed through it. A hundred yards away, across a field, two soldiers were watching them through binoculars. "The Russian sector. The Vopos watch us day and night. They're very interested in our radar station. They log everyone and everything that comes in and out of here. They're getting their first sight of you now. If they see you coming regularly, you might even get a code name." They walked back toward the car. "So, the first thing to remember is to behave at all times like a visitor to a radar station."

Leonard was about to ask about the men with the ball, but Glass was leading him around the side of the building and calling over his shoulder, "I was going to take you to your equipment, but what the hell. You might as well see the action." They turned a corner and passed between two roaring generator trucks. Glass held open a door for Leonard which gave onto a short corridor at the end of which was a door marked NO UNAUTHORIZED ENTRY. It was a warehouse after all, a vast concrete space dimly lit by dozens of bare light bulbs slung from steel girders. Bolted metal frame partitions separated the goods, wooden boxes and crates. One end of the warehouse was clear, and Leonard could see a forklift maneuvering across an oil-stained floor. He followed Glass toward it down an aisle of packaged goods stenciled FRAGILE.

"Some of your stuff is still here," Glass said. "But most of it is already in your room." Leonard did not ask questions. It was obvious that Glass was enjoying the slow unveiling of a secret. They stood by the clearing and watched the forklift. It had stopped by orderly piles of curved steel sections, about a foot wide and three feet long. There were scores of them, hundreds perhaps. Several were being lifted now.

"These are the steel liner plates. They've been sprayed with rubber solution to stop them banging around. We can follow these ones down." They walked behind the forklift as it began to descend a concrete ramp into the basement. The driver, a muscular little man in Army fatigues, turned and nodded at Glass. "That's Fritz. They all get called Fritz. One of Gehlen's men. You know who I mean?" Leonard's answer was choked by the smell that rose to meet them from below. Glass continued, "Fritz was a Nazi. Most of Gehlen's people were, but this Fritz was a real horror." Then he acknowledged Leonard's reaction to the smell with a deprecating smile, very much the flattered host. "Yeah, there's a story behind that. I'll tell you later."

The Nazi had driven his forklift over to one corner of the basement and turned the engine off. Leonard stood at the foot of the ramp with Glass. The smell came from the earth that covered two thirds of the basement floor and was piled to the ceiling. Leonard was thinking of his grandmother—not of her, exactly, but of the privy that stood at the bottom of her garden under a Victoria plum tree. It was gloomy in there, just as it was down here. The wooden seat was worn smooth at the rim, and was scrubbed near white. This was the smell that rose up through the hole—not altogether unpleasant, except in summer. It was earth, and a lurid dampness, and shit not quite neutralized by chemicals.

Glass said, "It's nothing like it was."

The forklift was parked near the rim of a well-lit hole that was twenty feet or so deep and as much in diameter. An iron-rung ladder was bolted to one of the pilings that had been driven into the floor of the shaft. At the base, cut into the wall of the shaft, was a round black hole: the entrance to a tunnel. Various lines and wires fed into it from above. A ventilation pipe was connected to a noisy pump set well back against the basement wall. There were field telephone wires, a thick cluster of electrical cable, and a hose streaked with cement, which fed into another, smaller machine which stood silent beside the first.

Grouped around the edge of the hole were four or five of the big men Leonard came to know as the tunneling sergeants. One of them was attending to a winch perched on the rim; another was talking into the field telephone. He raised his hand lazily in Glass's direction, then turned away to go on talking. "You heard what he said. You're right under their feet. Take it apart slowly, and for fuck's sake don't hit it." He listened and interrupted. "If you—listen to me, listen to me, no, listen, listen, if you want to get mad, come up here and do it." He put down the phone and spoke across the hole to

Glass. "Fucking jack's jammed again. Second time this morning."

Glass did not introduce Leonard to any of the men, and they took no interest in his presence. He was invisible as he moved around the shaft to get a better view. It was always to be like this, and he soon learned the habit himself: you did not speak to people unless their work was relevant to yours. The procedure evolved partly out of a concern for security, and partly, he discovered later, out of a certain virile cult of competence that permitted you to brush by strangers and talk past their faces.

He had moved around the edge of the hole to witness an exchange. A small wagon on rails had emerged from the tunnel into the shaft. On it was a rectangular wooden box filled with earth. The man pushing the wagon, who was naked to the waist, had called up to the man by the winch, who refused to let down the steel cable and hook. He called down that since the hydraulic jack was jammed, there was no point in sending the liner plates to the tunnel face, in which case the forklift in the basement could not be unloaded and could not carry away the box of earth if it was raised. So it might as well stay where it was.

The man in the shaft screwed up his face against the lights shining down on him. He had not heard clearly. The winch man repeated the explanation. The tunneler shook his head and put his hands, which were large, on his hips. The box could be winched up, he called, and set aside until the forklift was ready.

The winch man had his answer ready. He wanted to use the time to look at the winch's gearing mechanism. The man in the hole said what the fuck, that could be done when the box was up. No the fuck it couldn't, said the man by the winch.

The man said he was coming up there, and that was fine by the winch operator, who said he was ready for him.

The man in the hole glared up at the winch. His eyes were almost closed. Then he came bouncing up the rung ladder. Leonard felt sick at the prospect of a fight. He looked at Glass. He had folded his arms and cocked his head. The man was at the top of the ladder, and now he was walking around the rim, behind the equipment, toward the winch. The man there was making a point of not looking up from what he was doing.

Somehow, lazily, unintentionally, the other sergeants drifted into the diminishing space between the two men. There was a soothing confusion of voices. The tunneler strung out a sequence of obscenities at the winch man, who was turning a screwdriver into the machine and did not reply. This was the ritual defusion. The indignant man was being persuaded by the others to use the jack failure to his own advantage and take a break. At last he strode toward the ramp, muttering to himself and kicking at a loose stone.

When he was gone, the man at the winch spat into the shaft.

Glass took Leonard's elbow. "They've been on the job since last August, eight-hour shifts around the clock."

They walked to the administration building by way of a connecting corridor. Glass stopped by a window and once more pointed out the observation post beyond the perimeter wire. "I want to show you how far we've got. See, behind the Vopos there's a cemetery. Right behind that there are military vehicles. They're parked on the main road, the Schönefelder Chaussee. We're right under them, about to cross the road."

The East German trucks were about three hundred yards away. Leonard could make out traffic on the road. Glass walked on, and for the first time Leonard felt irritation at his methods.

"Mr. Glass—"

"Bob, please."

"Are you going to tell me what this is all for?"

"Sure. It's what concerns you most. On the far side of that road, buried in a ditch, are Soviet landlines that link with their high command in Moscow. All communications between East European capitals get routed into Berlin and out again. It's a legacy of the old imperial control. Your job is to dig upward and lay the taps. We're doing the rest." Glass was pressing on, through a set of swing doors into a reception area where there was fluorescent light, a Coca-Cola machine and the sound of typing.

Leonard caught hold of Glass's sleeve. "Look, Bob. I don't know anything about digging, and as for actually laying the . . . as for the rest of it . . ."

Glass whooped with glee. He had taken out a key. "Very funny. I meant the British, you idiot. This in here is your job." He unlocked the door, reached in and turned on the light and allowed Leonard to enter first.

It was a large, windowless room. Two trestle tables had been pushed against one wall. On them was some basic circuit-testing equipment and a soldering iron. The rest of the space was taken up by identical cardboard boxes piled right to the ceiling, ten deep.

Glass gave the nearest a gentle kick. "One hundred and

fifty Ampex tape recorders. Your first job is to unpack them and dispose of the boxes. There's an incinerator out back. That'll take you two or three days. Next, every machine has to have a plug, then it has to be tested. I'll show you how to order spare parts. You know about signal activation? Good. They've all got to be adapted. That'll take you a while. After that you might be helping with the circuits down to the amplifiers. Then the installation. We're still digging, so take your time. We'd like to see these rolling by April."

Leonard felt unaccountably happy. He picked up an ohm-meter. It was of German make, encased in brown bakelite. "I'll need a finer instrument than this for low resistances. And ventilation. Condensation could be a problem in here."

Glass raised his beard, as though in tribute, and gave Leonard a gentle thump on the back. "That's the spirit. Be outrageously demanding. We'll all respect you for it."

Leonard looked up to gauge Glass's expression for irony, but he had turned off the light and was holding the door open.

"Start tomorrow, 0900 hours. Now, the tour continues."

Leonard was shown only the canteen, where hot food was brought in from a nearby barracks, Glass's own office and finally the shower room and lavatories. The American's pleasure in revealing these amenities was no less intense. He warned solemnly of the ease with which the toilets became blocked.

They remained standing across from the urinals while he told a story, which faded skillfully into small talk on the two occasions someone came in. Aerial reconnaissance had shown that the best-drained land, and therefore the best land for tunneling, lay through the cemetery on the eastern side. After long discussion, the proposed route was abandoned. Sooner or later the Russians were going to discover the tunnel. There was no point in handing them a propaganda victory in the story of Americans desecrating German graves. And the sergeants would not care for coffins disintegrating above their heads. So the tunnel struck out to the north of the graveyard. But then, in the first month of digging, they had run into water. The engineers said it was a perched water table. The sergeants said come down and smell for yourselves. By trying to avoid the graveyard, the planners had routed the tunnel right through the drainage field of the establishment's own septic tank. It was too late to change course.

"You wouldn't believe what we were burrowing through, and it was all our very own. A putrefying corpse would have been light relief. And you should have heard the tempers then."

They ate lunch in the canteen, a bright room with rows of Formica tables and indoor plants under the windows. Glass ordered steak and french fries for them both. These were the biggest slabs of meat Leonard had ever seen outside a butcher's. His overhung the plate, and the following day his jaw still ached. He caused consternation when he asked for tea. A search was about to be mounted for the teabags the cook was certain were in the supplies. Leonard pleaded a change of mind. He had the same as Glass, freezing lemonade, which he drank out of the bottle like his host.

Afterward, as they were walking to the car, Leonard asked if he could take home circuit diagrams for the Ampex recording machines. He could see himself curled up on the Army issue sofa, reading in the lamplight while the afternoon gloom settled on the city. They were on their way out of the building.

Glass was genuinely irritated. He stopped to make his point. "Are you crazy? Nothing, nothing to do with this work ever goes home with you. Is that understood? Not diagrams, notes, not even a fucking screwdriver. You got that?"

Leonard blinked at the obscenity. He took work home in England, even sat with it on his lap, listening to the wireless with his parents. He pushed his glasses up his nose. "Yes, of course. Sorry."

As they stepped outside, Glass glanced around to make certain no one was close. "This operation is costing the government, the U.S. government, millions of dollars. You guys are making a useful contribution, especially with the vertical tunneling. You've also supplied the light bulbs. But you know something?"

They were standing on either side of the Beetle, looking at each other over its roof. Leonard felt obliged to make his face quizzical. He did not know something.

Glass had yet to unlock the driver's door. "I'll tell you. It's all political. You think we couldn't lay those taps ourselves? You think we don't have amplifiers of our own? It's for politics that we're letting you in on this. We're supposed to have a special relationship with you guys, that's why."

They got in the car. Leonard longed to be alone. The effort of being polite was stifling, and aggression was, for him, emotionally impossible.

He said, "It's very kind of you, Bob. Thank you." The irony fell dead.

"Don't thank me," Glass said as he turned the ignition. "Just don't screw up on security. Watch what you say, watch who you're with. Remember your compatriots, Burgess and Maclean."

Leonard turned aside to look out of his window. He felt the heat of anger in his face and across his neck. They passed the sentry hut and shuddered out onto the open road. Glass moved on to other topics—good places to eat, the high rate of suicide, the latest kidnapping, the local obsession with the occult. Leonard was sulkily monosyllabic. They passed the refugee shacks, the new buildings, and soon they were back among the devastation and reconstruction. Glass insisted on driving him all the way to Platanenallee. He wanted to learn the route, and he needed to see the apartment for "professional and technical reasons."

On the way they drove along a section of the Kurfürstendamm. Glass pointed out with some pride the brave elegance of new stores flanked by ruins, the crowds of shoppers, the famous Hotel am Zoo, the neon Cinzano and Bosch signs waiting to be turned on. By the Kaiser Wilhelm Memorial Church with its shorn spire there was even a small traffic jam.

Glass did not, as Leonard half expected, search the apartment for concealed listening devices. Instead he went from room to room, taking up a central position in each one and looking around before moving on. It did not seem right that he should go into the bedroom, with the bed unmade and yesterday's socks on the floor. But Leonard said nothing. He waited in the living room, and still thought he was about to hear a security assessment when Glass came in at last.

The American spread his hands. "It's incredible. It's beyond belief. You've seen where I live. How does a fucking technical assistant at the Post Office get a place like this?"

Glass glared across his beard at Leonard as though he really expected an answer.

Leonard had no ready means to respond to an insult. He had not received one in adult life. He was nice to people, and they were generally nice back to him. His heart beat hard, confusing his thoughts. He said, "I expect it was a mistake."

Without appearing to change the subject Glass said, "Look, I'll come by round about seven-thirty. Show you some places."

He was moving out of the room. Leonard, relieved that they were not to have a fistfight after all, accompanied his guest to the front door with earnest, polite thanks for the morning's tour and for the evening to come.

When Glass had gone he returned to the sitting room feeling sick with contradictory, unarticulated emotion. His breath tasted meaty, like a dog's. His stomach was still gaseous and tight. He sat down and loosened his tie.

3 TWENTY MINUTES LATER he was sitting at the dining room table filling his fountain pen. He wiped the nib with a rag he kept for the purpose. He squared a sheet of paper in front of him. Now that he had a workplace he was content, despite the confusion around Glass. His impulse was to set things in order. He was preparing to write the first shopping list of his life. He contemplated his needs. It was difficult to think about food. He was not at all hungry. He had everything he needed. A job, a place where he was expected. He would have a pass, he was part of a team, a sharer in a secret. He was a member of the clandestine elite, Glass's five or ten thousand, who gave the city its real purpose. He wrote *Salz*. He had seen his mother make her effortless lists on a sheet of Basildon Bond: 1 lb. mt, 2 lb. crts, 5 lb. pots. Such feeble encodings were not appropriate to a member of the intelligence community, one with level three clearance in Operation Gold. And he could not cook. He considered Glass's domestic arrangements, crossed out *Salz* and wrote *Kaffee und Zucker*. He consulted his dictionary for powdered milk: *Milchpulver*. Now the list was easy. As it grew longer he seemed to be inventing and defining himself. He would have no food in the house, no mess, no mundanity. At twelve deutsche marks to the pound, he could afford to eat in a *Kneipe* in the evening and at the Altglienicke canteen during the day. He looked in the dictionary again and wrote *Tee, Zigaretten, Streichhölzer, Schokolade*. The last was to keep his blood sugar level up when he worked late at night. He read the list through as he stood. He felt himself to be precisely what his list suggested: unencumbered, manly, serious.

He walked to Reichskanzlerplatz and found a line of

shops in a street near the *Kneipe* where he had eaten his supper. The buildings that had once faced directly onto the pavement had been blasted away to expose a second rank of structures sixty feet back, whose empty upper storeys had been sliced open to view. There were three-walled rooms hanging in the air, with light switches, fireplaces, wallpaper still intact. In one there was a rusted bed frame; in another a door opened onto empty space. Further along, only one wall of a room survived, a giant postage stamp of weather-stained floral paper on raised plaster, stuck onto wet brick. Next to it was a patch of white bathroom tiles intersected by the scars of waste pipes. On an end wall was the sawtooth impression of a staircase zigzagging five storeys up. What survived best were the chimney breasts, plunging through the rooms, making a community out of fireplaces that had once pretended to be unique.

Only the ground floors were occupied. An expertly painted board raised high on two posts and set by the edge of the pavement announced each shop. Well-traveled footpaths curved between rubble and regular stacks of bricks to entrances sheltering under the hanging rooms. The shops were well lit, almost prosperous, with as good a selection as any corner store in Tottenham. In each shop there was a small queue. Only instant coffee was unavailable. He was offered ground coffee. The lady in the *Lebensmittelladen* would only let him have two hundred grams. She explained why and Leonard nodded as though he had understood.

On the way home he had bockwurst and Coca-Cola at a pavement stall. He was back at Platanenallee, waiting for the lift, when two men in white coveralls passed him and began to climb the stairs. They were carrying paint cans, ladders and brushes. He met their glances, and there were mumbled *Guten Tag*'s as they edged past him. He was outside his own front door, searching for his key, when he heard the men talking on the landing below. The voices were distorted by the concrete steps and the glossy walls of the stairwell. The actual words were lost, but the rhythm, the lilt, was unmistakably London English.

Leonard left his shopping by his door and called down: "Hello . . ." At the sound of his own voice he recognized just how lonely he felt. One of the men had set down his ladder and was staring up. "Hello, hello?"

"You're English, then," Leonard said as he came down.

The second man had appeared from the apartment directly below Leonard's. "We thought you was a Kraut," he explained.

"I thought you were too." Now that Leonard was standing in front of the men, he wasn't sure what he wanted. They looked at him, neither friendly nor hostile.

The first man picked up his ladder again and carried it into the apartment. "Live here, do you?" he said over his shoulder.

It seemed all right to follow him in. "Just arrived," Leonard said.

This was a far grander place than his own. The ceilings were higher, and the hallway was a wide open space, where his own was little more than a corridor.

The second man was carrying in a pile of dustsheets. "Mostly they contract out to the Krauts. But we've got to do this one ourselves."

Leonard followed them into a large living room empty of furniture. He watched them spread their dustsheets over the polished wooden floor. They seemed happy to talk about themselves. They were in the Royal Army Service Corps, national servicemen who were in no particular hurry to go back home. They liked the beer and the sausages, and the girls. They were settling to their work, rubbing down the woodwork with sandpaper wrapped round rubber blocks.

The first man, who was from Walthamstow, said, "These girls—as long as you're not a Russian, you can't go wrong."

His friend, from Lewisham, agreed. "They hate the Russians. When they came in here, May '45, they behaved like animals, fucking animals. All these girls, now, see, they all got older sisters, or mums, or even their fucking grannies, raped, knifed. They all know someone, they all remember."

The first man was kneeling down to the baseboards. "We got mates who were here in '53, they were on duty down by Potsdamerplatz when they started shooting into the crowds, just like that, women with their nippers." He looked up at Leonard and said pleasantly, "They're scum, really." And then, "You're not military, then."

Leonard said he was a Post Office engineer come to work on the improvement of the Army's internal lines. This was the story agreed with Dollis Hill, and this was his first chance to use it. He felt mean-spirited in the face of the men's openness. He would have liked to tell them how he was doing his bit against the Russians. There was more desultory chat, and then the men were presenting their backs to him and bending to their work.

They said their goodbyes, and Leonard returned upstairs and took his shopping into the apartment. The task of finding places on the shelves for his purchases cheered him. He made tea for himself and was content to sit and do nothing in the deep armchair. If there had been a magazine, he might have read it. He had never been much interested in reading books. He fell asleep where he sat, and woke with only half an hour to prepare himself for his evening out.

4 THERE WAS ANOTHER MAN sitting in the front passenger seat of the Beetle when Leonard went down onto the street with Bob Glass. His name was Russell, and he must have been watching their approach in the rearview mirror, for he sprang out of the car as they approached it from behind and gave Leonard's hand a ferocious shake. He worked as an announcer for AFN, he said, and wrote bulletins for RIAS, the West Berlin radio service. He wore a gold-buttoned blazer of a shameless Post Office red, and cream-colored trousers with sharp creases, and shoes with tassels and no laces. After the introductions, Russell pulled a lever to fold down his seat and gestured Leonard into the back. Like Glass, Russell wore his shirt open to reveal a high-necked white T-shirt underneath. As they pulled away, Leonard fingered his tie knot in the darkness. He decided against removing the tie in case the two Americans had already noticed him wearing it.

Russell seemed to think it was his responsibility to impart as much information as possible to Leonard. His voice was professionally relaxed, and he spoke without fumbling a syllable or repeating himself or pausing between sentences. He was on the job, naming the streets as they passed down them, pointing out the extent of the bomb damage or a new office building going up. "We're crossing the Tiergarten now. You'll need to come by here in daylight. There's hardly a tree to be seen. What the bombs didn't destroy, the Berliners burned to keep warm in the Airlift. Hitler used to call this the east-west axis. Now it's Street of June 17, named for the uprising the year before last. Up ahead is the memorial to the Russian soldiers who took the city, and I'm sure you know the name of this famous edifice . . ."

The car slowed down as they passed West Berlin police and customs. Beyond them were half a dozen Vopos. One of them shone a torch at the license plate and waved the car into the Russian sector. Glass drove beneath the Brandenburg Gate. Now it was much darker. There was no other traffic. It was difficult to feel excitement, however, because Russell's travelogue continued without modulation, even when the car crashed through a pothole.

"This deserted stretch was once the nerve center of the city, one of the most famous thoroughfares in Europe. Unter den Linden . . . over there, the real headquarters of the German Democratic Republic, the Soviet embassy. It stands on the site of the old Hotel Bristol, once one of the most fashionable—"

Glass had been silent all this while. Now he interrupted politely. "Excuse me, Russell. Leonard, we're starting you in the East so you can enjoy the contrasts later. We're going to the Neva Hotel . . ."

Russell was reactivated. "It used to be the Hotel Nordland, a second-class establishment. Now it has declined further, but it is still the best hotel in East Berlin."

"Russell," Glass said, "you badly need a drink."

It was so dark they could see light from the Neva lobby slanting across the pavement from the far end of the street. When they got out of the car, they saw there was in fact another light, the blue neon sign of a cooperative restaurant opposite the hotel, the H.O. Gastronom. The condensation on the windows was its only outward sign of life.

At the Neva reception a man in a brown uniform silently directed them toward an elevator just big enough for three. It was a slow descent, and their faces were too close together under a single dim bulb for conversation.

There were thirty or forty people in the bar, silent over their drinks. On a dais in one corner a clarinetist and an accordion player were sorting through sheets of music. The bar was hung with studded, tasseled quilting of well-fingered pink which was also built into the counter. There were grand chandeliers, all unlit, and chipped gilt-framed mirrors. Leonard was heading for the bar thinking to buy the first round, but Glass guided him toward a table on the edge of a tiny parquet dance floor.

His whisper sounded loud. "Don't let them see your money in here. East marks only."

At last a waiter came and Glass ordered a bottle of Russian champagne. As they raised their glasses, the musicians began to play "Red Sails in the Sunset." No one was tempted onto the parquet. Russell was scanning the darker corners, and then he was on his feet and making his way between the tables. He returned with a thin woman in a white dress made for someone larger. They watched him move her through an efficient foxtrot.

Glass was shaking his head. "He mistook her in the bad light. She won't do," he predicted, and correctly, for at the end Russell made a courtly bow and, offering the woman his arm, saw her back to her table.

When he joined them he shrugged. "It's the diet here," and relapsing for a moment into his wireless propaganda voice, he gave them details of average calorie consumption in East and West Berlin. Then he broke off, saying "What the hell," and ordered another bottle.

The champagne was as sweet as lemonade and too gassy.

It hardly seemed a serious drink at all. Glass and Russell were talking about the German question. How long would the refugees flock through Berlin to the West before the Democratic Republic suffered total economic collapse because of a shortage of manpower?

Russell was ready with the figures, the hundreds of thousands each year. "And these are their best people; three quarters of them are under forty-five. I'll give it another three years. After that the East German state won't be able to function."

Glass said, "There'll be a state as long as there's a government, and there'll be a government as long as the Soviets want it. It'll be pretty damn miserable here, but the Party will get by. You'll see."

Leonard nodded and hmmed his agreement, but he did not attempt an opinion. When he raised his hand, he was rather surprised that the waiter came over for him just as he had for the others. He ordered another bottle. He had never felt happier. They were deep in the Communist camp, they were drinking Communist champagne, they were men with responsibilities talking over affairs of state. The conversation had moved on to West Germany, the Federal Republic, which was about to be accepted as a full member of NATO.

Russell thought it was all a mistake. "That's one crappy phoenix rising out of the ashes."

Glass said, "You want a free Germany, then you got to have a strong one."

"The French aren't going to buy it," Russell said, and turned to Leonard for support. At that moment the champagne arrived.

"I'll take care of it," Glass said, and when the waiter had gone he said to Leonard, "You owe me seven West marks."

Leonard filled the glasses and the thin woman and her girlfriend walked past their table, and the conversation took another turn. Russell said that Berlin girls were the liveliest and most strong-minded in all the world.

Leonard said that as long as you weren't Russian, you couldn't go wrong. "They all remember when the Russians came in '45," he said with quiet authority. "They've all got older sisters, or mothers, even grannies, who were raped and kicked around."

The two Americans did not agree, but they took him seriously. They even laughed at "grannies." Leonard took a long drink as he listened to Russell.

"The Russians are with their units, out in the country. The ones in town—the officers, the commissars—they do well enough with the girls."

Glass agreed. "There's always some dumb chick who'll fuck a Russian."

The band was playing "How Ya Gonna Keep 'Em Down on the Farm?" The sweetness of the champagne was cloying. It was a relief when the waiter set down three fresh glasses and a refrigerated bottle of vodka.

They were talking about the Russians again. Russell's wireless announcer's voice had gone. His face was sweaty and bright, reflecting the glow of his blazer. Ten years ago, Russell said, he had been a twenty-two-year-old lieutenant accompanying Colonel Frank Howley's advance party, which had set off for Berlin in May 1945 to begin the occupation of the American sector.

"We thought the Russians were regular guys. They'd suffered losses in the millions. They were heroic, they were big, cheerful, vodka-swilling guys. And we'd been sending them mountains of equipment all through the war. So they just had to be our allies. That was before we met up with them. They came out and blocked our road sixty miles west of Berlin. We got out of the trucks to greet them with open arms. We had gifts ready, we were high on the idea of the meeting." Russell gripped Leonard's arm. "But they were cold! Cold, Leonard! We had champagne ready, French champagne, but they wouldn't touch it. It was all we could do to make them shake us by the hand. They wouldn't let our party through unless we reduced it to fifty vehicles. They made us bivouac ten miles out of town. The next morning they let us in under close escort. They didn't trust us, they didn't like us. From day one they had us fingered for the enemy. They tried to stop us setting up our sector.

"And that's how it went on. They never smiled. They never wanted to make things work. They lied, they obstructed, they were cruel. Their language was always too strong, even when they were insisting on a technicality in some agreement. All the time we were saying, 'What the hell, they've had a crappy war, and they do things differently anyhow.' We gave way, we were the innocents. We were talking about the United Nations and a new world order while they were kidnapping and beating up non-Communist politicians all over town. It took us almost a year to get wise to them. And you know what? Every time we met them, these Russian officers, they looked so fucking unhappy. It was like they expected to be shot in the back at any moment. They didn't even enjoy behaving like assholes. That's why I could never really hate them. This was policy. This crap was coming from the top."

Glass poured more vodka. He said, "I hate them. It's not a passion with me, I don't go crazy with it like some guys. You could say it's their system you gotta hate. But there's no system without people to run it." When he set his glass down he spilled a little drink. He pushed his forefinger into the puddle. "What the Commies are selling is miserable, miserable and inefficient. Now they're exporting it by force. I was in Budapest and Warsaw last year. Boy, have they found a way of minimizing happiness! They know it, but they don't stop. I mean, look at this place! Leonard, we brought you to the classiest joint in their sector. Look at it. Look at the people here. Look at them!" Glass was close to shouting.

Russell put out his hand. "Take it easy, Bob."

Glass was smiling. "It's okay. I'm not going to misbehave."

Leonard looked around. Through the gloom he could see the heads of the customers bowed over their drinks. The barman and the waiter, who were standing together at the bar, had turned to face the other way. The two musicians were playing a chirpy marching song. This was his last clear impression. The following day he was to have no memory of leaving the Neva.

They must have made their way between the tables, ascended in the cramped elevator, walked past the man in the brown uniform. By the car was the dark window of a shopping cooperative, and inside a tower of tinned sardines, and above it a portrait of Stalin framed in red crepe paper with a caption in big white letters which Glass and Russell trans-

lated in messy unison: *The unshakable friendship of the So-*
viet and German peoples is a guarantee of peace and freedom.

Then they were at the sector crossing. Glass had switched
the engine off, torches were shone into the car while their
papers were being examined, there were sounds of steel-
tipped boots coming and going in the darkness. Then they
were driving past a sign that said in four languages YOU ARE
LEAVING THE DEMOCRATIC SECTOR OF BERLIN, toward another
that announced in the same languages YOU ARE NOW ENTER-
ING THE BRITISH SECTOR.

"Now we're in Wittenbergplatz," Russell called from the
front seat.

They drifted by a Red Cross nurse seated at the foot of a
gigantic model of a candle with a real flame on top.

Russell was attempting to revive his travelogue. "Collect-
ing for the *Spätheimkehrer,* the late homecomers, the hundreds of thousands of German soldiers still held by the
Russians . . ."

Glass said, "Ten years! Forget it. They ain't coming back
now."

And the next thing was a table set among scores of others
in a vast and clamorous space, and a band up on the stage
almost drowning the voices with a jazzed-up version of "Over
There," and a pamphlet attached to the menu, this time in
only German and English, with clumsy print that swayed and
danced. *"Welcome to the Ballhouse of technical wonders, the*
place of all places of entertainments. One hundred thousand
contacts are guaranteeing . . ." The word was an echo
Leonard could not place. *". . . are guaranteeing you the*
proper functioning of the Modern Table-Phone-System con-
sisting of two hundred and fifty Tablephone sets. The Pneu-

*matic-Table-Mail-Service is posting every night thousands of
letters or little presents from one visitor to the other—it is
unique and amusing for everyone. The famous RESI-Water-
Shows are magnificent in their beauty. It is amazing to
think, that in a minute eight thousand liters of water are
pressed through about nine thousand jets. For the play of
these changing light effects there are necessary one hundred
thousand colored lamps."*

Glass had his fingers in his beard and was smiling hugely.
He said something, and had to repeat it at a shout. "This is
better!"

But it was too noisy to begin a conversation about the
advantages of the Western sector. Colored water spouted up
in front of the band and rose and fell and lurched from side
to side. Leonard avoided looking at it. They were being sensible by drinking beer. As soon as the waiter had gone, a girl
appeared with a basket of roses. Russell bought one and presented it to Leonard, who snapped off the stem and lodged
the flower behind his ear. At the next table something came
rattling down the pneumatic tube, and two Germans in Bavarian jackets leaned forward to examine the contents of a
canister. A woman in a sequined mermaid suit was kissing
the bandleader. There were wolf whistles and cheers. The
band started up; the woman was handed a microphone. She
took off her glasses and began to sing "Too Darn Hot" with a
heavy accent. The Germans were looking disappointed. They
stared in the direction of a table some fifty feet away, where
two giggling girls were collapsing in one another's arms.
Beyond them was the packed dance floor. The woman sang
"Night and Day," "Anything Goes," "Just One of Those

Things," and finally "Miss Otis Regrets." Then everyone stood to cheer and stamp their feet and shout "Encore!"

The band took a break, and Leonard bought another round of beers. Russell took a good look around and said he was too drunk to pick up girls. They talked about Cole Porter and named their favorite songs. Russell said he knew someone whose father had been working at the hospital when they brought Porter in from his riding accident in '37. For some reason the doctors and nurses had been asked not to talk to the press. This led to a conversation about secrecy. Russell said there was far too much of it in the world. He was laughing. He must have known something about Glass's work.

Glass was serious in a punchy way. His head lolled back and he sighted Russell along his beard. "You know what the best course I ever took at college was? Biology. We studied evolution. And I learned something important." Now he included Leonard in his gaze. "It helped me choose my career. For thousands, no millions of years we had these huge brains, the neocortex, right? But we didn't speak to each other, and we lived like fucking pigs. There was nothing. No language, no culture, nothing. And then, suddenly, wham! It was there. Suddenly it was something we had to have, and there was no turning back. So why did it suddenly happen?"

Russell shrugged. "Hand of God?"

"Hand of God my ass. I'll tell you why. Back then we all used to hang out together all day long doing the same thing. We lived in packs. So there was no need for language. If there was a leopard coming, there was no point in saying, 'Hey man, what's coming down the track? A leopard!' Everyone could see it, everyone was jumping up and down and screaming, trying to scare it off. But what happens when someone goes off on his own for a moment's privacy? When he sees a leopard coming, he knows something the others don't. And he knows they don't know. He has something they don't, he has a *secret,* and this is the beginning of his individuality, of his consciousness. If he wants to share his secret and run down the track to warn the other guys, then he's going to need to invent language. From there grows the possibility of culture. Or he can hang back and hope the leopard will take out the leadership that's been giving him a hard time. A secret plan, that means more individuation, more consciousness."

The band was starting to play a fast, loud number. Glass had to shout his conclusion, "Secrecy made us possible," and Russell raised his beer to salute the theory.

A waiter mistook the gesture and was at his elbow, so a fresh round was ordered, and as the mermaid shimmered to the front of the band and the cheers rang out there was a harsh rattling at their table as a canister shot down the tube and smacked against the brass fixture and lodged there. They stared at it, and no one moved.

Then Glass picked it up and unscrewed the top. He took out a folded piece of paper and spread it out on the table. "My God," he shouted. "Leonard, it's for you."

For one confused moment he thought it might be from his mother. He was owed a letter from England. And it was late, he thought, he hadn't said where he was going to be.

The three of them were leaning over the note. Their heads were blocking out the light. Russell read it aloud. *"An den jungen Mann mit der Blume im Haar.* To the young man with the flower in his hair. *Mein Schöner,* I have been watch-

ing you from my table. I would like it if you came and asked
me to dance. But if you can't do this, I would be so happy if
you would turn and smile in my direction. I am sorry to
interfere. Yours, table number 89."

The Americans were on their feet casting around for the
table, while Leonard remained seated with the paper in his
hands. He read the German words over. The message was
hardly a surprise. Now it was before him, it was more a
matter of recognition for him, of accepting the inevitable. It
had always been certain to start like this. If he was honest
with himself, he had to concede that he had always known it
really, at some level.

He was being pulled to his feet. They turned him around
and faced across the ballroom. "Look, she's over there."
Across the heads, through the dense, rising cigarette smoke
backlit by stage lights, he could make out a woman sitting
alone. Glass and Russell were pantomiming a fuss over his
appearance, dusting down his jacket, straightening his tie,
fixing the flower more securely behind his ear. Then they
pushed him away, like a boat from a jetty. "Go on!" they said.
"Atta boy!"

He was drifting toward her, and she was watching his
approach. She had her elbow on the table, and she was supporting her chin with her hand. The mermaid was singing,
"Don't sit under zuh apple tree viz anyone else but me, anyone else but me." He thought, correctly as it turned out, that
his life was about to change. When he was ten feet away she
smiled. He arrived just as the band finished the song. He
stood swaying slightly, with his hand on the back of a chair,
waiting for the applause to die, and when it did Maria

Eckdorf said in perfect but sweetly inflected English, "Are we going to dance?"

Leonard touched his stomach lightly, apologetically, with his fingertips. Three entirely different liquids were sitting in there.

He said, "Actually, would you mind if I sat down?" And so he did, and they immediately held hands, and many minutes passed before he was able to speak another word.

5 HER NAME WAS MARIA LOUISE ECKDORF, she was thirty years old and she lived on Adalbertstrasse in Kreuzberg, a twenty-minute ride from Leonard's flat. She worked as a typist and translator at a small British Army vehicle workshop in Spandau. There was an ex-husband called Otto who appeared unpredictably two or three times in a year to demand money and sometimes smack her head. Her apartment had two rooms and a tiny curtained-off kitchen and was reached by five flights of a gloomy wooden staircase. On every landing there were voices through doors. There was no running hot water, and the cold tap was kept at a dribble in winter to stop the pipes freezing up. She had learned her English from her grandmother, who had been the German tutor at a school for English girls in Switzerland before and after the Great War. Maria's family had moved to Berlin from Düsseldorf in 1937, when she was twelve. Her father had been area representative for a company that made gearboxes for heavy vehicles. Now her parents lived in Pankow, in the Russian sector. Her father was a ticket collector on the railways, and these days her mother had a job too, packing light bulbs in a factory. They still resented their daughter for the marriage she had made at twenty against their wishes, and took no satisfaction in the fulfillment of all their worst predictions.

It was unusual for a childless woman to be living content-edly alone in a one-bedroom apartment. Accommodation was scarce in Berlin. The neighbors on her landing and on the one below kept their distance, but those on the lower floors, the ones who knew less about her, were at least polite. She had good friends among the younger women at the work-shop. The night she met Leonard she was with her friend

Jenny Schneider, who danced all evening with a French Army sergeant. Maria also belonged to a cycling club, whose fifty-year-old treasurer was forlornly in love with her. The April before someone had stolen her bike from the cellar of the apartment house. Her ambition was to perfect her English and to qualify one day as an interpreter in the diplomatic service.

A few of these facts Leonard came by after he had stirred himself to move his chair to exclude Glass and Russell from his view and order a Pimms and lemonade for Maria and another beer for himself. The rest were accumulated slowly and with difficulty over many weeks.

The morning after the Resi he was outside the gates at Altglienicke by eight-thirty, half an hour early, having walked the final mile from Rudow village. He was sick, tired, thirsty and still a little drunk. On his bedside table that morning he had found a scrap torn from a cigarette packet. On it Maria had written her address, and it was in his pocket now. On the U-Bahn he had taken it out several times. She had borrowed a pen from Jenny's friend, the French sergeant, and written it down using Jenny's back for support, while Glass and Russell waited in the car. In Leonard's hand was his radar station pass. The sentry took it and stared hard at his face.

When Leonard arrived at what he now thought of as his room, he found the door open and three men inside packing up their tools. From the look of them they had been working all night. The Ampex boxes had been piled in the center. Bolted to all the walls was shelving, deep enough to take an unpacked machine. A set of library steps provided access to the higher shelves. A circular hole had been cut in the ceiling for a ventilator duct, and a metal grill had just been screwed in place. From somewhere above the ceiling came the sound of an extractor fan. As Leonard stepped aside to let a fitter carry his ladder away, he saw a dozen boxes of electrical plugs and new instruments on the trestle table. He was examining them when Glass appeared at his side with a hunting knife in a green canvas sheath. His beard shone in the electric light.

He spoke without preliminaries. "Open them with this. Do ten at a time, get them on the shelves, then carry the cardboard round the back and burn it right down to ashes. Whatever you do, don't go round the front with it. They'll be watching you. Don't let the wind take anything away. You wouldn't believe it, but some genius has stenciled serial numbers on the boxes. When you're out of this room, keep it locked. This is your key, your responsibility. Sign for it here."

One of the workmen returned and began searching the room. Leonard signed and said, "That was a good evening. Thanks." He wanted Bob Glass to ask him about Maria, to acknowledge his triumph. But the American had turned his back and was looking at the shelves. "As soon as they're up, they'll need to go under dustsheets. I'll have some brought around." The fitter was on his hands and knees staring at the floor. With the toe of his brogues, Glass pointed to a bradawl.

"That really was quite a place," Leonard insisted. "In fact, I'm feeling a bit shaky this morning."

The man picked up the tool and left. Glass kicked the door shut after him. From the tilt of the beard, Leonard knew he was in for a telling-off.

"Listen to me. You think this is unimportant, opening boxes and burning the packing. You think it's something the janitor should do. Well, you're wrong. Everything, but *every-thing* on this project is important, every detail. Is there any good reason why you should let a craftsman know that you and I were out drinking together last night? Think it through, Leonard. What would a senior liaison officer be doing out with a technical assistant from the British Post Office? This craftsman is a soldier. He could be in a bar with his buddy, and they could be talking it over in a harmless, curious sort of way. Sitting on the next stool is a bright German kid who's learned to keep his ears open. There are hundreds of them all over town. Then he's straight down to the Café Prag or wherever with something to sell. Fifty marks' worth, twice that if he's lucky. We're digging right under their feet, we're in their sector. If they get wise they'll shoot to kill. They'd be well within their rights."

Glass came closer. Leonard was uncomfortable, and not only because of the other man's proximity. He was embarrassed for Glass. The performance was overdone, and Leonard felt the burden of being its sole audience. Once again, he was unsure how to set his face. He could smell the instant coffee on Glass's breath.

"I want you to get into a whole new state of mind on this. Anything you're about to do, pause and think of the consequences. This is a war, Leonard, and you're a soldier in it."

When Glass had gone, Leonard waited, then opened his door and looked both ways down the corridor before hurrying to the water fountain. The water was refrigerated and tasted of metal. He drank for minutes on end. When he returned to the room, Glass was there. He shook his head and held up the key Leonard had left behind. He pressed it into the Englishman's hand and closed his fingers around it and left without a word. Leonard blushed through his hangover. To steady himself, he reached into his pocket for the address. He leaned against the boxes and read it slowly. *Erstes Hinterhaus, fünfter Stock rechts, Adalbertstrasse 84.* He ran his hand along the surface of the box. The pale cardboard was almost skin color. His heart was a ratchet; with each thud he was wound tighter, harder. How would he open all these boxes in this state? He pressed his cheek against the cardboard. Maria. He needed relief, how else could he clear his mind? But the possibility of Glass returning again unexpectedly was equally unbearable. The absurdity, the shame, the security implications—he could not think which was worse.

With a moan, he put the scrap away and reached for a box on top of the pile and heaved it to the floor. He drew the hunting knife from its sheath and plunged it in. The cardboard yielded easily, like flesh, and he felt and heard something brittle shatter at the knife's tip. He experienced a thrill of panic. He cut away the lid, pulled clear handfuls of wood shavings and compressed sheets of corrugated paper. When he had cut away the cheesecloth wrapping around the tape recorder, he could see a long diagonal scratch across the area that would be covered by the spools. One of the control knobs had split in two. With difficulty he cut away the rest of the cardboard. He lifted the machine out, fitted a plug and carried it up the library steps to the topmost shelf. The broken knob he put in his pocket. He could fill in a form for a replacement.

Pausing only to remove his jacket, Leonard set about opening the next box. An hour later there were three more machines on the shelf. The sealing tape was easily cut, and so too were the lids. But the corners were heavily reinforced with layers of cardboard and staples that resisted the knife. He decided to work without a break until he had unpacked his first ten machines. He had them all on their shelves by lunchtime. There was a pile of flattened cardboard by the door five feet high and beside it a heap of wood shavings that reached up to the light switch.

The canteen was deserted but for one table of black tunneling sergeants, who paid him no attention. He ordered steak and french fries and lemonade again. The sergeants spoke in low murmurs and chuckles. Leonard strained to overhear. He discerned the word *shaft* several times and assumed they were being indiscreet by talking shop. He had just finished eating when Glass came in and sat down at his table and asked how the work was going. Leonard described his progress. "It's going to take longer than you thought," he concluded.

Glass said, "It sounds right to me. You'll do ten in the morning, ten in the afternoon, ten in the evening. Thirty a day. Five days. Where's the problem?"

Leonard's heart was racing because he had decided to speak his mind. He downed his lemonade. "Well, actually, as you know, my field is circuitry, not box opening. I'm prepared to do anything within reason because I know it's important. But I do expect to have some time to myself in the evenings."

At first Glass did not reply, nor did he show any expression. He watched Leonard, waiting for more. Finally he said, "You want to talk about hours? And job demarcation? Is this the British Commie trade union talk we keep hearing about? From the moment you got your clearance, your job here is to do what you're told. If you don't want the job, I'll cable

Dollis Hill and have them recall you." Then he stood and his expression relaxed. He touched Leonard on the shoulder and said before walking away, "Stick with it, pal."

And so for a week or more Leonard did nothing but stab open cardboard boxes and burn them and fit a plug on each machine, label it and stow it on the shelves. He worked a fifteen-hour day. He spent hours commuting. From Platanenallee he took the U-Bahn as far as Grenzallee, where he caught the 46 bus to Rudow. From there it was a twenty-minute walk along a charmless stretch of country road. He ate in the canteen and at a *Schnellimbiss* on Reichskanzlerplatz. He could think about her while he traveled or poked at burning cardboard boxes with his long pole or stood up to his diet of bratwurst. He knew that if only he had a little more leisure and were a little less tired he could be obsessed, he could be a man in love. He needed to sit down without dozing off and give the matter mental devotion. He needed that time edged with boredom in which fantasy could flourish. The work itself obsessed him; even the repetition of demeaning low-level tasks was mesmerizing for one of his orderly nature, and presented a genuine distraction.

Dressed like Father Time in a school play, in a borrowed bush hat, an Army cape that reached to his ankles, and overshoes, and equipped with a long wooden pole, he spent many hours tending his fire. The incinerator turned out to be a perpetual, feeble bonfire, inadequately protected on three sides against the wind and rain by a low brick wall. Nearby were two dozen dustbins and beyond them a workshop. Across a muddy track was a loading bay where Army trucks backed in and out all day with a grind of low gears. He was under strict instructions not to leave the fire until it had burned right down each time. Even with the help of gasoline, there were some sheets that could do little more than smolder.

In his room he was obsessed by the diminishing pile of boxes on the floor and the growing number of machines on the shelves. He persuaded himself he was emptying the boxes for Maria. This was the test of endurance, the labor he had to perform to be worthy. This was the work he dedicated to her. He tore into the cardboard with his hunting knife and destroyed it for her sake. He also thought how much bigger his room would be when his task was complete, and of how he would rearrange his work space. He planned lighthearted notes to Maria, suggesting with skillful unconcern that they meet in a pub near her flat. By the time he was home in Platanenallee, not so long before midnight, he was too tired to remember the precise order of words, and too tired to begin again.

Years later, Leonard had no difficulty at all recalling Maria's face. It shone for him, the way faces do in certain old paintings. In fact there was something almost two-dimensional about it; the hairline was high on the forehead, and at the other end of this long and perfect oval, the jaw was both delicate and forceful, so that when she tilted her head in a characteristic and endearing way, her face appeared as a disk, more of a plane than a sphere, such as a master artist might draw with one inspired stroke. The hair itself was peculiarly fine, like a baby's, and often wriggled free of the childish clips women wore then. Her eyes were serious, though not mournful, and were green or gray, according to the light. It was not a lively, animated face. She was a habitual daydreamer, often distracted by a line of thought she was unwilling to share, and her most typical expression was one of dreamy watchfulness, the head slightly lifted and tipped an inch or so to one side, the forefinger of her left hand playing with her lower lip. If one spoke to her after a silence, she might jump. It was the sort of face, the sort of manner, onto which men were likely to project their own requirements. One could read womanly power into her silent abstraction, or find a childlike dependency in her quiet attentiveness. On the other hand, it was possible she actually embodied these contradictions. For example, her hands were small, and she cut her fingernails short, like a child's, and never painted them. But she did take care to paint her toenails a lurid red or orange. Her arms were thin, and it was surprising what slight loads she could not raise, what unjammed windows she could not shift. And yet her legs, though slim, were muscular and powerful, perhaps from all the cycling she did before the gloomy treasurer scared her off and her bike was stolen from the communal cellar.

For the twenty-five-year-old Leonard, who had not seen her for five days, who struggled all day with cardboard and wood shavings, and whose only token was the smaller piece of cardboard bearing her address, the face was elusive. The more intensely he summoned it, the more provocative was its disintegration. In fantasy he had only an outline to play with, and even that wavered in the heat of his scrutiny. There were scenes he wanted to play out, approaches that had to be tested, and all his memory would permit was a certain presence, sweet and alluring, but invisible. And the inner ear was deaf to the way she had intoned an English sentence. He began to wonder if he would recognize her in the street. All he knew for certain was the effect on himself of spending ninety minutes with her at a table in a dance hall. He had loved the face. Now the face was gone and all that remained was the love, with too little to feed on. He had to see her again.

He had lost count of the days. It was on the eighth or ninth that Glass let him rest. All the machines had been unpacked, and twenty-six of them had been tested and fitted with signal activation. Leonard slept in an extra two hours, dozing in an erotic fug of bed warmth. Then he shaved and took a bath, and with only a towel around his waist strolled about the apartment, rediscovering it and feeling grand and proprietorial. He heard the scrape of the decorators' stepladder downstairs. It was a workday for everyone else, Monday perhaps. He had time at last to experiment with his ground coffee. It was not an outright success, with the grounds and undissolved milk powder rolling with the convection in the cup, but he was happy to be breakfasting alone on Belgian chocolate, poking his bare feet between the blades of the scalding radiator and planning his campaign. There was a letter from home to read. He opened it casually with a knife, as though receiving letters was what he did every morning at breakfast. *"Just a line to say thanks for yours and glad you're settling in . . ."*

He had it in mind to work on his undemanding note to Maria, but it did not seem right to start that until he was fully dressed. Then, when he was, and the letter was written *(You were kind enough to give me your address last week when we met at the Resi, so I hope you won't be troubled to hear from me, or feel obliged to reply . . .)*, the thought of waiting at least three days for her answer was more than he could bear.

By then he would be back in the dream world of his window-less room and fifteen-hour day.

He poured a second cup of coffee. The grounds had sunk. He had another plan. He would deliver a note for her to find when she came in from work. He would write that he happened to be passing and would be in a certain *Kneipe* on a certain nearby street at six o'clock. He could fill the blanks in later. He set to immediately. Half a dozen drafts later he was still not satisfied. He wanted to be eloquent and casual. It was important that she should think he had scribbled the note as he stood outside her door, that he had called by hoping to find her in and only then remembered that she went out to work. He did not want her to feel under pressure, and, more important, he did not want to appear earnest and foolish.

By lunchtime his attempts lay all about him and the final copy was in his hands. *I happened to be in your area so I thought I'd pop up and say hello.* He folded it into an envelope, which he sealed in error. He took the knife and opened it, imagining himself to be her, alone at her table, just in from work. He spread the letter out and read it twice, as she might. It was perfectly judged. He found another envelope and stood. There were all the hours of the afternoon before him, but he knew there was nothing he could do to stop himself leaving now. He was in the bedroom changing into his best suit. He was taking the worn scrap of cardboard from yesterday's trousers, even though he had memorized the address. He had the street plan opened out on the unmade bed. He was thinking of his bright red knitted tie. He was unbuttoning his traveling shoe-care kit and buffing his best black shoes as he studied his route.

To fill out the time and to savor the expedition, he walked to the Ernst-Reuter-Platz station before taking the U-Bahn to Kottbusser Tor in Kreuzberg. Almost too soon he was on Adalbertstrasse. No. 84 would be less than a five-minute walk. Here was the worst bomb damage he had seen. It would have been dismal enough without it. There were apartment-house facades drilled by small-arms fire, especially around the doors and windows. Every second or third building had a gutted interior and was without its roof. Whole structures had collapsed, and the rubble lay where it had fallen, with roof beams and rusted guttering poking from the heaps. After almost two weeks in the city, during which he had shopped, eaten, commuted and worked, his earlier pride in its destruction seemed puerile, repellent.

As he crossed Oranienstrasse and saw building work on a cleared site, he was pleased. He also saw a bar and went toward it. It was called Bei Tante Else, and it would do. He took out his note and inserted the name and the street in the blanks. Then, as an afterthought, he stepped inside. He paused beyond the leather curtain to accustom his eyes to the dark. It was a cramped and narrow place, almost a tunnel. Beyond the bar was a group of women drinking at one of the tables. One of them fingered the base of her neck to draw attention to Leonard's tie and pointed. *"Keine Kommunisten hier!"* Her friends laughed. For a moment he thought from their manner and faked glamour they might all have just come from a boisterous office party. Then he realized they were prostitutes. Elsewhere there were men asleep with their heads on the tables. As he backed out, another of the women called after him, and there was more laughter.

Back on the pavement, he hesitated. This was no place to

meet Maria. Nor did he wish to sit in there alone and wait for her. On the other hand, he could not alter his note without ruining its casual appearance, so he decided he would wait outside in the street, and when Maria came he would apologize and confess his ignorance of the area. It would be something to talk about. It might even strike her as funny.

No. 84 was an apartment building like all the others. A curving line of bullet marks above the tops of the ground-floor windows was probably machine-gun fire. A wide entrance brought him into a dark central courtyard. Weeds were growing between the cobblestones. Recently emptied dustbins lay on their sides. It was quiet. Kids were still at school. Indoors, late lunches or suppers were being prepared. He could smell cooking fat and onions. Suddenly he missed his daily steak and chips.

Across the courtyard was what he took to be the *Hinterhaus*. He walked to it and stepped through a narrow doorway. He was at the base of a steep wooden staircase. There were two doors on each landing. He rose through babies' cries, wireless music, laughter and, higher up, a man calling with a plaintive stress on the second syllable, "Papa? Papa? Papa?" He was an intruder. The elaborate dishonesty of his mission began to oppress him. He took the envelope from his pocket, ready to post it through the door and descend as quickly as he could. Her apartment was at the very top. Its ceiling was lower than the rest, and this too made him anxious to leave. Her door was a freshly painted green, unlike the others. He pushed the envelope through, and then he did an inexplicable thing, quite out of character.

His upbringing had instilled a simple faith in the inviolability of property. He never took a shortcut if it involved trespass, he never borrowed without first asking permission, and he never stole from shops like some of his friends at school. He was an overscrupulous observer of other people's privacy. Whenever he came across lovers kissing in a private place, he always felt it proper to avert his eyes, even though he longed to go closer and watch. So it made no sense now that without pausing to reflect, and without even a cursory knock on the door, he took hold of the handle and turned it. Perhaps he expected it to be locked, and perhaps therefore this was one of those meaningless little actions with which daily life is filled. The door yielded to him and swung open wide, and there she was, standing right before him.

6 THE APARTMENTS AT THE REAR of the old Berlin buildings were traditionally the cheapest and most cramped. They had once housed the servants, whose masters lived in the grander quarters at the front, facing the road. Those at the rear had windows facing onto the courtyard, or across a narrow space to the next building. It was a mystery, then, which Leonard never bothered to penetrate, how late-afternoon winter sunshine was able to spill out from the open bathroom door across the floor between them, a reddish-gold slanting pillar of light that picked out motes turning in the air. It could have been light reflected from an adjacent window; it did not matter. At the time it seemed an auspicious sign. Just in front of the wedge of sunlight lay the envelope. Beyond it, perfectly still, stood Maria. She wore a thick tartan skirt and a red cashmere sweater, American made, a present from the devoted treasurer which she had neither the selflessness nor the hardness of heart to return.

They stared at each other across the light, and neither of them spoke. Leonard was trying to formulate a greeting in the form of an apology. But how to explain away something so willed as the opening of a door? Confusing his responses was his joy in having her beauty confirmed. He had been right to be so disturbed. For her part, during the seconds before she recognized him, Maria had been immobilized by fear. This sudden apparition stirred ten-year-old memories of soldiers, usually in pairs, pushing open doors unannounced. Leonard misjudged her expression as the understandable hostility of a householder for an intruder. And he misread the quick faint smile of recognition and relief as forgiveness.

Testing his luck, he advanced a couple of steps and put out

his hand. "Leonard Marnham," he said. "You remember. The Resi?"

Even though she no longer felt she was in danger, Maria took a step backward and crossed her arms over her chest. "What do you want?"

It worked in Leonard's favor that he was so put out by such a direct question. He blushed, fumbled, and then for an answer picked up the envelope and handed it to her. She opened it, spread out the single sheet, and before reading glanced over the top to make sure he was coming no closer. The flash of the whites of those serious eyes! Leonard stood helpless. He remembered his father reading his mediocre end-of-term reports in his presence. Just as he had imagined, she read the note over twice.

"What does it mean, this 'pop up'? Just to open my door, is this a pop up?" He was about to offer an explanation, but she was beginning to laugh. "And you wish that I come to Bei Tante Else? Tante Else, the *Nuttenkneipe?*" To his amazement, she began to sing. It was from a number they were always playing on AFN, "Take Back Your Mink." What made him think that she was one of those girls? To be mocked by the impossible sweetness of a German girl's attempt at a Bronx accent—Leonard thought he might faint. He was miserable, he was exhilarated. Desperate for composure, he used his little finger to settle his specs on the bridge of his nose. "Actually," he began, but she was stepping round him to the door and saying mock sternly, "And why have you come to see me without the flower in the hair?" She closed the door and locked it. She was all smiles as she clasped her hands. It really seemed to be the case, she was delighted to see him. "Now," she said. "Isn't it time for tea?"

The room they were in was approximately ten feet by ten. Without standing on tiptoe, Leonard could press his palm against the ceiling. The view from the window was across the courtyard to a wall of similar windows. By standing up close and peering down, it was possible to see the dustbins lying on their sides. Maria had removed an advanced English grammar from the only comfortable chair so that he could sit while she busied herself in the curtained recess. Leonard could see his breath in the air, so he kept his coat on. He had grown used to overheated American interiors at the warehouse, and every room in his apartment had a ferocious radiator regulated from somewhere in the basement. He was shivering, but here even the cold was charged with possibility. He was sharing it with Maria.

By the window was a dining table on which stood a cactus in a bowl. Next to it was a candle in a wine bottle. There were two kitchen chairs, a bookcase and a stained Persian rug laid on bare boards. Pinned to the wall by what Leonard took to be the bedroom door was a black-and-white reproduction of Van Gogh's *Sunflowers,* cut out from a magazine. There was nothing else to look at apart from a jumble of shoes in a corner heaped around an iron cobbler's last. Maria's room could not have resembled less the polished and orderly clutter of the Marnham living room in Tottenham, with its mahogany radio/record player and the *Encyclopaedia Britannica* in a special case. This room made no claims. It would be possible to leave tomorrow without regret, taking nothing. It was a room that managed to be both spare and untidy. It was grubby and intimate. It might be possible to say exactly what you felt here. You could begin again with yourself. To one who had grown up edging round his mother's porcelain figurines, ever careful not to mark her walls with his fingers, it was strange and wonderful that this unfussy stripped-down room should belong to a woman.

She was emptying a teapot into the small kitchen sink where two saucepans balanced on top of a pile of dirty plates. He was sitting at the dining table watching the thick material of her skirt, how it moved in delayed motion, how the warm cashmere just covered the tops of the pleats and how she wore football socks inside carpet slippers. All this winter wool was reassuring to Leonard, who felt easily threatened by a provocatively dressed woman. Wool suggested undemanding intimacy, and body warmth, and a body hiding cosily, demurely, in the folds. She was making tea in the English style. She had a coronation caddy, and she was warming the pot. This too put Leonard at his ease.

In response to his question, she was telling him that when she had first started work at Twelve Armoured Workshops, REME, it had been her job to make tea three times a day for the CO and the second-in-command. She set down on the table two Army issue white mugs, exactly the same as the ones he had in his apartment. He had been entertained to tea a number of times by young women, but he had never met one who did not trouble to decant the milk into a jug.

She sat across from him and they warmed their hands around the big mugs. He knew from experience that unless he made a formidable effort, a pattern was waiting to impose itself: a polite inquiry would elicit a polite response and another question. Have you lived here long? Do you travel far to your work? Is it your afternoon off? The catechism would have begun. Only silences would interrupt the relentless tread of question and answer. They would be calling to each other over immense distances, from adjacent mountain peaks. Finally he would be desperate for the relief of heading away with his own thoughts, after the awkward goodbyes. Even now, they had already retreated from the intensity of their greeting. He had asked her about tea making. One more like that, and there would be nothing he could do.

She had set down her mug and had put her hands deep in the pockets of her skirt. She was tapping her slippered feet on the rug. Her head was cocked, with expectation perhaps, or was she marking time to the tune in her head? Was it still the song she had teased him with? He had never known a woman to tap her feet, but he knew he must not panic.

It was an assumption, lodged deep, beyond examination or even awareness, that the responsibility for the event was entirely his. If he could not find the easy words to bring them closer, the defeat would be his alone. What could he say that was neither trivial nor intrusive? She had taken up her mug again and was looking at him now with a half-smile that did not quite part her lips. "Aren't you lonely living here by yourself?" sounded too wheedlingly suggestive. She might think he was offering to move in.

Rather than tolerate more silence, he settled after all for small talk and began to ask, "Have you lived here long?"

But all in a rush she spoke over him, saying, "How do you look without your glasses? Show me, please." This last word she elongated beyond what any native speaker would have considered reasonable, unfurling a delicate, papery thrill through Leonard's stomach. He snatched the glasses from his face and blinked at her. He could see quite well up to three feet, and her features had only partially dissolved. "And so," she said quietly. "It is how I thought. Your eyes are beautiful, and all the time they are hidden. Has no one told you how they are beautiful?"

Leonard's mother used to say something of the sort when he was fifteen and he had his first pair, but that was hardly relevant. He had the sensation of rising gently through the room.

She took the glasses and folded down the sides and put them by the cactus.

His voice sounded strangled in his ears. "No, no one has said that."

"Not other girls?"

He shook his head.

"Then I am the first to discover you?" There was humor, but no mockery, in her look.

It made him feel foolish, immature, to be grinning so openly at her compliment, but he could do nothing about it.

She said, "And your smile."

She smoothed away a wisp of hair from her eyes. Her forehead, so high and oval, reminded him of how Shakespeare was supposed to look. He was not certain how to put this to her. Instead he took her hand as it completed its movement and they sat in silence for a minute or two, as they had at their first meeting. She interlocked her fingers with his, and it was at this moment, rather than later in the bedroom, or later still when they talked of themselves with greater freedom, that Leonard felt irrevocably bound to her. Their hands fitted well, the grip was intricate, unbreakable, there were so many points of contact. In this poor light, and without his glasses, he could not see which fingers were his own. Sitting in the darkening, chilly room in his raincoat, holding on to her hand, he felt he was throwing away his life.

The abandonment was delicious. Something was pouring out of him, through his palm and into hers; something was spreading back up his arm, across his chest, constricting his throat. His only thought was a repetition: so this is it, it's like this, so this is it . . .

Finally she pulled her hand away and folded her arms and looked at him expectantly. For no good reason other than the seriousness of her look, he began to explain himself. "I should have come sooner," he said, "but I've been working all hours of the day and night. And actually, I didn't know if you'd want to see me, or if you'd even recognize me."

"Do you have another friend in Berlin?"

"Oh no, nothing like that." He did not question her right to ask this question.

"And did you have many girlfriends in England?"

"Not many, no."

"How many?"

He hesitated before making a lunge at the truth. "Well, actually, none."

"You've never had one?"

"No."

Maria leaned forward. "You mean, you've never—"

He could not bear to hear whatever term she was about to use. "No, I never have."

She put her hand to her mouth to stifle a yelp of laughter. It was not so extraordinary a thing in 1955 for a man of Leonard's background and temperament to have had no sexual experience by the end of his twenty-fifth year. But it was a remarkable thing for a man to confess. He regretted it immediately. She had the laughter under control, but now she was blushing. It was the interlocking fingers that had made him think he could get away with speaking without pretense. In this bare little room with its pile of assorted shoes belonging to a woman who lived alone and did not fuss with milk jugs or doilies on tea trays, it should have been possible to deal in unadorned truths.

And in fact it was. Maria's blushes were brought on by shame at the laughter she knew Leonard would misunderstand. For hers was the laughter of nervous relief. She had been suddenly absolved from the pressures and rituals of seduction. She would not have to adopt a conventional role and be judged in it, and she would not be measured against other women. Her fear of being physically abused had receded. She would not be obliged to do anything she did not want. She was free, they both were free, to invent their own terms. They could be partners in invention. And she really had discovered for herself this shy Englishman with the steady gaze and the long lashes, she had him first, she would have him all to herself. These thoughts she formulated later in solitude. At the time they erupted in the single hoot of relief and hilarity which she had suppressed to a yelp.

Leonard took a long pull of his tea, set down the mug and said *Ah* in a hearty, unconvincing way. He put his glasses on and stood up. After the handclasp, nothing seemed bleaker than setting off back down Adalbertstrasse, descending into the U-Bahn and arriving at his apartment in the early evening darkness to find the breakfast coffee cup and the drafts of his foolish letter all over the floor. He saw it all before him as he adjusted the belt of his coat, but he knew that with his confession he had made a humiliating tactical error and he had to go. That Maria should blush for him made her all the sweeter, and hinted at the scale of his blunder.

She had stood too and was blocking his path to the door.

"I really ought to be getting back now," Leonard explained, "what with work and everything." The worse he felt, the lighter his tone became. He was stepping around her as he said, "You make a terrific cup of tea."

Maria said, "I want you to stay longer."

It was all he wanted to hear, but by now he was too low to enact a change of heart, too drawn to his own defeat. He was on his way to the door. "I have to meet someone at six." The lie was a hopeless commitment to his anguish. Even as it was happening, he was amazed by himself. He wanted to stay, she wanted him to stay, and here he was, insisting on leaving. It was the behavior of a stranger, and he could do nothing, he could not steer himself in the direction of his own interests. Self-pity had obliterated his habitual and meticulous good sense, he was in a tunnel whose only end was his own fascinating annihilation.

He was fumbling with the unfamiliar lock and Maria was right at his back. Though it still surprised her, she was to some extent familiar with the delicacy of masculine pride. Despite a surface assurance, men were easily offended. Their moods could swing wildly. Caught in the turbulence of unacknowledged emotions, they tended to mask their uncertainty with aggression. She was thirty; her experience was not vast, and she was thinking mostly of her husband and one or two violent soldiers she had known. The man scrabbling to leave by her front door was less like the men she had known and more like herself. She knew just how it felt. When you felt sorry for yourself, you wanted to make things worse. She was touching his back lightly, but he was not aware of it through his coat. He thought he had made his plausible excuses and was free to depart with his misery. To Maria, who had the liberation of Berlin and her marriage to Otto Eckdorf behind her, a display of vulnerability of any kind in a man suggested an approachable personality.

He opened the door at last and turned to say his goodbyes. Did he really believe that she was fooled by his politeness and the invented appointment, or that his desperation was invisible? He was telling her he was sorry he had to dash off, and expressing gratitude for the tea again, and offering his hand —a handshake!—when she reached up and lifted his glasses clear of his face and strode back into her living room with them. Before he had even started to follow her, she had slipped them under a chair cushion.

"Look here," he said, and, letting the door close behind him, took one step, then another, into the apartment. And that was it; he was back in. He had wanted to stay; now he had to. "I really do have to be going." He stood in the center of the tiny room, irresolute, still attempting to fake his hesitant English form of outrage.

She stood close so he could see her clearly. How wonderful it was, not to be frightened of a man. It gave her a chance to like him, to have desires that were not simply reactions to his. She took his hands in hers. "But I haven't finished looking at your eyes." Then, with the Berlin girl's forthrightness that Russell had praised, she added, *"Du Dummer! Wenn es für dich das erste Mal ist, bin ich sehr glücklich.* If this is your first time, then I am a very lucky girl."

It was her "this" that held Leonard. He was back with "this." What they were doing here was all part of "this," his first time. He looked down at her face, that disk, tipped way back to accommodate the seven-inch difference in their heights. From the top third of the neat oval, the baby hair fell back in loose curls and straggles. She was not the first young woman he had kissed, but she was the first who seemed to like it. Encouraged, he pushed his tongue into her mouth, the way, he had gathered, one was supposed to.

She drew her face back an inch or so. She said, "*Langsam.* Plenty of time." So they kissed with a teasing lightness. The very tips of their tongues just touched, and it was a greater pleasure. Then Maria stepped round him and pulled out from among the heap of shoes an electric heater. "There is time," she repeated. "We can pass a week with our arms just so." She embraced herself to show him.

"That's right," he said. "We could do that." His voice sounded high-pitched. He followed her into the bedroom.

It was larger than the room they had left. There was a double mattress on the floor—another novelty. One wall was taken up with a gloomy wardrobe of polished wood. By the window was a painted chest of drawers and a linen chest. He sat on the linen chest and watched her plug in the heater.

"It is too cold to be undressed. We go in like this." It was true, you could see the vapor on your breath. She kicked off her slippers; he untied his laces and took off his coat. They got under the eiderdown and lay with their arms round each other in the way she had prescribed, and kissed again.

It was not a week but several hours, just after midnight, before Leonard was able to define himself in strictest terms as an initiate, a truly mature adult at last. However, the line that divided innocence from knowledge was vague, and rapturously so. As the bed, and to a far lesser extent the room, warmed up, they set about helping each other undress. As the pile on the floor grew—sweaters, thick shirts, woolen underwear and football socks—so the bed, and time itself, grew more spacious. Maria, luxuriating in the possibility of shaping the event to her needs, said this was just the right moment for her to be kissed and licked all over, from the toes upward. This was how Leonard, halfway through a characteristically meticulous job, came to enter her first with his tongue. That surely was the dividing line in his life. But so too was the moment half an hour later when she took him into her mouth and licked and sucked and did something with her teeth. In terms of mere physical sensation, this was the high point of the six hours, and perhaps of his life.

There was a long interlude when they lay still, and in answer to her questions he told her about his school, his parents and his lonely three years at Birmingham University. She talked more reticently about her work, the cycling club and the amorous treasurer, and her ex-husband, Otto, who had been a sergeant in the army and was now a drunk. Two months before he had appeared after a year's absence and had hit her around the head twice with an open hand and demanded money. This was not the first time he had intimidated her, but the local police would do nothing. Sometimes they even bought him drinks. Otto had persuaded them he was a war hero.

This story temporarily erased desire. Gallantly, Leonard got dressed and went down to Oranienstrasse to buy a bottle of wine. People and traffic circulated, oblivious of the great changes. When he returned she was standing at the stove in a man's dressing gown and her football socks, cooking a potato and mushroom omelette. They ate it in bed with black bread. The Mosel was sugary and rough. They drank it in the tea mugs and insisted it was good. Whenever he put a piece of bread in his mouth, he smelled her on his fingers. She had brought in the candle in the bottle, and now she lit it. The cosy squalor of clothes and greasy plates receded into the shadows. The sulfur smell of the match hung in the air and mixed with the smell on his fingers. He tried to recall and recount in an amusing way a sermon he had once heard at school about the devil and temptation and a woman's body. But Maria misunderstood, or saw no reason why he should be telling her this or finding it funny, and she became cross and silent. They lay propped on their elbows in the gloom, sipping from their mugs. After a while he touched the back of her hand and said, "Sorry. A stupid story." She forgave him by turning her hand and squeezing his fingers.

She curled up on his arm and slept for half an hour. During that time he lay back, feeling proud. He studied her face—how scant her eyebrows were, how her lower lip swelled in sleep—and he thought what it would be to have a child, a daughter who might sleep on him like this. When she woke up she was fresh. She wanted him to lie on her. He cuddled up and sucked her nipples. They kissed, and it was acceptable this time when he was free with his tongue. They poured out the rest of the wine and she chinked his mug.

Of what followed he remembered only two things. The first was that it was rather like going to see a film that everybody else had been talking about: difficult to imagine in advance, but once there, installed, partly recognition, partly surprises. The encompassing slippery smoothness, for example, was much as he had hoped—even better, in fact—while nothing in his extensive reading had prepared him for the crinkly sensation of having another's pubic hair pressed against his own. The second was awkward. He had read all about premature ejaculation and wondered if he would suffer, and now it seemed he might. It was not movement that threatened to bring him on. It was when he looked at her face. She was lying on her back, for they were what she had taught him to call *auf Altdeutsch*. Sweat had restyled her hair into snaky coils and her arms were thrown up behind her head, with the palms spread, like a co nic-book representation of surrender. At the same time she was looking up at him in a knowing, kindly way. It was just this combination of abandonment and loving attention that was too good to be looked at, too perfect for him, and he had to avert his eyes, or close them, and think of . . . of, yes, a circuit diagram, a particularly intricate and lovely one he had committed to memory during the fitting of signal activation units to the Ampex machines.

7 IT TOOK FOUR WEEKS to test all the tape recorders and fit the signal activation units. Leonard was content working in his windowless room. The very repetitiveness of his routine absorbed him. When another ten machines were ready, a young serviceman came and loaded them onto a rubber-wheeled cart and took them along the corridor to the recording room. Already more people were working in there, some of them from England. But Leonard had not been introduced, and he avoided them. In his spare moments he liked to doze, and in the canteen he always took an empty table. Glass came by once or twice a week, always in a hurry. Like all the other Americans he chewed gum, but with a frenzy that was all his own. This and the livid semicircles under his eyes gave him the appearance of an anxious nocturnal rodent. There were no gray hairs in his beard, but it looked less black. It was dried out and shapeless.

His manner, though, was unchanged. "We're running on schedule, Leonard," he would say from the doorway, too busy to step in. "We're almost to the far side of the Schönefelder Chaussee. We got new people arriving every day. The place is humming!" And he would be gone before Leonard had time to put down his soldering iron.

It was true—after mid-February it became harder to find an unoccupied table in the canteen. In the noise of voices around him he could make out English accents. When he asked for his steak now, he was automatically handed a cup of tea into which three or four spoonfuls of sugar had already been stirred. For the benefit of the Vopos with their binoculars, many of the Englishmen wore American Army uniforms bearing the insignia of the Army Signal Corps. The vertical diggers had arrived, the specialists who knew how to tunnel upward to the telephone cables through soft earth without bringing the roof down on their heads. So too had men from the Royal Signals, who were to install the amplifiers near the head of the tunnel. There were faces Leonard recognized from Dollis Hill. A couple of these fellows nodded in his direction, but did not approach. It was possible they were being scrupulous about security, but it was more likely they considered a technical assistant beneath them. They had never spoken to him in London.

And security in the canteen was not tight. As the numbers eating there rose, so did the din of conversation. Glass would have been outraged. Small groups from all over the building talked shop in closed huddles. Leonard, eating alone, enfolded with his thoughts of Maria, still amazed at the changes that had come over his life, was sometimes drawn against his will into a story at a nearby table. His world had contracted to a windowless room and the bed he shared with Maria. Elsewhere in her apartment it was simply too cold. He had made himself an outsider here, and now he was becoming a reluctant eavesdropper, a spy.

He heard two vertical diggers at the next table reminisce with suppressed hilarity in front of their American colleagues. It appeared that the tunnel had a predecessor in Vienna. It had been dug in 1949 by MI6 and ran from a private house in the Schwechat suburb seventy feet out under a road, where it picked up the cables linking the headquarters of the Soviet occupation forces in the Imperial Hotel with the Soviet command in Moscow. "They needed a cover, see," one of the diggers said. A companion laid a hand on his arm, and the first man continued quietly, so that Leonard had to concentrate. "They needed a cover for all the coming and going while they installed the tap. So they opened up a Harris tweed import shop. They reckoned no one in Vienna would be too interested in that kind of thing. And what happened? The locals couldn't get enough Harris tweed. They were queuing up for it, and the first shipment was sold out in days. So there were these poor buggers filling out order forms all day and answering the phone instead of getting on with their business. They had to turn customers away and close the place down."

"And then," the American said when the laughter had died away, "our guy walked right into your act."

"That's right," the Englishman said. "That was Nelson, Nelson . . ." And it was this name, which Leonard was to hear again, that brought the group to the full awareness of its transgression. The conversation turned to sport.

Another time, a different group of tunnelers, vertical as well as horizontal, were comparing notes. The purpose of nearly all the stories Leonard heard was to entertain. The Americans recounted how they had had to shovel their way through the runoff of their own cesspit. Again there was loud laughter, and an English voice said to more laughter, "Digging through your own shit, that just about sums this business up." Then one of the American sergeants told how the sixteen of them, all hand-picked for the job, had been made to dig a practice tunnel in New Mexico before they started in Berlin. "Same kind of soil, was the idea. They wanted to figure out the optimum depth and check out if there was going to be any kind of slump on the surface, so we dug—" "And dug, and dug . . . " his friends joined in. "After fifty feet they had all they needed for the best depth, and there was no slump. But would they let us stop? You want a picture of futility? It's a tunnel in the desert, from nowhere to nowhere, four hundred and fifty feet long. Four hundred and fifty feet!"

One conversation the diners had frequently concerned how long it would take the Russians or the East Germans to smash through into the tap chamber, and what would happen when they did. Would the operators have time to get clear, would the Vopos shoot, would there be time to close the steel doors? There had once been a plan to install incendiary devices to destroy classified equipment, but the fire risks were thought too great. On one matter everybody was agreed, and Glass confirmed this too. There had even been a CIA study. If the Russians ever did break in, they would have to keep quiet about it. The embarrassment of having their top military lines tapped would be too great. "There are silences and silences," Glass had told Leonard. "But there's nothing like the great Russian silence."

There was another story Leonard heard several times. Its form changed only slightly with the retelling, and it worked best on newcomers, on people who were not yet acquainted with George. So in mid-February it was often heard in the canteen. Leonard first heard it while he was waiting in the queue. Bill Harvey, the head of the Berlin CIA base, a remote and powerful figure whom Leonard had never even glimpsed, occasionally visited the tunnel to check on progress. Because Harvey was conspicuous around Berlin, he came only at night. On one occasion he sat in the backseat of his car and overheard his driver and the GI beside him complain about their social life.

"I'm getting nowhere, and boy, am I ready for it," said one.

"Me too," said his friend. "But George is out there every afternoon, screwing by the fence."

"Lucky George."

The men at the warehouse were supposed to be kept in relative isolation. There was no telling what they might divulge to a fräulein in a moment of weakness. The extent of Harvey's anger when he arrived that night depended on the storyteller. In some versions he simply asked to see the duty officer; in others he stormed into the building in an alcohol-driven rage and the duty officer quivered before him. "Find this asshole George and get him out of here!" Inquiries were made. George was in fact a dog, a local mongrel adopted as the warehouse mascot. In further elaborations, Harvey was supposed to have responded with face-saving calmness. "I don't care what he thinks he is. He's making my men unhappy. Get rid of him."

At the end of four weeks Leonard's great task was over. The last four tape recorders to be fitted with signal activation were packed into two specially constructed cases with snap locks and canvas straps for extra security. The machines were to be used for monitoring purposes at the head of the tunnel. The cases were loaded onto the cart and taken down into the basement. Leonard locked his room and wandered down the corridor to the recording room. It was lit by hooded fluorescent lamps and was large, but not quite large enough to accommodate comfortably the 150 machines and all the men who were working around them. The recorders were stacked three high on metal shelves and arranged in five rows. Down the aisles there were people on their hands and knees tracing power cables and other circuits, and stepping over and around them were others with spools of tape, in and out trays, numbered signs and gummed paper. Two fitters were drilling into the wall with power tools, preparing to secure a twenty-foot-long set of pigeonholes to the wall. Someone else was already gluing pieces of card with code numbers under each compartment. By the door was a head-high pile of stationery and spare recording tape in plain white boxes. On the other side of the door, right in the corner, was a hole in the floor through which cables dropped down into the basement, down the shaft and along the tunnel to where the amplifiers were about to be installed.

Leonard was at the warehouse for almost a year before he understood the operating system in the recording room. The vertical diggers were scraping their way upward to a ditch on the far side of the Schönefelder Chaussee in which three cables lay buried. Each one contained 172 circuits carrying at least 18 channels. The twenty-four-hour babble of the Soviet command network consisted of telephone conversations and encoded telegraph messages. In the recording room only two or three circuits were monitored. The movements of the Vopos and the East German telephone repair crews were matters of immediate interest. If ever the tunnel was about to be discovered—if the beast, as Glass sometimes called the other side, was ready to break in and threaten the lives of our people—the earliest warnings would come over these lines. As for the rest, the taped telephone conversations were flown to London and the telegraph messages to Washington for decoding, all in military planes, under armed guard. Scores of workers, many of them Russian émigrés, toiled in small rooms in Whitehall and in the temporary huts that littered the way between the Washington Monument and the Lincoln Memorial.

Standing by the entrance to the recording room on the day he finished, Leonard was concerned only to find himself a new job. He teamed up with an older German, one of Gehlen's men, whom he had seen on his first day driving a forklift. Germans were no longer ex-Nazis, they were Maria's compatriots. So he and Fritz, who had once trained as an electrician and whose real name was Rudi, stripped wires and made connections at junction boxes, and fitted protective covers over power lines and secured them to the floor so that no one would trip on them. After an initial exchange of first names, they worked in comradely silence, passing the wire-strippers between them and making encouraging grunts whenever one small job was complete. Leonard took it as a sign of his new maturity that he could work contentedly alongside the man Glass had described as a real horror. Rudi's big fingers with splayed ends were swift and precise. The afternoon lights came on, coffee was brought. While the Englishman sat on the floor with his back against the wall, smoking a cigarette, Rudi kept at it and refused refreshment.

In the late afternoon people began drifting away. By six Leonard and Rudi had the room to themselves, and they worked faster to complete a final set of connections. At last Leonard stood up and stretched. Now he could allow himself to think again of Kreuzberg and Maria. He could be there in less than an hour.

He was fetching his jacket from the back of a chair when he heard his name being spoken from the door. A man too thin for his double-breasted suit was coming toward him with his hand extended. Rudi, who was on his way out, stepped aside and called *"Gute Nacht"* to Leonard over the stranger's shoulder. Leonard had his jacket half on and was returning the good night as he shook the man's hand. During this little flurry, Leonard was making the automatic, barely conscious appraisal of manner, appearance and voice by means of which one Englishman decodes another's status.

"John MacNamee. We've got someone fallen sick and I'll be needing another pair of hands at the tunnel head next week. It's all clear with Glass. I've got half an hour now if you want me to show you around." MacNamee had buck teeth, and very few of them—little pegs set far apart, and rather brown. Hence the slight lisp in a delivery from which the Cockney had not been fully expunged. The voice was almost chummy. A refusal was not expected. MacNamee was already leading the way out of the recording room, but his authority was lightly worn.

Leonard guessed that this was a senior government scientist. A couple of them had been his teachers at Birmingham, and there were one or two in and around the G.P.O. research laboratory at Dollis Hill. Theirs was a special generation of unpretentious, gifted men, brought into prominent government service in the forties by the necessities of modern scientific warfare. Leonard respected the ones he had met. They did not make him feel clumsy and short of the right word the way the public-school boys did—the ones who would not speak to him in the canteen and who were all set to rise through the hierarchies of command by dint of a reasonable grasp of Latin and ancient Greek.

Down in the basement they had to stand and wait by the shaft. Someone in front of them was having difficulty finding his pass for the guard. Near where they stood, the earth piled to the ceiling exuded its cold stench. MacNamee stamped his feet on the muddy concrete and clasped his bony white hands. On the way Leonard had taken from his room a greatcoat Glass had found for him, but MacNamee had only his gray suit.

"It'll be warm enough down there when we get those amplifiers running. It could even be a problem," he said. "Enjoying the work?"

"It's a very interesting project."

"You fitted out all the recorders. That must have got boring."

Leonard knew it was unwise to complain to a superior, even when prompted. MacNamee was showing his pass and signing for his guest. "It wasn't so bad, really."

He followed the older man down the ladder, into the pit. By the mouth of the tunnel MacNamee supported his foot against a railway line and bent to retie his lace. His voice was muffled, and Leonard had to stoop to hear. "What's your clearance, Marnham?" The guard at the edge of the shaft was looking down at them. Could he possibly believe, like the sentries on the gate, that he was guarding a warehouse, or even a radar station?

Leonard waited until MacNamee had straightened and they had stepped into the tunnel. The fluorescent striplights barely dispersed the blackness. The acoustic was dead. Leonard's voice sounded flat in his ears. "Actually, it's level three."

MacNamee was walking ahead of him, his hands deep in his trouser pockets for warmth. "Well, I suppose we might have to bring you into four. I'll see about that tomorrow."

They were making a shallow descent as they walked between the rails. There were puddles underfoot, and on the walls, where the steel plates had been bolted together to make a continuous tube, condensation glistened. There was a constant hum of a groundwater pump. On both sides of the tunnel sandbags were piled to shoulder height to support cables and pipes. A number of bags had split and were spilling their contents. Earth and water were pressing in on all sides, waiting to reclaim the space.

They arrived at a place where tight coils of barbed wire were stacked by a pile of sandbags. MacNamee waited for Leonard to draw level. "We're stepping into the Russian sector now. When they break in on us, which is bound to happen one of these days, we're meant to spread the wire across as we retreat. Make them respect the border." He smiled at his little irony, revealing his pitiful teeth. They teetered at all angles, like old gravestones. He caught Leonard's gaze. He tapped his mouth with his forefinger and spoke right into the younger man's embarrassment. "Milk teeth. The other lot never came through. I think perhaps I never wanted to grow up."

They continued along level ground. A hundred yards ahead a group of men stepped through a steel door and came toward them. They appeared deep in conversation, but as they came closer, Leonard realized they were making no sound. They jostled in and out of single file. When they were thirty feet away Leonard caught the sibilants of their whispers. Those ceased too as the two groups squeezed by each other with wary nods.

"The general rule is no noise, especially once you've crossed the border." MacNamee was speaking in a voice fractionally above a whisper. "As you know, low frequencies, men's voices, penetrate very easily."

Leonard whispered "Yes," but his reply was lost to the sound of the pumps.

Running along the tops of the twin banks of sandbags were power lines, the air-conditioning conduit and the lines from the recording room, encased in a lead sheath. Along the way there were telephones mounted on the wall, and fire extinguishers, fuseboxes, emergency power switches. At intervals there were green and red warning lights, like miniature traffic signals. It was a toytown, packed with boyish invention. Leonard remembered the secret camps, the tunnels through the undergrowth he used to make with friends in a scrap of woodland near his house. And the gigantic train set in Hamleys, the toy store—the safe world of its motionless sheep and cows cropping the sudden green hills that were no more than pretexts for tunnels. Tunnels were stealth and safety; boys and trains crept through them, lost to sight and care, and then emerged unscathed.

MacNamee murmured in his ear again. "I tell you what I like about this project. The attitude. Once the Americans decide to do a thing, they do it well, and hang the cost. I've had everything I wanted, never a murmur. None of this can-you-get-by-with-half-a-ball-of-string nonsense."

Leonard was flattered to be confided in. He tried to be humorous in agreement. "Look at all the trouble they take with the food. I love the way they do their chips."

MacNamee looked away. It seemed this puerile observation drifted with them down the tunnel until they reached the steel door.

Beyond it was air-conditioning equipment banked up on both sides to make a narrow corridor of the railway lines.

They edged past an American technician who was working there and opened a second door.

"Now," MacNamee said as he closed it behind him. "What do you think?"

They had entered a brightly lit section of the tunnel that was clean and well ordered. The walls were lined with plywood that had been painted white. The railway lines had disappeared under a concrete floor, which was covered with linoleum. From overhead came the rumble of traffic on the Schönefelder Chaussee. Wedged between racks of electronics were tidy workspaces, plywood surfaces with headsets and the monitoring tape recorders. Neatly stowed on the floor were the cases Leonard had sent down that day. He was not being asked to admire the amplifier. He knew the model from Dollis Hill. It was powerful, compact and weighed less than forty pounds. It was about the most expensive item in the lab where he had worked. It was not the machine, it was the sheer quantity of them, and the switching gear, all down one side of the tunnel, stretching ninety feet perhaps, stacked head high, like the interior of a telephone exchange. It was the quantity MacNamee was proud of, the handling capacity, the amplifying power and the feat of circuitry it implied. By the door, the lead-sheathed cables broke into multicolored strands, fanning out to junction points from which they emerged in smaller clusters held by rubber clips. Three men of the Royal Signals were at work. They nodded at MacNamee and ignored Leonard. The two men passed along the array at a stately pace, as though reviewing a guard of honor. MacNamee said, "Near on a quarter of a million pounds' worth. We're drawing off a tiniest fraction of the Russian signals, so we need the best there is."

Since his remark about the chips, Leonard was confining his appreciation to nods and sighs. He was thinking about an intelligent question he might put, and only half listened while MacNamee described the technicalities of the circuitry. Close attention was not necessary. MacNamee's pride in the bright white amplification room was impersonal. He liked to see the achievement afresh through the eyes of a newcomer, and any eyes would do.

Leonard was still working on his question as they approached a second steel door. MacNamee stopped by it. "This one is a double door. We're going to keep the tap room pressurized to stop the nitrogen leak." Leonard nodded again. The Russian cables would have nitrogen sealed within them to keep moisture out and to help monitor breaks. Pressurizing the air around the cables would make it possible to cut into them undetected.

MacNamee pushed open the doors, and Leonard followed him in. It was as though they had stepped inside a drum being beaten by a wild man. Road noise was filling the vertical tunnel and reverberating in the tap chamber. MacNamee stepped over empty sacks of sound insulation piled on the floor and took a torch from a table. They stood at the base of the access tunnel. Right up in its roof, picked out by the narrow beam, were the three cables, each four or five inches thick and caked in mud. MacNamee was about to speak, but the pounding intensified to a frenzy and they had to wait. When it subsided he said, "Horse and cart. They're the worst. When we're ready, we'll use a hydraulic jack to pull the cables down. Then we'll need a day and a half to cement the roof for support. We won't make the cut until all the backup is in shape. We'll bridge the circuits first and then break in and lead off. There's likely to be more than a hundred and fifty circuits in each cable. There'll be an MI6 technician laying the actual tap, and three standing by in case something goes wrong. We've one man off sick, so you might have to be in the support group."

While he was speaking, MacNamee rested his hand on Leonard's shoulder. They came away from the shaft to be out of the worst of the noise.

"Well, I have got a question," Leonard said, "but you might not want to answer it."

The government scientist shrugged. Leonard found that he wanted his approval. "Surely all the important military traffic will be encoded and telegraphed. How are we going to read it? These modern codes are meant to be virtually unbreakable."

MacNamee took a pipe from his jacket pocket and bit on its stem. Smoking, of course, was out of the question.

"This is what I wanted to speak to you about. You haven't been talking to anyone?"

"No."

"Have you heard of a man called Nelson, Carl Nelson? Worked for the CIA's Office of Communications?"

"No."

MacNamee was leading the way back through the double doors. He bolted them before they walked on. "This is level four now. We were going to let you in, I think. You're about to join an exclusive club." They had stopped again, this time by the first rack of amplifying equipment. At the far end the three men worked on in silence, well out of earshot. As MacNamee spoke he ran his finger along the front of an amplifier, perhaps to give the impression that he was discussing it. "I'll give you the simple version. It's been discovered that when you electrically encode a message and send it down the line, there's a faint electronic echo, a shadow of the original, of the clear text, that travels with it. It's so faint that it fades out after twenty miles or so. But with the right equipment, and if you can tap into the line within the twenty miles, you can have a readable message coming straight onto the teleprinter, no matter how well the material has been encoded. This is the basis for the whole operation here. We wouldn't be building something on this scale just to listen to low-priority telephone chat. It was Nelson's discovery, and the equipment was his invention. He was walking about in Vienna looking for a good place to try it out on the Russian lines when he walked right into a tunnel we had built to tap those same lines. So, very generously, we let the Americans into our tunnel, gave them facilities, let them make use of our taps. And you know what? They didn't even tell us about Nelson's invention. They were taking the stuff back to Washington and reading the clear text while we were knocking our brains trying to break the codes. And these are our allies. Bloody incredible, don't you think?" He paused for confirmation. "Now that we're sharing this project, they've let us in on the secret. But only the outline, mark you, not the details. That's why I can only give you the simplest account."

Two of the Royal Signals people were walking toward them. MacNamee steered Leonard back in the direction of the tap chamber. "On the need-to-know basis, you shouldn't be getting any of this. You're probably wondering what I'm up to. Well, they've promised to share whatever they come up with. And we have to take that on trust. But we're not prepared to live off the crumbs from their table. That's not our understanding of this relationship. We're developing our own version of Nelson's technique, and we've found some marvelous potential sites. We're not talking to the Americans about them. Speed is important because sooner or later the Russians are going to make the same discovery, and then they'll modify their machines. There's a Dollis Hill team working on it, but it would be useful to have someone here keeping his ears and eyes open. We think there might be one or two Americans here who know about Nelson's equipment. We need someone with a technical background, and not too highly placed. As soon as they see me, these people run a mile. It's the details we're after, odds and ends of electronics gossip, anything that might help things along. You know how careless the Yanks can be. They talk; things are left lying around."

They had stopped by the double steel doors. "So. What do you think?" It almost sounded like "fink."

"They're all very chatty in the canteen," Leonard said. "Even our own chaps."

"You'll do it, then? Good. We'll talk more later. Let's go up and have some tea. I'm freezing to death."

They went back along the tunnel, into the American sector, up the incline. It was hard not to feel proud of the tunnel. Leonard remembered before the war when his father built a small brick extension onto the kitchen. Leonard lent a child's token assistance, fetching a trowel, taking a list to the hardware shop and so on. When it was all finished, and before the breakfast table and chairs were moved in, he stood in the new space with its plaster walls, electrical fittings and homemade window, and he felt quite delirious with his own achievement.

Back in the warehouse, Leonard excused himself from tea in the canteen. Now that he had MacNamee's approval, his gratitude even, he felt confident and free. On his way out of the building he looked in at his room. The absence of tape recorders on the shelves was itself a small triumph. He locked the door and took the key to the duty officer's room. He crossed the compound, passed the sentry at the gate and set off for Rudow. The road was dark, but he knew every step of the way now. His greatcoat gave poor protection against the cold. He could feel the hairs in his nostrils stiffening. When he breathed through his mouth, the air stung his chest. He could sense the frozen flat fields around him. He passed the shacks where refugees from the Russian sector had set up home. There were kids playing in the dark, and as his steps rang out on the cold road, they shushed each other and waited until he had passed. Every yard away from the warehouse was a yard toward Maria. He had spoken to no one about her at work, and he could not talk to her about what he did. He was not certain whether this time spent traveling between his two secret worlds was when he was truly himself, when he was able to hold the two in balance and know them to be separate from himself; or whether this was the one time he was nothing at all, a void traveling between two points. Only on arrival, at this end or that, would he assume or be assigned a purpose, and then he would be himself, or one of his selves, again. What he did know for sure was that these speculations would begin to fade as his train approached his Kreuzberg stop, and that as he hurried across the courtyard and took the five flights of stairs two or even three at a time, they would have vanished.

8 LEONARD'S INITIATION HAPPENED to coincide with the coldest week of the winter. By Berlin's harsh standards, the old hands agreed, it was exceptional at minus twenty-five degrees. There were no clouds, and by day even the bomb damage, sparkling in rich orange light, looked almost beautiful. At night the condensation on the inside of Maria's windowpanes froze into fantastic patterns. In the mornings the top layer on the bed, usually Leonard's greatcoat, was stiff. During this time he rarely saw Maria naked, not all of her, all at once. He saw the gleam of her skin when he burrowed down into the humid gloom. Their winter bed, top-heavy with thin blankets, coats, bath towels, an armchair cover and a nursery quilt, was precarious, bound only by its own weight. There was nothing large enough to keep the whole together. One careless move and single items would slide away, and soon the ensemble would be in ruins. Then they would be standing facing each other across the mattress, shivering as they began the reconstruction.

So Leonard had to learn stealth as he burrowed down. The weather was enforcing an attention to detail. He liked to press his cheek against her belly, taut from all that cycling, or to push the tip of his tongue into her navel, as intricately convoluted as a sunken ear. Down here in the semidarkness —the bedclothes did not tuck under the mattress, and there was always light leaking in from the sides—in the closed and clotted space, he learned to love the smells: sweat like mown grass, and the moistness of her arousal with its two elements, sharp but rounded, tangy and blunt: fruit and cheese, the very tastes of desire itself. This synaesthesia was a kind of delirium. There were tiny blades of calluses the length of her little toes. He heard the rustle of cartilage in her knee joints. In the small of her back was a mole out of which grew two long hairs. Not until mid-March, when the room was warmer, did he see they were silver. Her nipples sprang erect when he breathed on them. On the earlobes were the marks left by her earring clasps. When he ran his fingers through her babyish hair he saw the roots parting in a three-armed whorl about the crown, and her skull looked too white, too vulnerable.

Maria indulged these *Erkundungen*, these excavations. She lay in a daydream, mostly silent, sometimes putting words around a stray thought and watching her breath ascend to the ceiling. "The Major Ashdown is a funny man . . . that's good, put your fingers between all the toes, yes, so . . . every four o'clock in his office he has a cup of hot milk and a boiled egg. He wants the bread cut one, two, three, four, five, like so, and do you know what he calls them, this military man?"

Leonard's voice was muffled. "Soldiers."

"Just so. Soldiers! Is this how you win the war? With these soldiers?" Leonard came up for air and she looped her arms around his neck. "*Mein Dummerchen*, my little innocent, what have you learned down there today?"

"I listened to your belly. It must be dinnertime."

She drew him in and kissed his face. Maria was free with her demands, and she allowed Leonard his curiosity, which she found endearing. Sometimes his inquiries were teases, forms of seduction. "Tell me why you like it halfway," he whispered, and she pleaded, "But I like it deep, really deep."

"You like it halfway, just here. Tell me why that is."

Leonard naturally inclined toward a well-ordered, hygienic existence. For four days after the inception of the first love affair of his life he did not change his underwear or socks, he had no clean shirt and he hardly washed. They had spent that first night in Maria's bed talking and dozing. Toward five A.M. they had cheese, black bread and coffee while a neighbor just through the wall was messily clearing his throat as he prepared to go to work. They made love again, and Leonard was pleased with his powers of recuperation. He was going to be all right, he thought, he was just like everyone else. After that, he fell into a dreamless sleep from which he was woken an hour later by the alarm clock.

He came up from under the bedclothes into a cold that contracted his skull. He lifted Maria's arm free of his waist, and shivering naked on all fours in the dark, he found his clothes beneath the ashtray, under the omelette plates, under the saucer with the burned-out candle. There was an icy fork in the arm of his shirt. He had thought to store his glasses in a shoe. The wine bottle had toppled, and the dregs had drained into the waistband of his underpants. His coat was spread over the bed. He pulled it clear and rearranged the covers over Maria. When he groped for her head and kissed it, she did not stir.

With his coat on he stood at the kitchen sink, moved a frying pan to the floor and splashed stinging cold water over his face. He remembered there was, after all, a bathroom. He turned on its light and went inside. For the first time in his life he used another person's toothbrush. He had never brushed his hair with a woman's hairbrush. He examined his reflection. Here was the new man. The day's growth of beard grew too sparsely to make for a dissolute stubble, and there was the hard red beginning of a pimple on the side of his nose. But he fancied that his gaze now, even in exhaustion, was steadier.

All day long he wore his tiredness well. It was just one aspect of his happiness. Lightweight and remote, the components of his day floated before him: the ride on the U-Bahn and the bus, the walk past a frozen pond and out between the white spiky fields, the hours alone with the tape recorders, the solitary steak and french fries in the canteen, more hours among the familiar circuits, the walk in the dark back to the station, the ride, then Kreuzberg again. It was pointless, wasting the precious workless hours by continuing past her district and heading for his own. That evening when he arrived at her door she was just back from work herself. The apartment was still a mess. Once again they got into bed to keep warm. The night repeated itself with variations, the morning was repeated without them. That was Tuesday morning. Wednesday and Thursday went the same way. Glass asked, rather coolly, if he was growing a beard. If Leonard needed proof of his dedication to a passion, it was in the matted thickness of his gray socks and the aroma of butter, vaginal juices and potatoes that rose from his chest when he loosened the top button of his shirt. The excessively heated interiors at the warehouse released from the folds of his clothes the scent of overused bedsheets and prompted disabling reveries in the windowless room.

It was not until Friday evening that he returned to his own apartment. It seemed like an absence of years. He went around turning on the lights, intrigued by the signs of a former self—the young man who had sat down to write these nervous, scheming drafts strewn across the floor, the scrubbed-clean innocent who had left scum and hairs round the bath and towels and clothes on the bedroom floor. Here was the inexpert coffee maker—he had watched Maria and knew all about it now. Here was the childish chocolate bar and beside it his mother's letter. He read it over quickly and found the little anxieties expressed on his behalf cloying, really quite irritating.

While the bath was filling, he padded around the place, luxuriating once more in space and warmth. He whistled and sang snatches of songs. At first he could not find the untamed number to carry his feelings. The crooning love songs he knew were all too courteously restrained. In fact, what suited him now was the raucous American nonsense he thought he despised. He recalled scraps, but they were elusive: "and make a something with the pots and pans. Shake, rattle and roll! Shake, rattle and roll!" In the bathroom's flattering acoustics, he boomed this incantation over and again. Bellowed in an English voice it sounded foolish, but it was the right sort of thing. Joyous and sexy, and more or less meaningless. He had never in his life felt so uncomplicatedly happy. He had solitude for the moment, but he was not alone. He was expected. He had time to clean himself up and tidy the flat, and then he would be on his way. "Shake, rattle and roll!" Two hours later he opened his front door. This time he took with him an overnight bag, and he did not return for a week.

During these early days, Maria would not come to Leonard's flat, despite his exaggerated description of its luxuries. She worried that if she started spending nights away, the neighbors would soon be telling each other that she had found a man and a better place to live. The authorities would hear about it, and then she would be out. In Berlin, demand even for a one-bedroom flat with no hot water was enormous. To Leonard it seemed reasonable she should want to be on home ground. They bundled up in bed, made dashes to the kitchen for hastily fried meals. To wash, it was necessary to fill a saucepan and wait in bed until it had boiled, then hurry to the bathroom to tip scalding water into the frozen basin. The plug leaked, and pressure in the single cold tap was unpredictable. For Leonard and Maria, work was where they got warm and ate decently. At home, there was nowhere else to be but bed.

Maria taught Leonard to be an energetic and considerate lover, how to let her have all her orgasms before he had his own. That seemed only polite, like letting a lady precede you through a door. He learned to make love in *der Hundestellung,* doggy fashion, which was also the quickest way to lose the bedclothes, and also from behind as she lay on her side, facing away from him, on the edge of sleep; and then on their sides, face to face, locked in tight, barely disturbing the bedclothes at all. He discovered there were no set rules for her preparedness. Sometimes he only had to look at her and she was all set to go. At others he worked away patiently, like a boy over a model kit, only to be interrupted by her suggesting cheese and bread and another round of tea. He learned that she liked endearments murmured in her ear, but not beyond a certain point, not once her eyes began their inward roll. She did not want to be distracted then.

He learned to ask for *Präservative* in the *Drogerie.* He found out from Glass that he was entitled to a free supply through the U.S. Army. On the bus he brought home four gross in a pale blue cardboard box. He sat with the package on his knees, aware of the passengers' glances, and somehow knew the color was a giveaway. Once, when Maria offered sweetly to put one on him herself, he said no too aggressively. Later he wondered what had troubled him. This was his first intimation of a new and troubling feature. It was hard to describe. There was an element of mind creeping in, of bits of himself, bits he did not really like. Once he was over the novelty of it all, and once he was sure he could do it just like everyone else, and when he was confident that he was not going to come too soon—when all that was cleared away, and once he was quite convinced that Maria genuinely liked and wanted him and would go on wanting him, then he started having thoughts that he was powerless to send away when he was making love. They soon grew inseparable from his desire. These fantasies came a little closer each time, and each time they continued to proliferate, to take new forms. There were figures gathering at the edge of thought; now they were striding toward the center, toward him. They were all versions of himself, and he knew he could not resist them.

It began on the third or fourth time with a simple perception. He looked down at Maria, whose eyes were closed, and remembered she was a German. The word had not been entirely prized loose of its associations after all. His first day in Berlin came back to him. German. Enemy. Mortal enemy. Defeated enemy. This last brought with it a shocking thrill. He diverted himself momentarily with the calculation of the total impedance of a certain circuit. Then: she was the defeated, she was his by right, by conquest, by right of unimaginable violence and heroism and sacrifice. What elation! To be right, to win, to be rewarded. He looked along his own arms stretched before him, pushing into the mattress, at where the gingerish hairs were thickest, just below the elbow.

He was powerful and magnificent. He went faster, harder, he fairly bounced on her. He was victorious and good and strong and free. In recollection these formulations embarrassed him and he pushed them aside. They were alien to his obliging and kindly nature, they offended his sense of what was reasonable. One only had to look at her to know there was nothing defeated about Maria. She had been liberated by the invasion of Europe, not crushed. And was she not, at least in their game, his guide?

But next time around the thoughts returned. They were irresistibly exciting, and he was helpless before their elaborations. This time, she was his by right of conquest, and then, *there was nothing she could do about it.* She did not want to be making love to him, but she had no choice. He summoned the circuit diagrams. They were no longer available. She was struggling to escape. She was thrashing beneath him, he thought he heard her call out "No!" She was shaking her head from side to side, she had her eyes closed against the inescapable reality. He had her pinioned against the mattress, she was his, there was nothing she could do, she would never get away. And that was it, that was the end for him, he was gone, finished. His mind was cleared and he lay back. His mind was clear and he thought about food, about sausages. Not bratwurst or bockwurst, but English sausages, fat and mild, fried brownish-black on all sides, and mashed potatoes, and mushy peas.

Over the following days, his embarrassment faded. He accepted the obvious truth that what happened in his head could not be sensed by Maria, even though she was only inches away. These thoughts were his alone, nothing to do with her at all.

Eventually, a more dramatic fantasy took shape. It recapitulated all the previous elements. Yes, she was defeated, conquered, his by right, could not escape, and now, *he was a soldier*, weary, battle-marked and bloody, but heroically rather than disablingly so. He had taken this woman and was forcing her. Half terrified, half in awe, she dared not disobey. It helped when he pulled his greatcoat further up the bed, so that by turning his head to the left or right he could catch sight of the dark green. That she was reluctant and he was inviolable were the premises of further elaborations. As he went about his business in a city full of soldiers, the soldier fantasy appeared ridiculous, but it was easy enough to put out of mind.

It was more difficult, however, when he found himself tempted to communicate these imaginings to her. Initially, he only squeezed her harder, bit her with considerable restraint, held her outstretched arms down and fantasized that he was preventing her from escaping. He slapped her buttocks once. None of this seemed to make much difference to Maria. She did not notice, or she pretended not to. Only his own pleasure was intensified. Now the idea was growing ever more urgent—he wanted her to acknowledge what was on his mind, however stupid it really was. He could not believe she would not be aroused by it. He slapped her again, bit and squeezed harder. *She had to give him what was his.*

His private theater had become insufficient. He wanted something between them. A reality, not a fantasy. Telling her somehow was the next inevitable thing. He wanted his power recognized and Maria to suffer from it, just a bit, in the most pleasurable way. He had no trouble keeping quiet once they had finished. Then he was ashamed. What was this power he wanted recognized? It was no more than a disgusting story in his head. Then, later, he wondered if she might not be excited by it too. There was, of course, nothing to discuss. There was nothing he was able, or dared, to put into words. He could hardly be asking her permission. He had to surprise her, show her, let pleasure overcome her rational objections. He thought all this, and knew it was bound to happen.

Toward the middle of March featureless white clouds covered the sky and the temperature rose sharply. The few inches of dirty snow melted in three days. On the walk between Rudow village and the warehouse there were green shoots in the slush, and on the roadside trees, fat sticky buds. Leonard and Maria emerged from their hibernation. They left the bed and the bedroom and brought the electric heater into the living room. They ate at a *Schnellimbiss* together, and went to a local *Kneipe* for a glass of beer. They saw a Tarzan film on the Kurfürstendamm. One Saturday evening they went to the Resi and danced to a German big band that alternated romantic American love songs with bouncy Bavarian numbers in strict oompah time. They bought sekt to toast their first meeting. Maria said she wanted to sit apart and send messages through the pneumatic tubes, but there were no vacant tables. They had a second bottle of sekt and just enough money left over to take a bus halfway home. As they walked to Adalbertstrasse, Maria yawned loudly and put her arm through Leonard's for support. She had put in ten hours overtime in the previous three days because one of the office girls was out with the flu. And the night before, she and Leonard had been awake until dawn, and even then they had had to remake the bed before they slept.

"Ich bin müde, müde, müde," she said quietly as they

began to climb the apartment stairs. Indoors, she went straight to the bathroom to prepare for bed. Leonard finished off a bottle of white wine while he waited in the living room. When she appeared he took a couple of paces toward her and stood blocking her way to the bedroom. He knew that if he acted confidently and was true to his feelings, he could not fail.

She went to take his hand. "Let's sleep now. Then we'll have all the morning."

He had moved his hand away and rested it on his hip. She gave off a childish smell of toothpaste and soap. She was holding the hairclip she had been wearing.

Leonard kept his voice level and, as he thought, expressionless. "Take off your clothes."

"Yes, in the bedroom." She went to step around him.

He held her by the elbow and pushed her back. "Do it here."

She was annoyed. He had anticipated that, he knew they would have to go through that. "I'm too tired tonight. You can see that." These last words were spoken in a conciliatory way, and it cost Leonard some effort of will to reach out and take her chin between his forefinger and thumb.

He raised his voice. "Do as you're told. In here. Now."

She shoved his hand away. She really was surprised, and now a little amused. "You're drunk. You drank too much at the Resi and now you are Tarzan."

Her laughter irritated him. He ran her against the wall, harder than he intended. The air was knocked from her lungs. Her eyes were wide. She got her breath and said, "Leonard . . ."

He knew that fear might come into it, and that they had

to get beyond that as soon as possible. "Do as I tell you and you'll be all right." He sounded reassuring. "Take it all off or I'll do it for you."

She pressed herself against the wall. She shook her head. Her eyes looked heavy and dark. He thought this might be the first indication of success. When she began to obey she would understand that this pantomime was all for pleasure, hers as well as his. Then the fear would disappear completely. "You'll do as I say." He managed to suppress the interrogative.

She dropped the clip and pressed her fingers against the wall behind her. Her head was still and a little bowed. She drew a deep breath and said, "Now I'm going to the bedroom." Her accent was more than usually pronounced. She had moved no more than a few inches from the wall before he pushed her back.

"No," he said.

She was looking up at him. Her jaw had dropped and her lips were parted. She was looking at him as though for the first time. It could have been wonder on her face, or even astonished admiration. At any moment it would all be different, there would be joyous compliance, and transformation. He hooked his fingers by the catch of her skirt and pulled hard. There was no going back. She yelped, and said his name twice quickly. She held her skirt up with one hand and the other was half raised, palm outward for protection. There were two black buttons on the floor. He took a fistful of material and jerked the skirt down. At that moment she made a lunge across the room. The skirt ripped along a seam and she tripped, scrabbled on the floor and fell again. He rolled her onto her back and pressed her shoulders down on the boards. They should be laughing, he thought. It was a game, an exhilarating game. She was wrong to overdramatize. He was kneeling by her, holding her with two hands. Then he let her go. He lay beside her awkwardly, propped on an elbow. With his free hand he pulled at her underwear and unbuttoned his fly.

She lay still and looked at the ceiling. She hardly blinked. This was the turning point. They were on their way. He wanted to smile at her, but he thought this might destroy for her the impression of his mastery. He kept a stern face as he positioned himself. If it was a game, it was a serious game after all. He was almost in place. She was tight. It was a shock when she spoke so calmly. She did not shift her gaze from the ceiling, and her voice was cold.

She said, "I want you to leave. I want you to go home."

"I'm staying here," Leonard said, "and that's that." He did not sound as forthright as he wanted.

She said, "Please . . ." Her eyes filled with tears. She continued to stare at the ceiling. At last she blinked and displaced a trickle. It ran straight down her temples and vanished into the hair above her ears. Leonard's elbow was stiff. She sucked her lower lip and blinked again. There were no more tears and she trusted herself to speak once more. "Just go."

He stroked her face, along the line of her cheekbone, down to where the hair was wet. She held her breath, waiting for him to stop.

He knelt up and rubbed his arm and buttoned his fly. The silence hissed around them. It was unjust, this unspoken blame. He appealed to an imaginary court. If this had been anything other than playfulness, if he had meant her harm, he would not have stopped when he did, the very moment he saw how upset she was. She was taking it literally, using it against him, and that was quite unfair. He did not know how to begin saying any of this. She had not moved from the floor. He was angry with her. And he was desperate for her forgiveness. It was impossible to speak. She let her hand go limp when he took it and squeezed. Half an hour before they had been walking arm in arm along Oranienstrasse. How would he ever get back to that? There came to him an image of a blue clockwork locomotive, a present on his eighth or ninth birthday. It used to pull a string of coal trucks round a figure-of-eight track until one afternoon, in a spirit of reverent experimentation, he had overwound it.

Finally Leonard stood and took a couple of steps back. Maria sat up and arranged her skirt over her knees. She too had a memory, but only ten years old and more burdensome than a broken toy train. It was of an air raid shelter in an eastern suburb of Berlin, near the Oberbaum bridge. It was late April, the week before the city fell. She was almost twenty. An advancing Red Army unit had installed heavy guns nearby and was shelling the city center. There were thirty of them in the shelter, women, children, old people, cowering in the din. Maria was with her uncle Walter. There was a lull in the firing, and five soldiers sauntered into the bunker—the first Russians they had ever seen. One of them pointed a rifle at the group while another mimed for the Germans: watches, jewelry. The collection was swift and silent. Uncle Walter pushed Maria deeper into the gloom, back to the first-aid station. She hid in a corner, wedged between the wall and an empty supply cupboard. On a mattress on the floor was a woman of about fifty who had been shot in both legs. Her eyes were closed and she was moaning. It was a high, continuous sound on one note. It attracted the attention of one of the soldiers. He knelt by the woman and took out a short-handled knife. Her eyes were still closed. The soldier lifted her skirt and cut away her underclothes. Watching over her uncle's shoulder, Maria thought the Russian was about to perform some crude battlefield surgery, removing a bullet with an unsterilized knife. Then he was lying on top of the wounded woman, pushing into her with jerking, trembling movements.

The woman's voice dropped to a low sound. Beyond her, in the shelter, people were turning away. No one made a sound. Then there was a commotion, and another Russian, a huge man in civilian clothes, was pushing through to the first-aid station. He was a political commissar, Maria learned later. His face was blotchy scarlet with a fury that stretched his lips across his teeth. With a shout he seized the soldier by the back of his jacket and pulled him off. The penis was vivid in the gloom, and smaller than Maria had expected. The commissar hauled the soldier away by the ear, shouting in Russian. Then it was silent again. Someone gave the wounded woman a drink of water. Three hours later, when it was certain that the artillery unit had moved on, they emerged from the shelter into the rain. They found the soldier lying face downward by the edge of the road. He had been shot in the back of the neck.

Maria stood. She supported her skirt with one hand. She pulled Leonard's greatcoat off the table and let it fall at his feet. He knew he was going because he could think of nothing to say. His mind was jammed. As he passed her, he placed his hand on her forearm. She stared down at the hand, and looked away.

He had no money, and had to walk to Platanenallee. The following day, after work, he called on her with flowers, but she was gone. The next day he learned from a neighbor she was with her parents in the Russian sector.

9 THERE WAS NO TIME FOR BROODING. Two days after Maria left, a hydraulic jack was brought to the head of the tunnel to pull the cables down. It was bolted in position under the vertical shaft. The double doors were sealed and the room was pressurized. John MacNamee was there, and Leonard and five other technicians. There was also an American in a suit, who did not speak. To adjust their ears to the rising pressure, they had to swallow hard. MacNamee passed around some boiled sweets. The American sipped water from a teacup. Traffic noise resonated in the chamber. Now and then they heard the roar of a heavy truck and the ceiling vibrated.

When a light flashed on a field telephone, MacNamee picked it up and listened. There had already been confirmations from the recording room, from the people running the amplifiers, and from the engineers responsible for the power generators and the air supply. The latest call was from the lookouts on the roof of the warehouse, who were watching the Schönefelder Chaussee through binoculars. They had been up there all through the digging. They used to bring work to a halt whenever Vopos were directly over the tunnel. MacNamee put down the phone and nodded at two men who were standing by the jack. One of them hung a wide leather strap over his shoulder and climbed a ladder to the cables. The strap was being passed behind the cables and attached to a chain, which was rubberized to stop it chinking. The man at the foot of the ladder fixed the chain to the jack and looked at MacNamee. When the first man was down and the ladder had been stowed, MacNamee picked up the phone again. He then put down the phone and nodded, and the man began to work the jack.

It was tempting to go and stand under the shaft to watch the cables being drawn down. They had calculated just how much slack there would be, and how much was safe to take up. No one knew for sure. But it would not be professional to show too much curiosity. The man turning the jack needed space. They waited in silence and sucked their sweets. The pressure was still rising; the air was sweaty and warm. The American stood apart. He glanced at his watch and made an entry in a notebook. MacNamee kept his hand on the phone. The man straightened from his work and looked at him. MacNamee went to the shaft and looked up. He stood on tiptoe and reached. When he brought his hand down, it was covered in mud. "Six inches," he said. "No more," and he went back to be by the phone.

The man who had been up the ladder brought a bucket of water and a cloth. His colleague unbolted the jack from the floor. In its place was lifted a low wooden platform. The man with the bucket took it over to MacNamee, who rinsed his hand. Then he carried it back to the shaft, hauled it onto the platform and washed the cables, which Leonard guessed were only six feet from the ground. A bath towel was passed up for the man to dry the cables with. Then one of the other technicians, who had been standing next to Leonard, took his place near the platform. In his hand was an electrician's knife and a pair of wire-strippers. MacNamee was on the phone again. "The pressure's good," he whispered to the room, and then he murmured some directions into the receiver.

Before the first cut was made, they allowed themselves their moment. There was just room on the steps for three men. They put their hands on the cables. Each one was as thick as an arm, dull black and cold, and still sticky from the moisture. Leonard could almost sense the hundreds of phone conversations and encoded messages flashing to and from Moscow beneath his fingertips. The American came and looked, but MacNamee hung back. Then only the technician with the knife remained on the platform, and he was starting work. To the others, standing watching him, he was visible from the waist down. He wore gray flannel trousers and polished brown shoes. Soon he passed down a rectangle of black rubber. The first cable had been exposed. When the other two had been cut, it was time for the tap. MacNamee was on the phone again, and nothing happened until he gave the signal. It was known that the East Germans kept a regular check on the integrity of their high-priority circuits by sending a pulse down the line which would bounce back if it encountered a break. The thin skin of concrete above the tap chamber could easily be smashed open. Leonard and all the others had learned the evacuation procedures. The last man was to close and bolt all the doors behind him. Where the tunnel crossed the border the sandbags and barbed wire were to be pulled into place, and so too the hand-painted wooden sign that sternly warned intruders in German and Russian that they were entering the American sector.

Supported on brackets along the plywood wall were the hundreds of circuits in neat multicolored bunches, ready to be clipped to the landline. Leonard and another man stood below and handed up wires as they were called for. The pattern of work was not as MacNamee had outlined it. The same man stayed on the platform, working at a speed Leonard knew he could not match. Every hour he took a ten-minute break. Ham and cheese sandwiches and coffee were brought from the canteen. One of the technicians sat at a table with a tape recorder and a set of headphones. In the third or fourth hour he raised his hand and turned to MacNamee, who went across and put one ear to the set. Then he handed it to the American, who was at his side. They had broken into the circuit used by the East German telephone engineers. There would be advance warning now of any alarm.

An hour later they had to evacuate the chamber. The moisture in the air was heavy enough to be condensing on the walls, and MacNamee was worried that it would interfere with the contacts. They left one man monitoring the engineers' circuit while the rest of them waited beyond the double doors for the moisture level to drop. They stood around in the short stretch of tunnel before the amplifiers with their hands in their pockets, trying not to stamp their feet. It was far colder out here. They all wanted to go back up to the top for a smoke. But MacNamee, who was chewing on his empty pipe, did not suggest it, and no one was prepared to ask. During the following six hours they left the chamber five times. The American left without a word. Finally MacNamee sent one of the technicians away. Half an hour later he dismissed Leonard.

Leonard passed unseen through the noiseless excitement round the racks of amplifiers and walked slowly along the tracks, back toward the warehouse. He had the long stretch to himself, and he knew he was delaying leaving the tunnel, leaving the drama and returning to his shame. He had stood outside Maria's apartment two nights before with his flowers, unable to come away. He persuaded himself that she had gone out shopping. Each time he heard footsteps on the stairs below, he peered over the rail and prepared to meet her. After an hour he posted the flowers, expensive hothouse carnations, through her door, one by one, and ran down the stairs. He went back the next evening, this time with marzipan-filled chocolates in a box whose lid featured puppies in a wicker basket. This and the flowers cost him almost a week's money. He was on the landing below Maria's when he met her neighbor, a gaunt, unfriendly woman whose apartment exhaled a carbolic breath through the open door behind her. She shook her head and her hand at Leonard. She knew he was foreign. *"Fort! Nicht da! Bei ihren Eltern!"* He thanked her. She repeated herself loudly when he continued up the stairs, and she waited for him to come down. The box would not fit through the door, so he posted the chocolates through, one by one. When he passed the neighbor on his way down, he offered her the box. She crossed her arms over her chest and bit her lip. The refusal cost her some effort.

As more time passed, the more unbelievable his attack on Maria seemed, and the less forgivable. There had been some logic, some crazed, step-by-step reasoning that he could no longer recall. It had made good sense, but all he could remember now was his certainty at the time, his conviction that ultimately she would approve. He could not recall the steps along the way. It was as if he were remembering the actions of another man, or of himself transformed in a dream. Now he was back in the real world—he was passing the underground border crossing and beginning to ascend the slope—and applying the standards of the world, his actions appeared not only offensive but profoundly stupid. He had chased Maria away. She was the best thing to have happened to him since . . . His mind ran over various childhood treats, birthdays, holidays, Christmases, university entrance, his transfer to Dollis Hill. Nothing remotely as good had ever happened to him. Unsummoned images of her, memories of her kindness, of how fond of him she had been, made him jerk his head to one side and cough to cover the sound of his agony. He would never get her back. He had to get her back.

He climbed the ladder out of the shaft and nodded at the guard. He made his way up to the next floor, to the recording room. No one had a drink in his hand, no one was smiling even, but the atmosphere of a celebration was unmistakable. The test row, the first twelve tape recorders to be connected, were already receiving. Leonard joined the group watching them. Four machines were running, then a fifth started, then a sixth; then one of the original four stopped, and immediately after it another. The signal activation units, the ones he had installed himself, were working. They had been tested, but never by a Russian voice, or a Russian code. Leonard sighed, and for the moment Maria receded.

A German who was standing close by put his hand on Leonard's shoulder and squeezed. Another of Gehlen's men, another Fritz, turned around and grinned at them both. There was lunchtime beer on their breath. Elsewhere in the room last-minute connections and alterations were being made. A handful of people with clipboards stood in a self-important cluster. Two Dollis Hill men were sitting close in on a third who was on the phone, listening intently, probably to MacNamee.

Then Glass came in, raised his hand to Leonard and strode toward him. He had not looked better in weeks. He had a different suit and a new tie knot. Lately Leonard had been avoiding him, but half-heartedly. The job for MacNamee had made him ashamed to spend time with the only American he could claim a friendship with. At the same time, he knew that Glass was likely to be a good source. Glass was tugging him by the lapel into a relatively deserted part of the room. The beard had resumed its old light-trapping forward thrust.

"This is a dream come true," Glass said. "The test row is perfect. In four hours the whole thing'll be rolling." Leonard started to speak, but Glass said, "Listen. Leonard, you haven't been completely open with me. You think I wouldn't know when you go behind my back?" Glass was smiling.

It occurred to Leonard that the tunnel might be bugged along its length. But surely MacNamee would know about it. "What are you talking about?"

"Come on. This is a small town. The two of you have been seen. Russell was in the Resi on Saturday, and he told me. His considered judgment was that you'd been the whole way many times. Is that true?"

Leonard smiled. He could not help his ludicrous pride. Glass was being mock stern. "That same girl, the one who sent the note? The one you said you got nowhere with?"

"Well, I didn't at first."

"That's amazing." Glass had his hands on Leonard's shoulders and was holding him at arm's length. His admiration and delight seemed so forceful that Leonard could almost forget recent events. "You quiet Englishmen—you don't horse around, you don't talk about it, you get in there fast."

Leonard wanted to laugh out loud; it was, it had been, quite a triumph.

Glass released him. "Listen, I phoned you every evening at your apartment last week. You moved in with her or what?"

"Only sort of."

"I thought we might have a drink, but now you've told me, why don't we make a double date? I have this nice friend,

Jean, from the U.S. embassy. She's from my hometown, Cedar Rapids. You know where that is?"

Leonard looked at his shoes. "Well, the fact is, we've had a sort of row. Quite a big one. She's gone off to stay with her parents."

"And where are they?"

"Oh, in Pankow somewhere."

"And when did she leave?"

"The day before yesterday."

Leonard was halfway through answering this last question when he understood that Glass had been on the job the whole time. Not for the first time in their acquaintanceship, the American had taken him by the elbow and was steering him somewhere else. Apart from Maria and his mother, no one had touched Leonard in his life more than Glass.

They were out in the quiet of the corridor. Glass took a notebook from his pocket. "You tell her anything?"

"Of course I didn't."

"You better give me her name and address."

The misplaced stress on the first syllable of this last word released in Leonard a surge of irritation. "Her name is Maria. Her address is none of your business."

A small display of feeling from the Englishman seemed to refresh Glass. He closed his eyes and breathed deeply, as though inhaling a fragrance. Then he said in a reasonable way, "Let me reorder the facts, then you tell me if it's worth my job to ignore them. A girl you've never seen before makes a highly unconventional approach to you at a dance hall. Finally you make it with her. She's chosen you, not you her. Right? You're doing classified work. You move in with her. The day before we lay the taps, she disappears into the Russian sector. What are we going to say to our superiors, Leonard? That you liked her a whole lot so we decided not to investigate? Let's have it."

Leonard felt physical pain at the thought of Glass with legitimate reason to be alone with Maria in an interrogation room. It started high in his stomach and spread downward to his bowels. He said, "Maria Eckdorf, Adalbertstrasse 84, Kreuzberg. *Erstes Hinterhaus, fünfter Stock, rechts.*"

"One of those cold-water walkups on the top floor? Not as classy as Platanenallee. Did she say she didn't want to stay at your place?"

"I didn't want her there."

"You see," Glass spoke as though Leonard had not replied, "she'd want you at her place if it was wired."

For the duration of a single pulse of sheer hatred, Leonard saw himself seizing Glass's beard with two hands and ripping it off, bringing face flesh with it, throwing the mess of red and black to the floor and stamping on it. Instead he turned and walked away without thought for his direction. He was back in the recording room. There were more machines running now. Up and down the room they were stopping and starting. All checked and fitted by him, all his own lonely, loyal work. Glass was at his side. Leonard started to head down one of the rows, but two technicians were blocking the way. He turned back.

Glass came up close and said, "I know it's tough. I've seen this before. And it's probably nothing. We just have to run through the procedure. One more question and I'll leave you in peace. Does she have a day job?"

No thought preceded the action. Leonard filled his lungs

and shouted. "A day job? A day job? You mean, as opposed to her night job? What are you trying to say?"

It was almost a scream. The air in the room hardened. Everyone stopped work and turned in his direction. Only the machines went on.

Glass pushed his palms downward, miming a lowering of volume. When he spoke, it was just louder than a whisper. His lips barely moved. "Everyone's listening, Leonard, including some of your own big boys over by the phone. Don't let them think you're a nut. Don't let them put you out of a job." It was true. Two of the Dollis Hill senior staff were watching him coolly. Glass went on with his ventriloquist's voice. "Do exactly as I say and we can save this. Bang me on the shoulder and we'll walk out of here together like good friends."

Everyone was waiting for something to happen. There was no other way out. Glass was his only ally. Leonard threw him a rough punch to the shoulder and immediately the American burst into loud, convincing laughter and put his arm around Leonard's shoulder, and once more walked him to the door. Between laughs he murmured, "Now it's your turn, you son of a bitch, save your ass and laugh."

"Heh-heh," the Englishman said croakily, and then louder, "Hahaha. Night job, that's a good one. Night job!"

Glass joined in, and behind them a low murmur of conversation, a friendly wave, swelled and bore them to the door.

They were back in the corridor, but this time they kept walking. Glass had his notebook and pencil out again. "Just give me the place of work, Leonard, then we'll have a drink in my room."

Leonard could not give it to him in one. The betrayal was

too great. "It's an Army vehicle workshop. British Army, that is." They walked on. Glass was waiting. "I think it's REME. It's in Spandau." Then, outside Glass's room, "The CO is a Major Ashdown."

"That'll do fine," Glass said, and unlocked the door and ushered him into the room. "You wanna beer? Or how about a Scotch?"

Leonard chose Scotch. He had been in here only once before. The desk was covered with papers. He was trying not to look too hard, but he could see that some of the material was technical.

Glass poured and said, "You want me to fetch some ice from the canteen?" Leonard nodded and Glass left. Leonard stepped toward the desk. He had, he estimated, a little under a minute.

10 EVERY EVENING LEONARD stopped off at Kreuzberg on his way home. He only had to set foot on Maria's landing to know she was not there, but he crossed it all the same and knocked. After the chocolates, he no longer posted gifts. He wrote no more letters after the third. The lady in the carbolic apartment downstairs sometimes opened her door to watch him come down. By the end of the first week her look was more pitying than hostile. He ate supper standing up at the *Schnellimbiss* on Reichskanzlerplatz and most evenings went to the bar in the narrow street to delay his return to Platanenallee. He had enough German now to know that the locals hunched at their tables were not discussing genocide. It was the usual pub grumble—the late spring, the government, the quality of the coffee.

When he was home he resisted the armchair and the torpid brooding. He was not going to let himself go. He made himself do jobs. He washed his shirts in the bathroom, scrubbing the cuffs and collars with a nailbrush. He did his ironing, polished his shoes, dusted the surfaces and pushed the squeaking carpet sweeper around the rooms. He wrote to his parents. Despite all his changes, he was unable to break with the flat tone, the stifling lack of information or affect. *Dear Mum and Dad, Thanks for yours. I hope you are well and over your colds. I've been very busy at work which is going very well. The weather* . . . The weather. He never gave the weather a second thought unless he was writing to his parents. He paused, then he remembered. *The weather has been very wet, but it's warmer now.*

What was beginning to oppress him, and it was an anxiety that his household chores could never quite silence, was the possibility that Maria would not return to her apartment. He would have to find out the address of Major Ashdown's unit. He would have to go out to Spandau and catch her coming out of work before she boarded her train for Pankow. Glass would already have spoken to her. She was bound to assume Leonard was trying to get her into trouble. She would be furious. The chances of winning her around on the pavement, in full view of the sentry, or in the homeward crush of the U-Bahn ticket hall, were slight. She would stride past him, or shout some German obscenity that everyone but himself would understand. To confront her he needed privacy and several hours. Then she could be furious, then accusatory, then sorrowful and finally forgiving. He could have drawn an emotional circuit diagram for her. As for his own feelings, they were beginning to be simplified by the righteousness of love. When she knew how much he loved her, she must forgive him. For the rest, the deed and its causes, the guilt, the evasion, he tried hard not to brood. That would solve nothing. He tried to be invisible to himself. He scrubbed out the bath, washed the kitchen floor and fell asleep just past midnight with tolerable ease, faintly comforted by a sense of being misunderstood.

One evening during the second week of Maria's disappearance Leonard heard voices from the empty apartment downstairs. He put down his iron and went out onto his landing to listen. Up the elevator shaft came the sound of furniture scraping on the floor, footsteps and more voices. Early the next morning he was descending in the elevator when it stopped at the floor below. The man who stepped in nodded and faced away. He was in his early thirties and carried an attaché case. His beard was trimmed neatly in the naval style, and he gave off a scent of cologne. Even Leonard could tell that the dark blue suit was well made. The two men rode down in silence. The stranger allowed Leonard to precede him out of the lift with an economical movement of his open palm.

They met again on the ground floor by the lift shaft two days later. It was not quite dark. Leonard had come in from Altglienicke by way of Kreuzberg and his customary two liters of lager. The lights in the lobby had not been turned on. When Leonard reached the man's side, the lift had just risen to the fifth floor. In the time it took to come back down, the man offered his hand, and without smiling or, as far as Leonard could tell, altering his expression at all, said, "George Blake. My wife and I live right under your feet."

Leonard gave his name and said, "Do I make a lot of noise?"

The lift came and they stepped inside. Blake pushed the fourth and fifth buttons, and when they were moving looked from Leonard's face to his shoes and said in a neutral way, "Carpet slippers would help."

"Well, sorry," Leonard said with as much aggression as he dared. "I'll get some."

His neighbor nodded and pressed his lips together, as if to say, *That's the spirit.* The door slid back and he went off without another word.

Leonard reached his apartment resolved to pound the floors harder than ever. But he could not quite bring himself to it. He hated to be in the wrong. He trod heavily along his hall and took his shoes off in the kitchen.

Over the months that followed he occasionally saw Mrs. Blake about the place. She had a beautiful face and a very straight back, and although she smiled at Leonard and said hello, he avoided her. She made him feel shabby and awkward. He overheard her talking in the lobby and thought she sounded intimidating. Her husband became a little friendlier over the summer months. He said he worked for the Foreign Office at the Olympic Stadium, and he was politely interested when Leonard told him he worked for the Post Office, installing internal lines for the Army. Thereafter, he never failed to say on the few occasions they passed each other in the lobby or shared the lift, "How are the internal lines?" with a smile that made Leonard wonder if he was being mocked.

At the warehouse the tap had been declared a success. One hundred and fifty tape recorders stopped and started day and night, triggered by the amplified Russian signals. The place emptied rapidly. The horizontal diggers, the tunneling sergeants, had long departed. The British vertical men had left just as the excitement was growing, and no one noticed them go. All kinds of other people—experts whose fields, it seemed, were known only to themselves—drifted away, as did the senior Dollis Hill staff. MacNamee called in once or twice a week. All that remained were the men monitoring or distributing the take, and these were the busiest and least communicative. There were also a few technicians and engineers keeping the systems running, and the security people. Leonard sometimes found himself eating in an empty canteen. His instructions were that he should stay on indefinitely. He carried out routine checks on the integrity of the circuits and replaced faulty valves in the tape recorders.

Glass stayed away from the warehouse, and at first Leonard was relieved. Until he was reconciled with Maria, he did not want to hear news of her through Glass. He did not want Glass to have the power of an intermediary over him. Then he began to find excuses to walk past the American's office several times a day. Leonard was often at the water fountain. He was certain that Maria would be cleared, but he had his doubts about Glass. The interviews would be opportunities for seduction, surely. If Maria was still angry and Glass was sufficiently energetic, the worst might be happening even as Leonard stood outside the locked room. Several times he almost phoned Glass from home. But what was he to ask? How would he bear the confirmation, or believe the denial? Perhaps the very question would seem to Glass a form of incitement.

As the weather grew warmer in May, the off-duty Americans set up softball games in the rough ground between the warehouse and the perimeter fence. They were under strict instructions to wear the insignia of radar operatives. The Vopos over by the cemetery watched the games through field glasses, and when a long ball sailed over the sector boundary they ran forward willingly and lobbed it back. The players cheered, and the Vopos waved good-naturedly. Leonard sat out with his back to the wall watching the games. One reason he refused to join in was that softball looked like nothing more than rounders for grown-ups. The other reason was that he was useless at any game with a ball. In this one the throws were hard and low and pitilessly accurate, and the catches were all taken in an obligatory offhand manner.

Every day now there were hours of idleness. He often leaned against the wall in the sun below an open window. One of the Army clerks propped a wireless on the sill and broadcast AFN to the players. When a lively song came up, the pitcher might pat out a rhythm on his knees before a throw, and the men out on the bases would snap their fingers and practice little shuffles. Leonard had never seen popular music taken so seriously. Only one performer could temporarily halt the game. If it was Bill Haley and the Comets, and especially if it was "Rock Around the Clock," there would be shouts for more volume, and players would drift toward the window. For two and a half minutes no one could strike out. To Leonard, the unrestrained exhortation to dance for hours on end seemed puerile. It was a counting song that girls with a skipping rope might chant in the playground. It was "Hickory Dickory Dock," it was "One potato, two potato, three potato, four. . . ." But with repetition, the thumping rhythm and the virile insistence of the guitar began to stir him, and he moved from hating the song to pretending to hate it.

Soon he was glad when the mail clerk crossed his office at a cue from the announcer and turned up the volume. More than half a dozen players would come and stand around where he was sitting. They were mostly sentries in their late teens, clean and huge, with bristling heads. All of them knew his first name by now, and they were always friendly. For them the song seemed to have more than musical importance. It was an anthem, a rite; it bound these players and separated them from the older men who stood waiting on the field. This state of affairs lasted only three weeks before the song lost its power. It was played loudly, but it did not interrupt the game. Then it was ignored altogether. A replacement was needed, but it did not come until April of the following year.

It was at the height of Bill Haley's triumph at the warehouse, just as the young Americans were jostling around the open window one afternoon, that John MacNamee came looking for his spy. Leonard saw him walking from the administration offices toward the din. MacNamee had not yet seen him, and there was just time to dissociate himself from what the government scientist was bound to despise. However, he felt a certain defiance, and a degree of loyalty to the group. He was an honorary member. He compromised by standing and pushing his way through to the edge of the crowd, where he waited. As soon as MacNamee saw him, Leonard went toward him, and together they set off for a walk along the perimeter fence.

MacNamee had his lit pipe between his baby teeth. He leaned toward his charge. "I suppose you've had no luck."

"Not really," Leonard said. "I've been in five different offices with time to look around. Nothing. I've made approaches to various technical people. They're all very security-conscious. I couldn't press too hard."

The truth was he had had one unsuccessful minute in Glass's office. He did not find it easy to fall into conversation with strangers. He had tried a couple of locked doors, that was all.

MacNamee said, "Did you have a go at that chap Weinberg?"

Leonard knew the one, a whippet-shaped American with a skullcap who played chess with himself in the canteen. "Yes. He didn't want to talk."

They stopped and MacNamee said, "Ah well . . ." They were looking toward the Schönefelder Chaussee, more or less along the line of the tunnel. "That's too bad," MacNamee said. He spoke with an unfamiliar tightness, Leonard thought, a deliberation that seemed more than disappointment.

Leonard said, "I did try."

MacNamee looked away while he spoke. "We've got other possibilities, of course, but you keep trying." His flat emphasis on this last word, an echo of Leonard's, suggested skepticism, an accusation of some sort.

With a farewell grunt, MacNamee set off for the administration section. There came to Leonard an image of Maria walking away from him too, across the rough ground. Maria and MacNamee, showing him their backs. Across the grass the Americans were already back at their game. He felt his failure as a weakness in his legs. He had been about to walk back to his place by the window, but for the moment he did not feel like it, and remained where he was, out by the wire.

11

LEONARD STEPPED OUT of the lift onto his landing the following evening and found Maria waiting for him by his door. She was standing in the corner, her coat buttoned up, both hands on the strap of her handbag, which hung down in front of her, covering her knees. It might have been an attitude of contrition, but she held her head up and her eyes were on his. She defied him to assume that by seeking him out she had forgiven him. It was almost dusk, and very little natural light reached the landing through the east-facing window. Leonard had pushed the timed light switch at his elbow, and it had begun to tick. The sound resembled the panicked heartbeat of a minute creature. The doors slid shut behind him and the lift sank away. He said her name, but he made no move toward her. The single overhead light made deep shadows under her eyes and nose and gave her face a hard appearance. She had not spoken yet, she had not moved. She was staring at him, waiting for whatever he had to say. The buttoned coat and formal grip on the handbag hinted that she was ready to leave if she was not satisfied.

Leonard was flustered. Too many half-sentences were crowding before him. He had been handed a gift he could easily destroy in the unwrapping. The light-switch mechanism by him raced softly, making it harder to settle on a coherent thought. He said her name again—the sound simply left his throat—and took a half-step toward her. From the shaft came the rumble of the cables hauling their burden upward, the sigh of the lift settling on the floor below, then the doors opening and Mr. Blake's voice, urgent and muted. It was abruptly cut off by the sound of his front door closing.

Nothing in her expression had changed. Finally he said, "Did you get those letters?"

She blinked in acknowledgment. The three letters of love and breathless apology and the chocolates and the flowers were not to be considered here. He said, "What I did was very stupid." She blinked again. This time the lashes touched for a fraction longer, suggesting a softening, a form of encouragement. He had his tone now, simplicity. It was not so difficult. "I ruined everything. I've been desperate since you went. I wanted to come and find you in Spandau, but I was ashamed. I didn't know how you would ever be able to forgive me. I was ashamed of approaching you in the street. I love you very much, I've been thinking about you all the time. I'll understand if you can't forgive me. It was a horrible and stupid thing . . ."

Leonard had never in his life spoken about himself and his feelings in such a way. Nor had he even thought in this manner. Quite simply, he had never acknowledged in himself a serious emotion. He had never gone much further than saying he quite liked last night's film, or hated the taste of lukewarm milk. In fact, until now, it was as though he had never really had any serious feelings. Only now, as he came to name them—shame, desperation, love—could he really claim them for his own and experience them. His love for the woman standing by his door was brought into relief by the word, and sharpened the shame he felt for assaulting her. As he gave it a name, the unhappiness of the past three weeks was clarified. He was enlarged, unburdened. Now that he could name the fog he had been moving through, he was at last visible to himself.

But he was not in the clear. Maria had not shifted her

position or her gaze. He said, after a pause, "Please forgive me." At that moment the time mechanism clicked and the light went out. He heard Maria breathe in sharply. When his eyes had adjusted he could see the gleam of the window behind him reflected on the clasp of her handbag and in the whites of her eyes as she seemed to glance away. He took a risk and came away from the light switch without pressing it. His elation gave him confidence. He had behaved badly; now he was going to put things right. What was demanded of him was truth and simplicity. He would no longer sleepwalk through his misery, he would name it accurately and in that way dispel it. And with the opportunity provided by this near darkness, he was about to re-establish by means of touch the old bond between them, the simple, truthful bond. The words could come later. For now, all that was required, he was convinced, was that they should hold hands, perhaps even kiss lightly.

As he crossed toward her she moved at last, back into the corner of the landing, deeper into the shadows. When he came close he put out his hand, but she was not quite there. He had brushed her sleeve. Again, he caught sight of the whites of her eyes as her head appeared to duck away. He found her elbow and held it gently. He whispered her name. Her arm was crooked tight and unyielding, and through the material of her coat he could feel her trembling. Now he was close, he was aware of her breathing fast and shallow. There was a sweaty taste in the air. For an instant he thought that she had mounted swiftly to the extremities of sexual arousal, a thought rendered instantly blasphemous when he moved his hand to her shoulder and she half called out, half screamed an inarticulate sound, followed by *"Mach das Licht an. Bitte!*

Turn on the light!" and then, "Please, please." He placed a second hand on her shoulder. He shook her gently, reassuringly. All he wanted to do was wake her from this nightmare. He had to remind her who he was really, the young innocent she had sweetly coaxed and brought on. She screamed again, this time at full strength and piercingly. He backed off. A door opened on the floor below. There were rapid footsteps on the stairs that ran around the lift shaft.

Leonard pressed the light switch just as Mr. Blake rounded the corner of the half-landing. He took the final flight of stairs three at a time. He was in shirtsleeves and without a tie, and he had silver armbands around his biceps. His face was hard, emanating ferocious military competence, and his hands were tensed and open at the ready. He was prepared to do someone a lot of harm. When he arrived at the top of the stairs and took in Leonard, his face did not relax. Maria had let her handbag drop to the floor and had raised her hands to cover her nose and mouth. Blake took up a position between Leonard and Maria. His hands were on his hips. He already knew he was not going to have to hit anyone, and this added to his ferocity.

"What's going on here?" he demanded of Leonard, and without waiting for a reply he turned away impatiently and confronted Maria. His voice was kindly. "Are you hurt? Has he tried to hurt you?"

"Of course I haven't," Leonard said.

Blake called over his shoulder, "Shut up!" and turned back to Maria. His voice was immediately kind again. "Well?"

He was like an actor in a wireless comedy, Leonard thought, doing all the voices. Because he did not like Blake standing between them like a referee, Leonard crossed the landing, pressing the light switch on his way to give them another ninety seconds. Blake was waiting for Maria to speak, but he seemed to know that Leonard was coming up behind. He put out an arm to stop Leonard walking around him and going to Maria. She had said something Leonard had not caught, and Blake was replying in competent German. Leonard disliked him more. Was it out of loyalty to Leonard that Maria answered in English?

"I'm sorry to make this noise and bring you from your house. It's something between us, that's all. We can make it better." She had taken her hands from her face. She picked up her handbag. Having it in her hands seemed to restore her. She spoke around Blake, though not quite to Leonard. "I'll go inside now."

Leonard took out his key and stepped around Maria's savior to open the door. He leaned in and turned on his hall light.

Blake had not moved. He was not satisfied. "I could phone a taxi for you. You could sit with my wife and me until it comes."

Maria crossed the threshold and turned to thank him. "You're very kind. I'm okay now, see. Thank you." She walked confidently along the hall of the apartment she had never visited, stepped into the bathroom and closed the door.

Blake stood at the head of the stairs with his hands in his pockets. Leonard felt too vulnerable, and too irritated by his neighbor, to offer further explanations. He stood irresolutely by his door, restrained from going indoors until the other man had gone away.

Blake said, "Women generally scream like that when they think they're about to be raped."

The ludicrous knowingness of the remark called for an elegant rebuttal. Leonard thought hard for several seconds. What impeded him was that he was being mistaken for a rapist when in fact he had almost been one. In the end he said, "Not in this case." Blake shrugged to indicate his skepticism and descended the stairs. From then on, whenever the two men met by the lift, they did so in cold silence.

Maria had locked the bathroom door and washed her face. She lowered the lid on the toilet and sat there. She had surprised herself by her scream. She did not really believe that Leonard had wanted to assault her again. His awkward and sincere apologies had been adequate guarantee. But the sudden darkness and his quiet approach, the possibilities, the associations, had been too much for her. The delicate equilibrium she had developed during three weeks in her parents' stuffy apartment in Pankow had come apart at the touch of Leonard's hand. It was like a madness, this fear that someone pretending affection should want to do her harm. Or that a malice she could barely comprehend should take on the outer forms of sexual intimacy. Otto's occasional assaults, dreadful as they were, did not inspire anything like this sickness of fear. His violence was an aspect of his impersonal hatred and sodden helplessness. He did not wish to do her harm *and* long for her. He wanted to intimidate her and take her money. He did not want to get inside her, he did not ask her to trust him.

The trembling in her arms and legs had ceased. She felt foolish. The neighbor would despise her. In Pankow she had come slowly to the decision that Leonard was not malicious or brutal, and that it was an innocent stupidity that had made him behave the way he had. He lived so intensely within himself that he was barely aware of how his actions appeared to others. This was the benign judgment she had reached by way of much harsher evaluations and emphatic resolutions never to see him again. Now, with her scream in the dark, her instincts seemed to have overridden her forgiveness. If she could no longer trust him, and even if her mistrust was irrational, what was she doing in his bathroom? Why had she not accepted the neighbor's offer of a taxi? She still wanted Leonard; she had realized that in Pankow. But what kind of man was it who crept up in the dark to apologize for a rape?

By the time she emerged ten minutes later, she had decided to talk to Leonard one more time and see what happened. She was not committed either way. She kept her coat on, buttoned up. He was in the living room. The overhead lights were on, and so were the Army issue standard and table lamps. He had taken up a position in the center of the room and looked, she thought as she came in, like a boy who had just had his backside thrashed. He gestured toward a chair. Maria shook her head. Someone was going to have to speak first. Maria did not see why it should be her, and Leonard was wary of making another mistake. She came further into the room and he took a couple of steps back, unconsciously granting her more space and light.

Leonard had the outlines of a speech in mind, but he was not certain how it would go down. If Maria were to absolve him of the responsibility for further explanation by turning on her heel and slamming the front door on her way out, he would be relieved, at least initially. When he was alone, there was a sense in which he ceased to exist. Here, now, he had to take control of a situation without destroying it. Maria was watching him expectantly. She was offering another chance.

Her eyes were bright. He wondered if she had been crying in the bathroom.

He said, "I didn't mean to frighten you." He was tentative; it was almost a question. But she did not have an answer for him, yet. In all this time she had not spoken a word to him. She had spoken only to Mr. Blake. Leonard said, "I wasn't going to . . . to do anything. I only wanted . . ." He was sounding implausible. He fumbled. To get up close in the dark and hold her hand, that was all he had wanted, to illuminate with the old terms of touch. It was his unexamined assumption that he was safer under cover. He could not tell her, he hardly knew it himself, that the chance darkness on the landing was one with the gloom under the covers in the coldest week of winter, back in the old familiarity when everything had been new. The blade of calluses on her toe, the mole with two hairs, the minuscule dents on her lobes. If she went, what was he going to do with all these loving facts, these torturing details? If she wasn't with him, how would he bear all this knowledge of her alone? The force of these considerations drove the words out of him, they came as easily as breath. "I love you," he said, and then he said it again, and repeated it in German until he had expunged the last traces of self-consciousness, the wincing foolishness of the formula, until it was clean and resonant, as though no one in life or in films had ever uttered it before.

Then he told her how miserable he had been without her, how he had thought about her, how happy he had been before she went away, how happy he thought they both had been, how precious and beautiful she was, and what an idiot, a selfish, ignorant fool, he had been to frighten her. He had never said so much in one go. In the pauses, when he was searching for the unfamiliar, intimate phrases, he pushed his glasses up his nose, or took them off, examined them closely and replaced them. His height seemed to work against him. He would have sat down if only she had.

It was almost unbearable to watch this clumsy, reticent Englishman who knew so little about his feelings lay himself open. He was like a prisoner in a Russian show trial. Maria would have told him to stop, but she was fascinated, the way she had been once as a girl when her father had removed the back of a wireless set and shown her the bulbs and sliding metal plates responsible for human voices. She had not lost touch with her fear, even though it was diminishing with each halting intimacy. So she listened, betraying nothing by her expression while Leonard told her once more that he did not know what had come over him, that he had not meant her harm, and that it would never, ever, happen again.

Finally he ran out. The only sound was that of a scooter on Platanenallee. They listened to it changing down at the end of the road and pulling away. The silence made Leonard think he was doomed. He could not bring himself to look at her. He took off his glasses and polished them on his hankie. He had said too much. It had sounded dishonest. If she went now, he thought, he would take a bath. He wouldn't drown himself. He glanced up. Around the elongated blur that represented Maria in his field of vision there was discernible movement. He returned the glasses to his face. She was unbuttoning her coat, and then she was crossing the room toward him.

12

LEONARD WAS WALKING along the corridor from the water fountain to the recording room, a route that took him past Glass's office. The door was open and Glass was behind his desk. Immediately he was on his feet and waving Leonard in.

"Good news. We ran the checks on that girl. She's cleared. She's okay." He was pointing at a chair, but Leonard remained leaning in the doorway.

"I told you that in the first place."

"That was subjective. This is official. She's a nice-looking girl. The CO and the second-in-command out at this toytown repair outfit have both got the hots for her in their own British way. But she plays it very straight."

"You met her, then." Leonard already knew from Maria about the three interviews with Glass. He did not like it. He hated it. He had to hear about it.

"You bet. She told me that you two were having some trouble and that she was staying out of your way. I told her, 'What the fuck, we're spending valuable man-hours checking you out because you're stepping out with one of our guys, the closest we've ever seen to a genius, godammit, who's doing very important work for his country and mine.' This was after I knew she was okay. I said, 'You just propel your ass around to his apartment and make it up. Herr Marnham isn't the kind of guy you mess around with. He's the best we got, so you better count yourself a privileged lady, Frau Eckdorf!' Did she come back?"

"The day before yesterday."

Glass whooped and started to laugh in a theatrical way.

"There, see? I did you a big favor, I built you up, you got her back. Now we're even."

All very childish, Leonard thought, this locker-room treatment of his private life. He said, "What happened at these interviews?"

The speed of Glass's transition from hilarity to seriousness was in itself a kind of mockery. "She told me you started acting rough. She had to run for her life. Listen, I keep underestimating you, Leonard. That's quite an act you keep hidden there. At work you're Mr. Meek and Mild, then you go home and wham! It's King Kong."

Glass was laughing again, genuinely this time. Leonard was irritated.

Last night Maria had told him all about the security check, which had rather impressed her. Now Glass was back behind his desk, and still Leonard could not dispel his doubts. Could he really trust this man? It was undeniable: one way or another, Glass had climbed into bed with them.

When the laughter had stopped Leonard said, "It's not something I'm proud of." Then he added, with what seemed the correct degree of menace, "Actually, I'm pretty serious about this girl."

Glass stood up and reached for his jacket. "I would be too. She's a honey, a real honey." Leonard stood aside while he locked his office. "What is it I heard one of your people saying once—a proper little darling?"

Glass put his hand on the Englishman's shoulder and walked with him along the corridor. The Cockney imitation was halfhearted, deliberately appalling, Leonard thought. "C'mon, cheer up. Let's go an' 'ave a nice cuppa tea."

13

LEONARD AND MARIA began again on different terms. As the summer of 1955 got under way, they were dividing their time more equally between his apartment and hers. They synchronized their arrivals home from work. Maria cooked, Leonard washed the dishes. On the weekday evenings they walked to the Olympic Stadium and swam in the pool, or, in Kreuzberg, walked along the canal, or sat outside a bar near Mariannenplatz, drinking beer. Maria borrowed bicycles from a cycling club friend. On weekends they rode out to the villages of Frohnau and Heiligensee in the north, or west to Gatow to explore the city boundaries along paths through empty meadows. Out here the smell of water was in the air. They picnicked by Gross-Glienicke See under the flightpath of RAF planes, and swam out to the red-and-white buoys marking the division of the British and Russian sectors. They went on to Kladow by the enormous Wannsee and took the ferry across to Zehlendorf and cycled back through ruins and building sites, back into the heart of the city.

Friday and Saturday evenings they went to the pictures on the Ku'damm. Afterward they jostled with the crowds for a table outside Kempinski's, or they went to their favorite, the smart bar at the Hotel am Zoo. Often they ended up late at night eating a second dinner at Aschinger's, where Leonard liked to gorge himself on yellow pea soup. On Maria's thirty-first birthday they went to the Maison de France for dinner and dancing. Leonard did the ordering in German. Later the same night they went on to Eldorado to see a transvestite cabaret in which completely convincing women sang the usual evergreens to a piano and bass accompaniment. When they got home, Maria, still tipsy, wanted Leonard to squeeze into one of her dresses. He was having none of that.

In their evenings at home, at his place or hers, they kept the radio tuned to AFN for the latest American rhythm and blues. They loved Fats Domino's "Ain't That a Shame" and Chuck Berry's "Maybellene" and Elvis Presley's "Mystery Train." This kind of song made them feel free. Sometimes they heard Glass's friend Russell giving five-minute lectures on the democratic institutions of the West, how the second chamber worked in different countries, the importance of an independent judiciary, religious and racial tolerance, and so on. They found nothing to disagree with in anything he said, but they always turned down the volume and waited for the next song.

There were light, rainy evenings when they stayed in and sat apart without talking for as long as an hour, Maria with one of her romantic novels, Leonard with a two-day-old copy of *The Times*. He could never read a paper, especially this one, without feeling he was imitating someone else, or in training for adulthood. He followed the Eisenhower-Khrushchev summit and later on gave Maria an account of the proceedings and issues in the urgent tones of one who was personally responsible for the outcome. It gave him great satisfaction to know that if he lowered the page, his girl would be there. It was a luxury to ignore her. He felt settled, proud, truly grown-up at last.

They never discussed Leonard's work, but he sensed that she was impressed. The word *marriage* was never mentioned, and yet it was the case that Maria dragged her feet past store window furniture displays on the Ku'damm, and Leonard did put up a crude shelf in the Kreuzberg bathroom so that his shaving stuff could stand by her one jar of moisturizing cream and their toothbrushes could lean together, side by side in a mug. All this was cosy and companionable. With Maria's prompting, Leonard was working at his German. His mistakes made her laugh. They teased each other, giggled a great deal and sometimes had tickling fights on the bed. They made love merrily enough, and rarely missed a day. Leonard kept his thoughts under control. They felt themselves to be in love. When they were out walking, they compared themselves favorably with other young couples they saw. At the same time, it gave them pleasure to think how they resembled them, how they were all part of one benign, comforting process.

Unlike most of the courting couples they saw on the banks of the Tegeler See on a Sunday afternoon, however, Leonard and Maria were already living together, and had already suffered a loss that was not mentioned because it was not at all defined. They could never regain the spirit of February and early March, when it had seemed possible to make their own rules and thrive independently of those quiet, forceful conventions that keep men and women in their tracks. They had lived hand to mouth in lordly squalor, out at the extremes of physical delight, happy as pigs, beyond all consideration of domestic detail or personal cleanliness. It was Leonard's naughtiness—this was the word Maria had used one evening in a glancing reference, thereby bestowing the final forgiveness—his *Unartigkeit,* that had ended all that and forced them back. It was blissful ordinariness they settled for now. They had cut themselves off from the world and ended by making themselves miserable. Now it was the orderliness of going to and from work, of keeping their places tidy and buying an extra chair in a *Trödelladen* for Maria's living room, of linking arms in the street and joining the queues to see *Gone With the Wind* for the third time.

Two events marked the summer and autumn of 1955. One morning in mid-July Leonard walked along the tunnel to the tap chamber, where he was to make a routine check of the equipment. Along the last fifty feet or so, before the antipersonnel door that sealed off the chamber, he found his way blocked. A new man, an American for sure, was supervising the removal of the plugs in the steel liner plates. He had two men working for him, and the amplifiers made it impossible to squeeze around. Leonard cleared his throat loudly and waited patiently. A plug was removed, and the three men made way for him. It was Leonard's "Good morning" that prompted the new man to say in a friendly way, "You guys really screwed up." Leonard went on through to the pressurized tap chamber and spent an hour going over the equipment and its connections. He replaced, as he had been asked, the microphone installed in the ceiling of the vertical shaft, the one that would alert the warehouse to a break-in by the Vopos. On his way back past the amplifiers he found the men drilling with hand-turned bits into the concrete that had been pumped through the liner holes during construction. Another half-dozen plugs had been removed further up the tunnel. No one spoke as he went by this time.

Back in the warehouse he found Glass in the canteen. Leonard waited until the man sitting with him had wandered off before asking what was going on in the tunnel.

"It's your Mr. MacNamee. His calculations were all wrong. Way back he gave us a pile of crappy math to show that the air-conditioning would take care of the heat coming off the amps. Now it looks like he was way off. We brought in a specialist from Washington. He's measuring the soil temperature at different depths."

"What's the harm," Leonard said, "if the earth warms up a bit?"

The question irritated Glass. "Christ! Those amps are right under the road, right under Schönefelder Chaussee. The first frost of fall is going to melt in a handy little block. This way, you guys, there's something going on under here we want you to see!" There was a silence, then "I really don't understand why we let you people in on this. You're not serious the way we are."

"That's nonsense," Leonard said.

Glass did not hear him. "This joker MacNamee. He should be at home with his train set. You know where he did his calculations for the heat output? On the back of an envelope. An envelope! We would have had three independent teams. If they hadn't come up with the same result, we would have wanted to know why. How can the guy think straight with teeth like that?"

"He's an eminent man," Leonard said. "He worked on radio-beam navigation and radar."

"He makes mistakes. That's all that matters. We should have done this thing alone. Collaboration leads to errors, security problems, you name it. We got our own amps. What are we doing with yours? We let you in on this for politics, for some half-assed tradeoff we'll never know anything about."

Leonard felt hot. He pushed his hamburger away. "We're in on this because we have a right. No one fought Hitler for as long as we did. We saw the whole war through. We were

Europe's last and best chance. We gave it everything, so we have the right to be in on everything, and that includes the security of Europe. If you don't understand that, you belong on the other side."

Glass had raised his hand. He was laughing through his apology. "Hey, nothing personal."

Indeed, there was something personal. Leonard was still preoccupied with Glass's time with Maria, and Glass's boast that he had sent Maria back. Maria herself insisted there had been no such exhortation. According to her, she had mentioned the separation in the most general terms and Glass had simply noted it down. Leonard was still unsure, and the uncertainty made him angry.

Glass was saying, "Leonard, don't get me wrong. When I say 'you,' I'm talking about your government. I'm glad *you're* here. And it's true, what you say. You guys were great in the war, you were formidable. It was your moment. And this is my point." He placed a hand on Leonard's arm. "That was your moment, now this is ours. Who else is going to face down the Russians?"

Leonard looked away.

The second event took place during the Oktoberfest. They went down to the Tiergarten on Sunday and for the following two evenings. They saw a Texan rodeo, visited all the sideshows and drank beer and watched a whole pig roasting on a spit. There was a choir of children with blue neckerchiefs singing traditional songs. Maria winced and said they put her in mind of the Hitler Youth. But the songs were wistful, quite beautiful, Leonard thought, and the children were so confident with the difficult harmonies. The next evening they agreed to stay at home. The crowds were tiring after a day's work, and they had already spent next week's going-out money.

As it happened, Leonard had to stay on at the warehouse that evening for an extra hour. A row of eight machines in the recording room had suddenly failed. It was clearly a fault in the power circuits, and it took him and one of the senior American staff half an hour to trace, and as long to put right. He arrived at Adalbertstrasse at seven-thirty. Even as he began to climb the last set of stairs but one, he sensed something different. It was quieter. It was the muted, cautious atmosphere one might expect after an eruption. There was a woman mopping the stairs and an unpleasant smell. On the landing below Maria's a small boy saw him coming up and ran indoors shouting, *"Er kommt, er kommt!"*

Leonard took the last flight at a run. Maria's door was ajar. A small rug just inside the door was askew. In the living room there was broken china across the floor. Maria was in the bedroom, sitting on the mattress in the dark. She was facing away from him, holding her head in her hands. When he put on the light, she made a sound of protest and shook her head. He turned it off and sat by her and put his hand on her shoulder. He said her name and tried to turn her toward him. She resisted him. He eased himself along the mattress to face her. She put her hands across her face and turned away again. "Maria?" he said again, and pulled at her wrist. There was snot on her hand, and blood. It was just visible by the light from the living room. She let him take her hands. She had been crying, but she wasn't now. Her left eye was swollen and closed. The left side of her face had a pulpy texture and was ballooning out. There was a tear, a quarter-inch gash, in the corner of her mouth. The sleeve of her blouse was ripped to the shoulder.

He had known he would have to face it one day. She had told him about the visits. Otto came once, perhaps twice in a year. So far it had been shouted threats, demands for money and, last time, a swipe to the head. Nothing had prepared Leonard for this. Otto had hit her in the face with a closed fist and with all his strength, once, twice, and then again. As he went to fetch cotton wool and a bowl of water, Leonard was thinking through the nausea of shock that he knew nothing about people, what they could do, how they could do it. He knelt in front of her and washed first the wound on her lip. She closed her good eye and whispered, *"Bitte, schau mich nicht an."* Please don't look at me. She wanted him to say something to her.

"Beruhige dich. Ich bin ja bei dir." I'm here with you. Then, remembering his own behavior months before, he could not speak at all. He pressed the cotton wool to her cheek.

14 LEONARD RETURNED HOME for Christmas, having failed to persuade Maria to accompany him. She thought that a divorced older woman, a German, to whom Leonard was not even engaged would not be welcomed by Leonard's mother. He thought she was being too scrupulous. He could not honestly say that his parents lived by such precise and limiting codes. Once he had been home twenty-four hours, he realized she had been right. It was difficult. His bedroom with its single bed and the framed certificate proclaiming him winner of the sixth-form maths prize was a child's room. He was changed, he was transformed, but it was impossible to convey this to his parents. Twisted crepe paper crisscrossed the living room, the holly was in place, framing the mantelpiece mirror. They heard out his enthusiastic account on his first evening home. He told them about Maria and her work and what she was like, about her apartment and his, about the Resi, the Hotel am Zoo, the lakes, and the edginess and excitement of the half-ruined city.

There was a roast chicken in his honor, and more roast potatoes than he could eat these days. There were perfunctory questions, his mother asking how he did for laundry and his father referring to "this girl you're seeing." Maria's name evinced a barely conscious hostility, as though, assuming they would never have to meet her, they could brush her aside. He avoided reference to her age or marital status. Otherwise, their remarks had the effect of grinding away at the difference between here and there. Nothing he said aroused curiosity or wonder or disgust, and soon Berlin was loosened from its strangeness and was nothing more than an outlying stretch of Tottenham, confined and known, interesting in itself, but not for long. His parents did not know he was in love.

And Tottenham, and all of London, was sunk in Sunday torpor. People were drowning in ordinariness. In his street the parallel walls of Victorian terraces were the end of all change. Nothing that mattered could ever happen here. There was no tension, no purpose. What interested the neighbors was the prospect of renting or owning a television. The H-shaped aerials were sprouting on the rooftops. On Friday evenings his parents popped into the house two doors down to watch, and they were saving hard, having sensibly set their hearts against hire-purchase. They had already seen the set they wanted, and his mother had shown him the corner of the living room where it would one day stand. The great struggle to keep Europe free was as remote as the canals of Mars. Down at his father's pub, none of the regulars had even heard of the Warsaw Pact, the ratification of which had caused such a stir in Berlin. Leonard paid for a round and, prompted by one of his father's friends, gave a slightly boastful account of the bomb damage, the fabulous money made by smugglers, the kidnappings—men dragged shouting and kicking into saloon cars and driven off into the Russian sector, never to be seen again. These were all things, the company agreed, that everyone should do without, and the conversation reverted to football.

Leonard missed Maria, and he missed the tunnel almost as much. Daily for almost nine months he had been padding along its length, securing his lines against moisture penetration. He had come to love its earth-water-and-steel smell, and the deep, smothering silence, unlike any silence on the surface. Now he was away from it, he was aware of just how daring, how extravagantly playful, it was to steal secrets from under the feet of East German soldiers. He missed the perfection of the construction, the serious, up-to-the-minute equipment, the habits of secrecy and all the little rituals that went with it. He was nostalgic for the quiet brotherliness of the canteen, the unity of purpose and the competence of all the people there, the generous portions of food, which seemed at one with the whole enterprise.

He fiddled with the living room wireless, trying to find the music to which he was now addicted. "Rock Around the Clock" was here, but that was old hat. He had specialized tastes now. He wanted Chuck Berry and Fats Domino. He needed to hear Little Richard singing "Tutti Frutti," or Carl Perkins's "Blue Suede Shoes." This music played in his head whenever he was alone, tormenting him with everything he was away from. He took the back off the wireless and found a way of boosting the receptor circuits. Through a wail and warble of interference he found AFN and thought he heard Russell's voice. He could not explain his excitement to his mother, who was watching the partial dismantling of the family's Grandvox with despair.

On the street he listened for American voices and never heard any. He saw someone getting off a bus who looked like Glass, and felt disappointment when the man turned his way. Even at the height of his homesickness, Leonard could not delude himself that Glass was his closest friend, but he was a kind of ally, and Leonard missed the near rudeness of the American's speech, the hammer-blow intimacy, the absence of the modifiers and hesitancies that were supposed to mark out a reasonable Englishman. There was no one in the whole of London who would want to seize Leonard's elbow or squeeze his arm to make a point. There was no one, apart from Maria, who cared so much what Leonard did or said.

Glass had even given Leonard a Christmas present. It was at the canteen party, which had centered on a colossal side of beef and dozens of bottles of sekt—a seasonal contribution, it was announced, from Herr Gehlen himself. Glass had pressed a small gift-wrapped box into Leonard's hands. Inside was a silver-plated ballpoint pen. Leonard had seen them around, but he had never used one before.

Glass said, "Developed for Air Force pilots. Fountain pens don't work at high altitudes. One of the lasting benefits of warfare."

Leonard was about to speak his thanks when Glass put his arms around him and squeezed. It was the first time Leonard had been embraced by a man. They were all well on the way to being drunk. Then Glass proposed a toast, "to forgiveness," and looked at Leonard, who took Glass to be referring to the screening of Maria and drank deeply.

Russell had said, "We're doing Herr Gehlen the kindness of drinking his wine. You can't get more forgiving than that."

Under a framed photograph of Tottenham Grammar School's upper sixth, 1948, Leonard sat on the edge of his bed and wrote to Maria with his pen. It flowed beautifully, as though a miniature bolt of bright blue cloth were being pressed into the page. It was a piece of tunnel equipment he held in his hands, a fruit of war. He was sending a letter each day. Writing was a pleasure, and so, for once, was composition. His dominant mode was a jokey tenderness—*I long to suck your toes and play upon your clavicle.* He made a point of not complaining about Tottenham. After all, he might want to entice her here one day. During the first forty-eight hours at home he had found the separation excruciating. In Berlin he had grown so fond, so dependent, and at the same time had felt so grown-up. Now the old, familiar life engulfed him. He was suddenly a son again, not a lover. He was a child. Here was his room again, and his mother worrying over the state of his socks. Early on his second day he woke from a nightmare in which his Berlin life seemed long in the past. *There's no point going back to that town now,* he heard someone say, *it's all different there these days.* He sat on the edge of his bed, cooling his sweat, making plans to have a telegram sent that would urgently recall him to the warehouse.

By the fourth day he was calmer. He could contemplate Maria's qualities, and look forward to seeing her in just over a week. He had given up trying to make his parents see how she had changed his life. She was a secret he carried around with him. The prospect of seeing her at Tempelhof again made everything tolerable. It was during this period of comfortable longing and expectation that he decided he must ask her to marry him. Otto's attack had pushed them even closer together, and had made their lives even less adventurous and more companionable. Maria never stayed alone in her flat now. If they agreed to meet there after work, Leonard made a point of arriving first. While he was in England, she was to stay a few days in Platanenallee, and then move to Pankow for Christmas. They stood back to back, ready to face their common enemy. When they went out together they always walked close, arm in arm, and in bars and restaurants they sat in tight, with a good view of the door. Even when Maria's face had healed and they had stopped talking about him, Otto was always with them. There were times when Leonard was angry with Maria for marrying him.

"What are we going to do?" he asked her. "We can't go around like this forever."

Maria's fear was lightened by contempt. "He's a coward. He'll run when he sees you. And he drinks himself to death. The sooner the better. Why do you think I always give him money?"

In fact the precautions became a habit, part of their intimacy. It was cosy, this common cause of theirs. There were times when Leonard thought it was rather fine, having a beautiful woman rely on him for protection. He had vague plans to get himself in better shape. He found out from Glass that he had the right to U.S. Army gymnasium facilities. Weight-lifting might be of use, or judo, although there would be no room to throw Otto in Maria's flat. But he was not in the habit of taking physical exercise, and each evening it seemed more sensible to go home.

He had fantasies of confrontation that made his heart race. He saw himself in movie style, the peaceable tough guy, hard to provoke, but once unleashed, demonically violent. He delivered a blow to the solar plexus with a certain sorrowful grace. He disarmed Otto of his knife, and in the same movement broke his arm with fastidious regret and "I warned you not to get rough." Another fantasy evoked the irresistible power of language. He would take Otto aside, to a *Kneipe* perhaps, and win him over with a kindly but unflinching reasonableness. They would be man to man, and Otto would depart at last in a mood of mellowed acceptance and dignified acknowledgment of Leonard's position. Perhaps Otto would become a friend, a godfather to one of their children, and

Leonard would use some recently acquired influence to secure the ex-drunk a job at one of the military bases. In other wistful sequences Otto simply never appeared again, having fallen out of a train, or died from his habit, or met the right girl and married again.

All these daydreams were driven by the certainty that Otto would be back and that whatever happened would be unpredictable and unpleasant. Leonard had occasionally seen fights in pubs and bars in London and Berlin. The reality was that his arms and legs went watery at the sight of violence. He had always marveled at the recklessness of fighting men. The harder they struck out, the more vicious were the blows they provoked, but they did not seem to mind. One good kick seemed worth the risk of a life in a wheelchair or with one eye.

Otto had years of brawling experience. He had nothing against hitting a woman in the face with all his strength. What would he want to do with Leonard? Maria's account had made it clear that Leonard was now fixed in his mind. Otto had arrived at her flat fresh from an afternoon's Oktoberfest drinking. He had run out of money and had come by to collect a few marks and remind his ex-wife that she had ruined his life and stolen everything he had. The extortion and the ranting would have been the sum of the visit had Otto not lurched into the bathroom to relieve himself and seen Leonard's shaving brush and razor. He took his piss and came out sobbing and talking of betrayal. He rushed past Maria into the bedroom and saw a shirt of Leonard's folded on the chest. He pulled the pillows off the bed and found Leonard's pajamas. The sobs became shouts. First he pushed Maria around the flat, accusing her of whoring. Then he took hold of her hair in one hand and beat her face with the other. On his way out he swept some cups onto the floor. Two flights below he was sick on the stairs. As he staggered down he shouted more insults up the stairwell for all the neighbors to hear.

Otto Eckdorf was a Berliner. He had grown up in the Wedding district, the son of the owner of a local *Eckkneipe*— one of the reasons Maria's parents had opposed the marriage so bitterly. Maria was vague about Otto's war. She guessed he had been called up in 1939, when he would have been eighteen. He was in the infantry for a while, she thought, and had been part of the victorious procession into Paris. Then he was injured, not in combat but in an accident involving an Army truck overturned by a drunken friend. After a couple of months in a hospital in northern France, he was transferred to a signals regiment. He was on the eastern front, but always well back from the front lines. Maria said, "When he wants you to know how brave he is, he tells you about all the fighting he's seen. Then when he is drunk and he wants to let you know how clever he is, he tells you how he kept out of the fighting by getting sent to the field headquarters as a telephonist."

He had returned to Berlin in 1946 and met Maria, who was working in a food distribution center in the British sector. The answer to Leonard's question was that she had married him because everything at that time had come apart and it did not really matter much what you did, because she had fallen out with her parents, and because Otto was good-looking and seemed kind. A young single woman was vulnerable in those days, and she had wanted protection.

In the gray days after Christmas Leonard took long walks alone and thought about marrying Maria. He walked to Finsbury Park, through Holloway to Camden Town. It was important, he thought, to reach a decision rationally, and not be influenced by separation and longing. He needed to concentrate on whatever counted against her and decide how important it was. There was Otto, of course. There was his lingering suspicion of Glass, but that surely was a matter of his own jealousy. She had told Glass more than she had needed to, that was all. There was her foreignness; perhaps that was an obstacle. But he liked speaking German—he was even getting good, with her encouragement—and he preferred Berlin to any place he had ever been. His parents might object to her. His father, who had been wounded in the Normandy landings, used to say he still loathed the Germans. After a week at home, Leonard accepted that that would be his parents' problem, not his. While his father had been lying in the hollow of a sand dune with a bullet in his heel, Maria had been a terrified civilian, cowering from the nightly bombing.

In effect, there was nothing standing in his way, and when he reached the Regent's Park canal and stopped on the bridge, he abandoned his rigorous scientific procedure and permitted all that was lovely about her to invade his thoughts. He was in love, and he was about to be married. Nothing could be simpler, more logical or more satisfying. Until he had asked Maria, there was no one he could tell. There was no one to confide in. When it was time to break the news, the only friend he could imagine being truly pleased for him, and who would spare nothing to show it, would be Glass.

The surface of the canal showed tiny disturbances, the first signs of rain. The thought of walking northward all the way home, back along the line of his meditation, tired him. He would take a bus from Camden High Street instead. He turned and walked quickly in that direction.

15 AMERICAN SONGS WERE what marked out the weeks and months for Leonard and Maria now. In January and February of 1956 they favored Screamin' Jay Hawkins's "I Put a Spell on You," and "Tutti Frutti." It was the latter, sung by Little Richard at the outer limit of effort and joy, that started them jiving. Then it was "Long Tall Sally." They were familiar with the moves. The younger American servicemen and their girls had been dancing that way at the Resi for a long time. Until now, Leonard and Maria had disapproved. The jivers took up too much space and bumped into the backs of the other dancers. Maria said she was too old for that sort of thing, and Leonard thought it was showy and childish, typically American. So they had clung to each other through the quicksteps and waltzes. But this would not do for Little Richard. Once they had succumbed to the music, there was nothing for it but to turn up the volume of Leonard's wireless set and try the steps, the passes and crossovers and turns, having first made sure that the Blakes downstairs were out.

It was an exhilarating exercise in reading the other's mind, in guessing your partner's intentions. There were many collisions in their first attempts. Then a pattern emerged, devised consciously by neither of them, the product not so much of what they did but of who they were. There was tacit agreement that Leonard should lead and that Maria, by her own movements, should indicate just how he should do so.

Soon they were ready for the dance floor. There was nothing like "Long Tall Sally" to be heard at the Resi or the other dance halls. The bands played "In the Mood" and "Take the 'A' Train," but by now the movements were enough in themselves. Beyond the excitement Leonard took satisfaction in dancing in a way his parents and their friends did not, and could not, and in liking music they would hate, and in feeling at home in a city where they would never come. He was free.

In April came a song that overwhelmed everybody, and that marked the beginning of the end of Leonard's Berlin days. It was no use at all for jiving. It spoke only of loneliness and irresolvable despair. Its melody was all stealth, its gloom comically overstated. He loved it all, the forlorn, sidewalk tread of the bass, the harsh guitar, the sparse tinkle of a barroom piano, and most of all the tough, manly advice with which it concluded: "Now if your baby leaves you, and you've got a tale to tell, just take a walk down Lonely Street . . ." For a time AFN was playing "Heartbreak Hotel" every hour. The song's self-pity should have been hilarious. Instead, it made Leonard feel worldly, tragic, bigger somehow.

It formed the background to the arrangements for the engagement party Leonard and Maria were giving at Platanenallee. It was playing in Leonard's mind when he was buying drinks and peanuts in the Naafi. In the gift section he came across a young officer languidly stooped over a glass counter display of watches. It took several seconds to recognize him as Lofting, the lieutenant who had given him Glass's number on his first day. Lofting too had difficulty in placing Leonard. When he did, he became talkative and a lot friendlier than before. Without preamble, he told how he had finally located a wide open site, persuaded a civilian contractor to clear and level it, and, through someone in the mayor of Berlin's office, had it seeded, ready for use as a cricket pitch. "The speed this grass grows! I've arranged a twenty-four-hour sentry to keep kids off. You must come and look."

He was lonely, Leonard decided, and before he had thought the matter through, he was telling Lofting about his engagement to a German girl and inviting him to the party. They were, after all, rather short of guests.

In the late afternoon before the party *(Drinks 6–8 P.M.),* Leonard was half humming, half singing "Heartbreak Hotel" as he carried a sackful of kitchen rubbish down to the dustbins out the back. The lift was out of order that day. On his way up, Leonard bumped into Mr. Blake. They had not spoken since the scene on Leonard's landing the previous year. Enough time had passed to neutralize that, for when Leonard nodded, Mr. Blake smiled and said hello. Again without reflection, and because he was feeling expansive, Leonard said, "Would you and your wife like to drop in for a drink this evening? Anytime after six."

Blake was searching in his overcoat pocket for his key. He took it out and stared at it. Then he said, "That would be pleasant. Thank you."

"Heartbreak Hotel" was playing on the wireless while Leonard and Maria waited for the first guest. There were peanuts in saucers and, on a table pushed against a wall, bottles of beer and wine, lemonade, Pimms, tonic and a liter of gin, all duty free. There were ashtrays for everyone. Leonard had wanted pineapple chunks and cheddar cheese on toothpicks, but Maria had laughed so hard at this mad concoction that the matter was dropped. They held hands while they surveyed their preparations, conscious that their love was about to begin its public existence. Maria wore a layered white dress that rustled when she moved, and pale blue dancing pumps. Leonard had his best suit on, and—the daring touch—a white tie.

". . . he's been so long on Lonely Street . . ." The door-bell rang, and Leonard went. It was Russell from AFN. Leonard did not know why he should feel foolish that his wireless was tuned to that station. Russell did not seem to notice. He had taken Maria's hand and was holding on to it far too long. But her friends from work, Jenny and Charlotte, were suddenly there too, giggling and holding out presents. Russell stood back as the German girls swept the bride-to-be away in embraces and slangy Berlin exclamations and camped down with her on the sofa. Leonard made a gin and tonic for Russell, and Pimms and lemonade for the girls.

Russell said, "She's the one who sent the message down the tube?"

"That's right."

"She really knows her mind. You want to introduce me to her friends?"

Glass arrived, followed immediately by Lofting, whose attention was drawn by a burst of feminine laughter from the sofa. So Leonard fixed the drinks and took the radio announcer and the lieutenant across. When the introductions had been made, Russell began a breezy flirtation with Jenny, telling her he just knew he had seen her someplace before and that she had the sweetest face. Lofting, more in Leonard's style, engaged Charlotte in tortured small talk. When he said, "That's fascinating. And just how long does it take you to get out to Spandau in the morning?" she and her friends had a fit of the giggles.

Glass had agreed to give a speech. Leonard was touched that his friend had taken the trouble to type it out on cards. He tinkled a bottle opener against the gin for silence. Glass started with an amusing account of Leonard with a rose behind his ear and the message coming down the pneumatic tube. He hoped that one day he too would be delivered from bachelorhood with a similarly dramatic approach, and by a girl as gorgeous and as wonderful in every way as Maria. Russell called out "Hear, hear." Maria shushed him.

Then Glass paused to indicate a change in tone. He was drawing breath to begin again when the doorbell rang. It was the Blakes. While everyone waited, Leonard poured their drinks. Mrs. Blake took an armchair. Her husband remained standing by the door, staring expressionlessly at Glass, who tilted his beard in acknowledgment that the interruption was over.

He spoke quietly. "We all of us in this room, German, British, American, in our different kinds of work, have committed ourselves to building a new Berlin. A new Germany. A new Europe. I know that's the grand way politicians talk, even if it is true. I know that at seven o'clock on a winter's morning, when I'm getting dressed for work, I don't think too hard about building a new Europe." There was a murmur of laughter. "We all know the kinds of freedom we want and like, and we all know what threatens them. We all know that the place, the only place, to start making a Europe free and safe from war is right here, with ourselves, in our hearts. Leonard and Maria belong to countries that ten years ago were at war. By engaging to be married, they are bringing their own peace, in their own way, to their nations. Their marriage, and all others like it, bind countries tighter than any treaty can. Marriages across borders increase understanding between nations and make it slightly harder each time for them to go to war ever again."

Glass looked up from his postcards and grinned, suddenly

disowning his seriousness. "That's why I'm always watching out for a nice Russian girl to take back home to Cedar Rapids. To Leonard and Maria!"

They raised their glasses, and Russell, who had his arm around Jenny's waist, called out, "Come on, Leonard. Speech!"

The only time Leonard had spoken in public was at school, where as a sixth-form monitor in his final year he was obliged once every two weeks to take his turn at reading out the announcements at morning assembly. As he started now, he found that his breathing was too rapid and shallow. He had to speak in clusters of three or four words.

"Thank you, Bob. Speaking for myself, I can't guarantee to rebuild Europe. It's as much as I can do to put up a shelf in the bathroom." His joke went down well. Even Blake smiled. Across the room Maria was beaming at him, or was she half crying too? Leonard blushed. His success made him light. He wished he had another ten jokes to tell. He said, "Speaking for us both, all we can promise, to you and to each other, is to be happy. Thank you very much for coming."

There was applause, and again encouraged by Russell, Leonard crossed the room and kissed Maria. Russell kissed Jenny, then they all settled down to drink.

Blake came across to shake Leonard's hand and offer his congratulations. He said, "The American with the beard. How is it you know him?"

Leonard hesitated. "He's at my work."

"I didn't know you were working for the Americans."

"Ah yes. It's an intersector thing. Telephone lines."

Blake gave Leonard a long stare. He walked with him into a quiet corner of the room. "I want to give you some advice.

That fellow there—Glass, isn't it?—works for Bill Harvey. If you're telling me you work with Glass, you're telling me what it is you do. Altglienicke. Operation Gold. I don't need to know that. You're making a security error there."

Leonard would have liked to say that Blake too had breached security by indicating that he too was part of the intelligence community.

Blake said, "I don't know who these other people here are. I do know that in these matters this is a very small town. It's a village. You shouldn't be seen in public with Glass. It's a giveaway. My advice is that you keep your professional and social lives well separated. Now, I'm going to give my best wishes to your intended, then we'll take our leave."

The Blakes left. Leonard stayed apart for a while with his drink. A part of him—a nasty part, he thought—wanted to see if anything passed between Maria and Glass. They were ignoring each other completely. Glass was the next to leave. Lofting had had several drinks and was making better progress with Charlotte. Jenny was sitting on Russell's lap. The four of them had decided to go to a restaurant, and then to a dance hall. They tried hard to persuade Leonard and Maria to go with them. When they were convinced that they could not succeed, they left with kisses, embraces and goodbyes shouted up the stairwell.

There were abandoned glasses on every surface, and cigarette smoke hung in the air. The apartment was peaceful.

Maria put her bare arms around Leonard's neck. "You made a beautiful speech. You didn't tell me you were good at that." They kissed.

Leonard said, "It's going to take you a long time to find

out all the things I'm good at." He had addressed a crowd of eight. He felt different, capable of anything.

They put their coats on and went out. The plan was to eat in Kreuzberg and spend the night at Adalbertstrasse, thereby including both homes in the celebrations. The bedroom there had been prepared by Maria with fresh sheets, new candles in bottles and a potpourri emptied into two soup bowls.

They dined on *Rippchen mit Erbsenpüree,* spare ribs and pease pudding, in a pub on Oranienstrasse that had become their local. The owner knew about the engagement and brought them glasses of sekt on the house. It was like a bedroom where they were, almost like a bed. They were deep in the recesses of the place, at a table of dark stained wood two inches thick, boxed in by high-backed pews worn smooth by backsides. A tablecloth of thick brocade hung heavily on their laps. Over this a waiter spread a cloth of starched white linen. There was dim light from a red glass lantern that hung from the low ceiling by a heavy chain. A warm, moist air enclosed them further in a fug of Brazilian cigars, strong coffee and roasted meat. Half a dozen old men sat around the *Stammtisch,* the regulars' table, drinking beer and *Korn,* and nearer there was a game of skat.

One of the old fellows paused in his stagger past Leonard's and Maria's table. He looked theatrically at his watch and said, *"Auf zur Ollen!"*

When he had gone, Maria explained. It was a Berlin phrase: "Back to the old woman. Is this you in fifty years?"

He raised his glass. "To my *Olle.*"

There was another celebration coming up, one he could not talk to her about. In three weeks the tunnel would be one year old, calculating, as had been agreed, from the date of the first interception. It had also been agreed that something must happen to mark the event, something that would not violate security, but flamboyant all the same, and symbolic. An ad hoc committee was formed. Glass made himself chairman. There were also a U.S. Army sergeant, a German liaison officer and Leonard. To emphasize the collaboration of three nations, the contributions would reflect something of each national culture. It had seemed to Leonard a little unfair the way Glass had divided the responsibilities, but he said nothing. The Americans would take care of the food, the Germans would provide the drink, and the British would offer a surprise entertainment, a party turn.

With a budget of thirty pounds, Leonard had visited the noticeboards in the YMCA and the Naafi and Toc H clubs, searching for the act that would do his country honor. There was the wife of a corporal in the RAOC who read tea leaves. There was a singing dog, for sale rather than rent, property of an AKC manager, and there was an incomplete morris-dancing team, an offshoot of the RAF rugby club. There was a Universal Aunt who met children and senile relatives off airplanes and trains, and there was a "top-notch" conjuror, for under-fives only.

It was the very morning of his engagement party that Leonard had followed up a lead and made contact with a sergeant in the Scots Greys who promised to supply, in return for a thirty-pound contribution to the sergeant's mess fund, a piper in full regimental dress—tartan, feathers, sporran, the lot. This, and his short speech and its successful joke, and the sekt, and the gin that had preceded it, and the new language he was beginning to master, and the *Gaststätte* where he felt so at home, and above all his beautiful fiancée, who was clinking her glass against his—all this made Leonard reflect that he had never really known himself at all, he was far more interesting and, well, civilized than he had ever dared suspect.

Maria had curled her hair for the event. Artfully disordered wisps lay across the high Shakespearean forehead, and just below the crown was a new white clip, the childish touch she was reluctant to abandon. She was looking at him now with patient amusement, that same regard, both proprietorial and abandoned, that had forced him in their early days to divert himself with circuitry and mental arithmetic. She was wearing the silver ring they had bought from an Arab on the Ku'damm. Its very cheapness was a celebration of their freedom. Outside the big jewelry stores, young couples were eyeing engagement rings that cost more than three months' wages. After Maria's hard bargaining, with Leonard, too embarrassed to listen, standing several paces off, they got theirs for less than five marks.

The meal was all that stood between them and Maria's flat, the prepared bedroom and the consummation of their engagement. They wanted to talk about sex, so they were talking about Russell. Leonard was trying out a tone of responsible caution. It did not quite suit his mood now, but the force of habit was strong. He had a warning for Maria to pass on to her friend Jenny. Russell was a fast mover—an operator, as Glass would say—who had once claimed that in his four years in Berlin he had chalked up more than 150 girls. Leonard said in German, "Apart from the fact that he's bound to have the clap"—den Tripper; he had recently learned the word from a poster in a public lavatory—"he is not going to take Jenny seriously at all. She ought to know that."

Maria had put her hand over her mouth and laughed at Tripper. *"Sei nicht doof!* You're . . . *schüchtern.* How do you say it in English?"

"A prude, I think," Leonard was forced to say.

"Jenny looks after herself. Do you know what she was saying when the Russell came in the room? She said, 'That's the one I want. I don't get paid till the end of next week and I want to go to a restaurant. Then I want to go dancing. And,' she said, 'he has a beautiful jaw, like Superman.' So, she goes to work, and Russell thinks he did it all by himself."

Leonard put down his knife and fork and wrung his hands in mock anguish. "My God! Why am I so ignorant?"

"Not ignorant. Innocent. And now you marry the first and only woman you ever knew. Perfect! It's women who should marry the virgins, not men. We want you fresh—"

Leonard pushed his plate aside. It was not possible to eat while you were being seduced.

"—we want you fresh so we can show you how to please us."

"Us?" said Leonard. "You mean there's more than one of you?"

"There's just me. That's all you have to think about."

"I need you," Leonard said. He waved at the waiter. It was not the conventional exaggeration. If he did not lie down with her soon he thought he might be sick, for there was a cold upward pressure on his stomach and on the pease pudding in there.

Maria raised her glass. He had never seen her so beautiful. "To innocence."

"To innocence. And Anglo-German cooperation."

"It was a terrible speech," Maria said, although from her look he thought she did not really mean it. "Does he think I'm the Third Reich? Is that what he thinks you are marrying? Does he really think that people represent countries? Even the major makes a better speech at the Christmas dinner."

But when they had paid and put on their coats and were walking toward Adalbertstrasse, she resumed more seriously. "I don't trust this one. I didn't like him when he was asking me questions. His mind is too simple and too busy. These are the dangerous ones. He thinks you must love America or you must be a spy for the Russians. These are the ones who want to start another war."

Leonard was pleased to hear her say she did not like Glass, and he was reluctant to start an argument now. All the same he said, "He takes himself very seriously, but he's not so bad, really. He's been a good friend to me in Berlin."

Maria pulled him closer to her. "Innocence again. You like anyone who's kind to you. If Hitler buys you a drink, you say he's a decent fellow!"

"And you'd fall in love with him if he told you he was a virgin."

Their laughter sounded loud in the empty street. As they came up the stairs at No. 84, their hilarity echoed on the bare wood. On the fourth floor someone opened a front door a few inches, then slammed it shut. They made almost as much noise the rest of the way up, shushing each other and giggling.

To make a welcome, Maria had left all the lights on in her flat. The electric heater was on in the bedroom. While she was in the bathroom, Leonard opened the wine that had been left ready. There was a smell in the air he could not quite place. It was of onions, perhaps, and something else. There was an association there he could not make. He filled their glasses and turned on the wireless. He was ready now for another dose of "Heartbreak Hotel," but all he could find was classical music of some sort, and jazz, both of which he loathed.

He forgot to mention the smell when Maria came out of the bathroom. They took their glasses through to the bedroom and lit cigarettes and talked quietly about the success of their party. The smell, which had been in this room too, and the fragrance of the potpourri, were lost to the smoke. They were returning to the urgency they had felt at dinner, and as they talked they began to undress, and touch and kiss. Accumulated excitement and unrestrained familiarity made everything so easy. By the time they were naked, their voices had dropped to whispers. Beyond the room came the subsiding rumble of a city beginning to take itself to bed. They got under the covers, which were lighter again now that spring was here. For five minutes or so they luxuriated in the postponement of their pleasure with a long embrace. "Engaged," Maria whispered, *verlobt, verlobt.* The very word was a form of invitation, incitement. They began lazily. She was lying beneath him. His right cheek was pressed against hers. His view was of the pillow and of her ear, and hers was over his shoulder, of the ripple and pull of small muscles in his back, and then, the darkened room beyond the candlelight. He closed his eyes and saw an expanse of smooth water. It might have been the Wannsee in summer. With each stroke he was drawn down the shallow curve of his descent, further and deeper, until the surface was liquid silver far above his head. When she stirred and whispered something, the words poured like mercury droplets, but fell like feathers. He grunted. When she said it again, into his ear, he opened his eyes, though he still had not heard. He lifted himself onto his elbow.

Was it ignorance or innocence that made him think that the accelerating thud of her heart against his arm was excitement, or that the wide stare of her eyes, the seed pearls of moisture on her upper lip, the difficulty she was having moving her tongue to repeat her words, were all for him? He dropped his head closer. What she was saying was framed in the quietest whisper imaginable. Her lips were brushing his ear, the syllables were furred. He shook his head. He heard her tongue unglue itself and try again. What at last he heard her say was, "There's someone in the wardrobe."

Then his heart was racing hers. Their ribcages were touching, and they could feel, but not hear, the arrhythmic clatter, like horses' hooves. Against this distraction he was trying to listen. There was a car drawing away, there was something in the plumbing, and behind that nothing, nothing but silence and inseparable darkness, and scratchy silence too hastily scanned. He went back over it, searching the frequencies and watching her face for a cue. But every muscle there was already tight; her fingers were pinching his arm. She was still hearing it, she was willing his attention toward it, forcing him to attend to the band of silence, the narrow sector where it lay. He had shrunk to nothing inside her. They were separate people now. Where their bellies touched was wet. Was she drunk, or mad? Either would have been preferable. He cocked his head, straining, and then he heard it, and knew he had been hearing it all along. He had been searching for something else, for sounds, for pitch, for the friction of solid objects. But this was only air, air pulled and pushed; this was muted breathing in an enclosed space. He rose on all fours, and turned. The wardrobe was by the door, by the light switch. He found his glasses on the floor. They did nothing to clarify the large dark mass. His instinct was that he could do nothing, confront nothing, submit to nothing, unless he was covered. He found his underpants and put them on. Maria was sitting up. She had her hands cupped over her nose and mouth.

The thought came to Leonard, and perhaps it was a habit from all his time at the warehouse, that they should do nothing to betray their awareness of the presence. A pretended conversation was not possible. So Leonard stood in the dark in his underpants and began to hum through a constricted throat his favorite song while he tried to think, in his terror, what to do next.

16 MARIA REACHED FOR her skirt and blouse. Her movement made the candle gutter, but it did not quite die. Leonard took his trousers from a chair. He had increased the tempo of his humming, transforming it into a cheerful tune of dotted rhythms. His only thought now was to be dressed. Once his trousers were on, he felt the bareness of his chest pricking in the dark. When his shirt was on, his feet were vulnerable. He found his shoes, but not his socks. While he was tying the laces he fell silent. They stood on either side of the bed, the engaged couple. The rustle of fabric and Leonard's song had obscured the breathing. Now they heard it again. It was faint, but deep and steady. To Leonard it suggested some unflinching purpose. Maria's body blocked the candle's light and threw a giant shadow toward the door and wardrobe. She looked at him. Her eyes were sending him to the door.

He went quickly, and tried to tread quietly on the bare boards. It took four steps. The light switch was right against the wardrobe. It was impossible not to sense the presence, to feel on his fingers and his scalp the force field of a human presence. They were about to give themselves away, make it known that they knew. His knuckles brushed against the polished surface as he snatched at the light. Maria was behind him; he felt her hand on the small of his back. The explosion of light was surely more than sixty watts. He screwed his eyes up against the brightness. He had his hands up, ready. The wardrobe doors would be bursting open now. Now.

But there was nothing. The wardrobe had two doors. One opened onto a set of drawers and was firmly closed. The other door, the one that opened onto the coat space, a space big enough for a man to stand in, was slightly ajar. The catch was not engaged. It was a big brass ring that turned a worn spindle. Leonard put his hand out toward it. They could hear the breathing. It was not a mistake. They were not going to be laughing about this in two minutes. It was breathing, human breathing. He got his fingers and thumb on the ring and lifted it without making a sound. Still holding on, he shuffled backward. Whatever was going to happen, he wanted there to be space. The greater the distance, the more time he would have. These geometrical thoughts came in hard little packets, tightly bound. Time to do what? The question too was wrapped tight. He squeezed harder on the ring, and yanked the door open wide.

There was nothing. Only the blackness of a serge coat, and a smell, a miasma, sucked outward by the door's movement, of alcohol and pickle. Then the face, the man, was right down by the floor in a sitting position, with his knees drawn up, asleep. The sleep of a drunk. It was beer and *Korn* and onions, or sauerkraut. The mouth hung open. Along the lower lip was a trail of whitish scum, interrupted in the center, at right angles, by a big black split of congealed blood. A cold sore, or a whack on the mouth from another drunk. They stepped back, out of the immediate path of the sweet stench.

Maria whispered, "How did he get in?" Then she answered herself. "He could have taken a spare key. When he came last time."

They stared in at him. The immediate danger was subsiding. What was taking the place of fear was disgust, and a sense of violation, householderly outrage. It did not seem an improvement. This was not how Leonard had expected to confront his enemy. He had a chance to size him up. The head was small, the hair was thinning on top and was of the sandy, tobacco-stained kind, almost greenish at the roots, that Leonard had noticed frequently around Berlin. The nose was big and weak-looking. Along its sides were ruptured vessels under tight shiny skin. Only the hands gave an impression of strength—raw red, and bony and big at the knuckles and joints. The head was small, and so were the shoulders. It was hard to tell with him slumped down, but this was beginning to look like a runt, a bully and a runt. The threat he had represented, the way he had knocked Maria around, had magnified him. The Otto of Leonard's thoughts had been a weathered Army tough, a survivor of a war Leonard had not been old enough to fight.

Maria pushed the wardrobe door shut. They turned out the bedroom light and went into the living room. They were too agitated to sit. Maria's voice grated with a bitterness he had never heard before.

"He's sitting on my dresses. He's going to piss on them."

This had not occurred to Leonard, but now she had spoken it appeared the most pressing problem. How were they to prevent this further violation? Lift him out, carry him to the toilet?

Leonard said, "How are we going to get rid of him? We could get the police." He had a brief bright thought of two *Polizisten* carrying Otto out through the front door, and the rest of the evening resuming after a calming drink and a good laugh.

But Maria shook her head. "They know about him, they even buy him beers. They won't come." She was distracted. She muttered something else in German and turned away, changed her mind and turned back. She was going to speak, and thought better of it.

Leonard still held to the possibility of rescuing their celebration. It was simply a matter of getting rid of a drunk. "I could carry him out, drag him down the stairs, put him out in the street. I bet he wouldn't even wake . . ."

Maria's distraction was settling into anger. "What was he doing in my bedroom, in our bedroom?" she demanded, as though Leonard had put him there. "Why aren't you thinking about that? Why is he hiding in the wardrobe? Go on, tell me what you think."

"I don't know," he said. "I don't care for now. I just want him out."

"You don't care! You don't want to think about it." She sat down suddenly on one of the kitchen chairs. She was by the heap of shoes piled up around the cobbler's last. She snatched a pair and pulled them on.

It occurred to Leonard that they were about to have a row. It was their engagement night. It was not his fault and they were having a row. Or at least she was.

"It matters to me. I was married to this pig. It matters to me that when I am making love to you, this pig, this piece of human shit, is hiding in the cupboard. I know him. Do you understand that?"

"Maria—"

This time she raised her voice. "I know him." She was trying to light a cigarette and making a mess of it.

Leonard wanted one too. He said soothingly, "Come on now, Maria . . ."

She got hers alight and inhaled. It did not do her any good, she was still close to shouting. "Don't talk to me like this. I don't want to be calmed down. And why are you so peaceful? Why aren't you angry? There is a man spying on you in your own bedroom. You should be breaking the furniture. And what are you doing? Scratching your head and saying nicely we should get the police!"

It seemed to him that everything she was saying was correct. He had not known how to react, he had not even thought about it. He did not know enough. She was older than him, she had been married. This was how you were when you found someone hiding in your bedroom. At the same time it irritated him, what she was saying. She was accusing him of not being a man. He had hold of the cigarettes now. He took one out. She was still going on at him. Half of it was in German. She had the lighter in her fist and she was barely conscious of him taking it away from her.

"You're the one who should be shouting at me," she said. "It's my husband, isn't it? Aren't you angry, just one little bit?"

This was too much. He had filled his lungs; now he expelled the smoke with a shout. "Shut up! For God's sake, shut up for one minute!"

She was instantly quiet. They both were. They smoked their cigarettes. She remained in the chair. He went and stood as far away as was possible in the tiny room. Presently she looked at him and smiled an apology. He kept his face neutral. She had wanted him to be a little angry with her; well, he would be, for a bit.

She spent some time stubbing out her cigarette and at first did not look up from what she was doing when she spoke. "I'll tell you why he's in there. I'll tell you what Otto wants. I wish I didn't know, I hate knowing why. But, so . . ."

When she began again, her tone was brighter. She had a theory. "When first you know Otto, he is kind. This was before the drinking began, seven years ago. At first he is kind. He does everything he can think of to please. This was when I married him. Then slowly you see that this kindness is possession. He's possessive, he thinks all the time you are looking at other men, or they are looking at you. He is jealous, he starts hitting me, and making up stories, stupid stories about me and men, people he knows, or people in the street, it doesn't matter. He always thinks there's something. He thinks one half of Berlin has been to bed with me, and the other half is waiting. About this time the drinking gets worse. And finally, after all this time, I see it."

She was reaching for another cigarette, but she shuddered and changed her mind. "This thing, me and another man, he *wants* this. It makes him angry, but he wants it. He wants to watch me with another man, or he wants to talk about it, or he wants me to talk about it. It excites him."

Leonard said, "He's . . . he's a sort of pervert." He had never actually said the word before. It was satisfying.

"Exactly so. He discovers about you, that's when he hits me. Then he goes away and thinks about it, and can't stop thinking about it. This is all his dreams come true, and this time it's real. He thinks and he drinks, and all the time he has a key from somewhere. Then tonight he drinks even more than usual, comes up here and waits . . ."

Maria was beginning to cry. Leonard crossed the room and put his hand on her shoulder.

"He waits, but we are late and he falls asleep. Perhaps he was going to jump out while, when . . . it was happening and accuse me of something. He still thinks he owns me, he thinks I am going to feel guilty . . ."

She was crying too much to speak. She was fumbling in her skirt for a handkerchief. Leonard gave her his big white one from his trouser pocket. When she had blown her nose, she breathed deeply.

Leonard started to speak, but she spoke over him. "I hate him, and I hate knowing about him."

Then he said what he had been going to say. "I'll take a look." He went into the bedroom and turned on the light. To open the wardrobe he had to close the bedroom door behind him. He stared at the voyeur. Otto's position was unchanged. Maria called from next door. He opened the bedroom door an inch or so. "It's all right," he told her. "I'm just looking at him."

He continued to stare. Maria had actually chosen this man as her husband. That was what it came down to. She might say she hated him, but she had chosen him. And she had also chosen Leonard. The same taste exercised. He and Otto had both appealed to her, they had that in common—aspects of personality, appearance, fate, something. Now he did feel angry with her. She had bound him by her choices to this man whom she was pretending to disown. She was making out it was all an accident, as if it really had nothing to do with her. But this voyeur was in their bedroom, in the wardrobe, asleep, drunk, about to piss on all the clothes because of the choices she had made. Yes, now he really was angry. Otto was her responsibility, her fault, he was hers. And she had the nerve to be angry with him, Leonard.

He turned out the bedroom light and went back into the

living room. He felt like leaving. Maria was smoking. She smiled nervously.

"I'm sorry I shouted."

He reached for the cigarettes. There were only three left. When he chucked the pack down, it slid to the floor, by the shoes.

She said, "Don't be angry with me."

"I thought that's what you wanted."

She looked up, surprised. "You *are* angry. Come and sit down. Tell me why."

"I don't want to sit down." He was enjoying his scene now. "Your marriage to Otto is still going on. In the bedroom. That's why I'm angry. Either we talk about how we get rid of him, or I'm going back to my place and you two can carry on."

"Carry on?" Her accent gave the familiar phrase a strange lilt. The menace she intended was not there. "What are you trying to say?"

It irritated him that she was coming back at him with anger, instead of allowing him his scene. He had let her have hers. "I'm saying that if you don't want to help me get rid of him, then you can spend the evening with him. Talk over old times, finish the wine, whatever. But count me out."

She put her hand to her beautiful high forehead and spoke across the room to her imagined witness. "I don't believe this. He's jealous." Then to Leonard. "You too? Just like Otto? You want to go home now and leave me with this man? You want to be at home and think about Otto and me, and perhaps you'll lie on the bed and think about us . . ."

He was genuinely horrified. He did not know she could talk like this, or that any woman could. "Don't talk such bloody nonsense. Just now I was for dragging him out into the street and leaving him there. But you just want to sit here and give me a loving description of his character, and cry into my hankie."

She balled the handkerchief up and threw it at his feet. "Take it. It stinks!"

He did not pick it up. They both went to speak, but she got there first. "You want to throw him in the street, why don't you just do that? Do it! Why can't you just act? Why do you have to stand around and wait for me to tell you what to do? You want to throw him out, you're a man, throw him out!"

His manliness again. He strode across the room and grabbed her by the front of her blouse. A button came off. He put his face up close to hers and shouted, "Because he's yours! You chose him, he was your husband, he got your key, he's your responsibility." His free hand was in a fist. She was frightened. She had dropped her cigarette into her lap. It was burning, but he didn't care, he didn't give a damn. He shouted again. "You want to sit by while I sort out the mess you've made of your past—"

She shouted back, right into his face. "That's right! I've had men screaming at me, hitting me, trying to rape me. Now I want a man to look after me. I thought it was you. I thought you could do it. But no, you want to be jealous and scream and hit and rape like him and all the rest—"

Just then Maria burst into flames.

From where the cigarette had smoldered leaped a single finger of flame, which instantly crossed and wreathed itself around others springing from the folds of white fabric. These flames were multiplying outward and upward even before she had drawn her first breath to scream. They were blue and yellow, and quick. She scrambled to her feet, beating with her hands. Leonard reached for the wine bottle and the half-full glass that stood beside it. He emptied the glass over her lap and it made no difference. As she stood and began a second long scream he was trying to pour the wine from the bottle over her. But it would not come quick enough. There was a moment when her skirt was like a flamenco dancer's, all oranges and reds, with in-woven blue, and to a crackling sound she was turning, thrashing, pirouetting as though she might rise up and out of it. This was a moment, a fraction of an instant before Leonard hooked both hands into the waistband and tore the skirt away. It all came in one piece, and blazed afresh on the floor. He stamped on it, glad of his shoes, and as the flames gave way to thick smoke he was able to turn and see her face.

It was relief he saw there, stunned relief, not physical pain. There was a lining, a stitched-in petticoat of satin or some natural material that had been slow to catch. It had protected her. It was under his feet now, browned but intact.

He could not stop what he was doing. He had to go on stamping as long as there were flames. The smoke was bluish-black and thick. He needed to open a window, and he wanted to put his arms around Maria, who was standing motionless, perhaps in shock, naked but for her blouse. He needed to fetch her dressing gown from the bathroom. He would do that first, when he was certain that the carpet would not catch fire. But when at last he was satisfied and had stepped away, it was natural that he should turn and embrace her first. She was shivering, but he knew she was going to be all right. She was saying his name over and over. And he kept saying, "Oh God, Maria, oh my God."

At last they pulled away a little, only a few inches, and looked at each other. She had stopped trembling. They kissed, then again, and then her eyes shifted from his and widened. He turned. Otto was leaning by the bedroom door. The remains of the smoldering skirt lay between them. Maria stepped behind Leonard. She said something quick in German which Leonard did not catch. Otto shook his head, more to clear his thoughts, it looked, than to deny what she had said. Then he asked for a cigarette, a familiar phrase that Leonard only just managed to understand. Whatever the improvements in Leonard's German lately, it was going to be hard following the conversation of this once-married couple.

"Raus," Maria said. Get out.

And Leonard said in English, "Clear off, before we call the police."

Otto stepped over the skirt and came to the table. He was wearing an old British Army jacket. There was a V shape of darker material where a corporal's stripe had been. He was sifting through the ashtray. He found the largest stub and lit it with Leonard's lighter. Because he was still covering Maria, Leonard was unable to move. Otto took a drag as she stepped around them and made for the front door. It hardly seemed possible that he was about to step out of their evening. And it was not. He reached the bathroom and went inside. As soon as the door closed, Maria ran to the bedroom. Leonard filled a saucepan with water and poured it over the skirt. When it was drenched through, he lifted it into the wastepaper basket. From the bathroom came the sound of a terrible hawking and spitting, a thick and copious expectoration through the medium of an obscene shouting noise. Maria came back, fully dressed. She was about to speak when they heard a loud crash.

She said, "He's knocked down your shelf. He must have fallen onto it."

"He did it deliberately," Leonard said. "He knows I put it up."

Maria shook her head. He did not see why she should be defending him.

She said, "He's drunk."

The door opened and Otto was before them again. Maria retreated to her chair by the pile of shoes, but she did not sit. Otto had doused his face and had only partially dried himself. Lank, dripping hair hung over his forehead, and a droplet had formed at the end of his nose. He wiped it with the back of his hand. Perhaps it was mucus. He was looking toward the ashtray, but Leonard blocked his way.

Leonard had folded his arms and set his feet well apart. The destruction of his shelf had got to him, it had set him calculating. Otto was six inches or so shorter and perhaps forty pounds lighter. He was either drunk or hung over, and he was in bad physical shape. He was narrow and small. Against that, Leonard would have to keep his glasses on and was not used to fighting. But he was angry, incensed. That was something he had over Otto.

"Get out now," Leonard said, "or I'll throw you out."

From behind him Maria said, "He doesn't speak English." Then she translated what Leonard had said. The threat did not register on Otto's pasty face. The gash in his lip was oozing blood. He probed it with his tongue and at the same time reached into first one and then another of his jacket pockets. He brought out a folded brown envelope, which he held up.

He spoke around Leonard to Maria. His voice was deep for such a small frame. "I've got it. I've got the something from the office of something-something" was all Leonard could make out.

Maria said nothing. There was a quality, a thickness to her silence that made Leonard want to turn around. But he did not want to let the German through. Otto had already taken a step forward. He was grinning, and some muscular asymmetry was pulling his thin nose to one side.

At last Maria said, *"Es ist mir egal, was es ist."* I don't care what you've got.

Otto's grin widened. He opened the envelope and unfolded a single sheet that had seen much handling. "They have our letter of 1951. They found it. And our something, signed by both of us. You and me."

"That's all in the past," Maria said. "You can forget about that." But her voice wavered.

Otto laughed. His tongue was orange from the blood he had licked.

Without turning around, Leonard said, "Maria, what's going on?"

"He thinks he has a right to this apartment. We applied for it when we were still married. He's been trying this one for two years now."

Suddenly, to Leonard, it seemed a solution. Otto could take this place, and they would live together in Platanenallee, where he could never find them. They would be married soon, they did not need two places. They would never see Otto again. Perfect.

But Maria, as if reading his thoughts, or warning him off them, was spitting out her words. "He has his own place, he has a room. He only does this to make trouble. He still thinks he owns me, that's what it is."

Otto was listening patiently. His eyes were on the ashtray, he was waiting for his chance.

"This is my place," Maria was saying to Otto. "It's mine! That's the end of it. Now get out!"

They could be packed up in three hours, Leonard thought. Maria's stuff would fit into two taxis. They could be safe in his apartment before dawn. However tired, they might still resume their celebration, in triumph.

Otto flicked the letter with his fingernail. "Read it. See for yourself." He took another half-step forward. Leonard squared up to him. But perhaps Maria should read it.

Maria said, "You haven't told them we're divorced. That's why they think you have a right."

Otto was gleeful. "But they do know. They do. We have to appear together before a something-something, to see who has the greater need." Now he glanced at Leonard, then round him to Maria again. "The Englishman has a place, and you have a ring. The something-something will want to know about that."

"He's moving in here," Maria said. "So that's the end of the matter."

This time Otto held Leonard's gaze. The German was becoming stronger, less the derelict and drunk, more the operator now. He thought he was winning. He spoke through a smile. *"Ne, ne. Die Platanenallee 26 wäre besser für euch."*

It was as Blake had said. Berlin was a small town, a village.

Maria shouted something. It was certainly an insult, an effective one. The smile went from Otto's face. He shouted back. Leonard was in the crossfire of a marital row, an old war. In the volleys he caught only verbs, piling at the ends of staccato sentences like spent ammunition, and the traces of some obscenities he had learned, but inflected into new, more violent shapes. They were shouting at the same time. Maria was ferocious, she was a fighting cat, a tiger. He had never guessed she could be so passionate, and he felt momentary shame that he himself had never aroused her this way. Otto was straining forward. Leonard put his hand out to hold him back. The German hardly noticed the contact, and Leonard did not like what he felt. The chest was hard and heavy to the touch, like a sandbag. The man's words came vibrating up Leonard's arm. Otto's letter had put Maria on the defensive, but whatever she was saying now was striking home. *You never could, you didn't have, you aren't capable* . . . She was going for the weaknesses, the drink perhaps, or sex, or money, and he was shaking, he was shouting. His lip was bleeding more. His saliva spotted Leonard's face. He was pushing forward again. Leonard caught his upper arm. It was hard too, impossible to deflect from its movements.

Then Maria said something intolerable, and Otto tore from Leonard's grip and went for her, straight for her throat, cutting off her words and any possible sound. His free hand was raised, the fist was clenched. Leonard caught it in both hands just as it began the trajectory to Maria's face. The lock on her windpipe was tight, her tongue was forced out, purplish-black, her eyes were big and beyond pleading. The blow still carried Leonard forward, but he pulled down on Otto's arm, swung it up and round his back, against the joint, where it should have cracked. Otto was forced to turn to his right, and as Leonard firmed his two-handed grip on the man's wrist and pushed the arm higher up the spine, Otto let Maria go and spun to free his arm and face his attacker. Leonard released him and took a step back.

Now his expectations were fulfilled. This was the thing he had dreaded. He stood to be seriously hurt, disabled forever. If the front door had been open, he might have made a run for it. Otto was little, and strong and vicious beyond belief. All his hatred and anger were on the Englishman now, everything that should have been Maria's. Leonard pushed his glasses up his nose. He did not dare remove them. He had to see what was about to happen to him. He put his fists up, the way he had seen boxers do it. Otto had his hands by his side, like a cowboy ready to draw. His drunk's eyes were red. What he did was simple. He drew back his right foot and kicked the Englishman's shin. Leonard dropped his guard. Otto punched out, straight for his Adam's apple. Leonard managed to turn aside, and the blow caught him on the collarbone. It hurt, it really hurt, beyond reason. It could be broken. It would be his spine next. He raised his hands, palms outward. He wanted to say something, he wanted Maria to say something. He could see her over Otto's shoulder, standing by the pile of shoes. They could live in Platanenallee. It would be all right with her, if she would only think it through. Otto hit him again, hard—very hard—on the ear. There was a ringing sound, an electric bell sound from every corner of the room. It was so venomous, so . . . unfair. This was Leonard's last thought before they went into the clinch.

They had their arms around each other. Should he pull the tight, hard, disgusting little body in closer, or push it away where it might hit him again? He felt the disadvantage of his height. Otto was right into him, and suddenly he understood why. Hands were groping between his legs, and finding his testicles and closing around them. The grip that had been around Maria's throat. Burnt ocher blossomed in his vision, and there was a scream. Pain was not a big enough word. It was his whole consciousness in a terrible corkscrewed reverse. He would do anything, give anything, to be free, or dead. He folded over, and his head came level with Otto's, his cheek grazed his, and he turned and opened his mouth and bit deep into Otto's face. It was not a fighting maneuver, it was the agony that clenched his jaw until his teeth met and his mouth was filled. There was a roar that could not have been his own. The pain was diminished. Otto was struggling to be away. He let him go and spat out something of the consistency of a half-eaten orange. He did not taste a thing. Otto was howling. Through his cheek you could see a yellow molar. And blood, who would have thought there was so much blood in a face? Otto was coming again. Leonard knew there would be no escape now. Otto was coming with his bleeding face, and there was something else too, something coming from behind, black and high up on the periphery of vision. To protect himself from this as well, Leonard stretched up his right hand, and time slowed as his fingers closed around something cold. He could not sway it from its course, he could only take hold and participate, let it carry on down, and down it came, all force and iron, the sign of the kicking feet, down it dropped like justice, with his hand on it, and Maria's hand, the full weight of a judgment, the iron foot crashed down on

Otto's skull, and pierced the bone toe-first and went deeper still and dropped him to the floor. He went down without a sound, face forward and he was stretched full out.

The cobbler's last still protruded from his head, and the whole city was quiet.

17

AFTER THEIR ENGAGEMENT PARTY, the young couple stayed up all night and talked. This was how he was trying to see it two hours after dawn, as he waited in line with the rush-hour crowd for his bus out to Rudow. He needed a sequence, a story. He needed order. One thing after another. He boarded the bus and found a seat. His lips were forming the words as he carried through the actions. He found a seat and sat down. After the fight, he brushed his teeth for ten minutes. Then they put a blanket over the body. Or was it, they covered the body with a blanket, and then he went in the bathroom and brushed his teeth for ten minutes. Or twenty. His toothbrush was on the floor, among the broken glass, under the shelf that had crashed down. The toothpaste had fallen in the basin. The drunk knocked down the shelf and the toothpaste fell in the basin. The toothpaste knew it would be needed, the toothbrush didn't. The toothpaste was in charge, the toothpaste was the brains . . .

They did not, could not, remove the last. It stuck up under the blanket. Maria laughed. It was still there now. They covered up the last, and it was still there. The quick and the last. The quick found a seat, the last had to stand. As they moved along Hasenheide the bus filled. There was standing room only. Then the driver called down to the pavement that there was no more room at all. That was comforting somehow; no one else could get on. For the moment they were safe. As they dropped southward, against the rush-hour flow, the bus began to empty. By the time they reached Rudow village, there was only Leonard, exposed among the lines of seats.

He began the familiar walk. There was more building going on than he remembered. He had not been this way since yesterday. Yesterday morning, before he was engaged. They took a blanket off the bed and spread it over. It was not respect, why had he ever thought it had to do with respect? They had to protect themselves from the sight of it. They had to be able to think. He was going to pull the last out. Perhaps that was respect. Or concealment. He knelt down and took hold. It moved under his touch, like a stick in thick mud. That was why he could not pull it out. Was he going to have to wipe it off, rinse it under the bathroom tap?

They tried to cover up the lot, and it looked silly, a worn-out shoe at one end, at the other the mystery shape looming up, pinching all the blanket that should have been the shoe's. Maria started laughing, horrible fall-about laughing, full of fear. He could have joined in. She did not try to meet his eye, the way laughing people do. She was alone with it. She was not trying to stop, either. If she had stopped she would have started crying. He could have joined in, but he did not dare. Things could get out of hand. In films, when women laughed like that you were supposed to slap them hard round the face. Then they were silent as they grasped the truth, then they started crying and you comforted them. But he was too tired. She might complain or tell him off or hit him back. Anything might happen.

It already had. Before or after the blanket, he did his teeth. The toothbrush was not enough; as a tool it was insufficient. When he asked her, she fetched him the toothpicks. That was what he had to use to remove what was trapped between an incisor and a canine. He was not sick. He thought of Tottenham and Sunday lunch and his father and himself with the toothpicks, before pudding. His mother never used them. Somehow women did not. He did not swallow the morsel and add to his crimes. Now, every little thing was a plus. He washed it away under the tap and hardly saw it, just a glimpse of something shredded and palest pink, and then he spat and spat again and rinsed his mouth.

And then they had a drink. Or he had already had one to help him lift the last. The wine was gone, the good Mosel was in the skirt. There was nothing but the Naafi gin. No ice, no lemon, no tonic. He took it into the bedroom. She was hanging up the clothes. Not pissed on—there was another plus.

She said, *Where's mine?* So he gave her his and went back for another. He was by the table pouring it, trying not to look, when he looked. It had moved. There were two shoes now, and a black sock. They had not turned it over, they had not actually checked to see if it was dead. He watched the blanket for a sign of breathing. It had started with the breathing. Was there a tremor, a little rise and fall? Would it be worse if there were? Then they would have to call an ambulance, before they'd had a chance to talk, to sort out the story. Or they would have to kill him again. He watched the blanket, and watching it made it move.

He took his drink into the bedroom and told her. She would not come and look. She was not having it. She had her mind made up. It was dead. The clothes were all hung up and she shut the wardrobe door. She went next door to find the cigarettes, but he knew she had gone to look. She came back and said she could not find them. They sat on the bed and drank their drinks.

When he sat down, his testicles hurt. And his ear, and his collarbone. Someone ought to look after him. But they had to talk, and to talk they had to think. To do that they needed a drink and a sit-down, and that hurt, and so did his ear. He had to get out of these too fast, too tight circles. So he drank the gin. He looked at her as she looked at the ground in front of her feet. She was beautiful, he knew that, but he could not feel it. Her beauty did not affect him the way he wanted it to. He wanted to be moved by her, and for her to remember how she felt about him. Then they could face this together, and decide what it was they were going to tell the police. But looking at her, he did not feel a thing. He touched her arm and she did not look up.

They had to get together so they could be sure they were believed. The police might think she was beautiful, they might even feel it. He only knew it for a fact. If they felt it, they might understand, and that might be the way through. *It was self-defense,* she would tell them, and that would be all right.

He took his hand off her arm and said, *What are we going to tell the police?* She did not speak, she did not even look up. Perhaps he had not spoken. He had meant to, but he had not heard anything himself. He could not remember.

He was walking past the refugee shacks. It hurt to walk. His collarbone only hurt when he lifted his arm, his ear when he touched it, but his testicles hurt when he sat down and when he walked. When he was out of sight of the shacks, he would stand still. He saw a kid with ginger hair, a carrot-top. He had short trousers and scabby knees. He looked like a little bruiser. He looked like an English kid. Leonard had seen him often enough before on his way to work. In all this time they had never spoken or even waved. They just stared, as if they had known each other in a previous life. Today, to bring himself luck, Leonard raised his hand in greeting and half smiled. It hurt when he raised his hand. The kid would not have cared if he had known that, he just stared. The grown-up had broken the rules.

He walked on around the corner and stopped to lean against a tree. Across the road they were building an apartment house. Soon this would not be countryside any longer. The people who lived here would not know what it had once looked like. He would come back and tell them. *It never did look very good here,* he would say. *So it's all right. Everything is all right.* Except the thoughts, on and on.

There was nothing he could do. He touched her arm again, or it was the first time. He asked his question again, or he asked it for the first time and took care that the words were actually spoken.

I know, she said, meaning *I share your question, I share your worry.* Or perhaps *You've asked me this already, and I heard you.* Or perhaps *I answered you just now.*

To keep things going he said, *It was self-defense, it was self-defense.*

She sighed. Then she said, *They know him.*

Yes, he said. *So they'll understand.*

She said in a rush, *They liked him, they thought he was a war hero, he told them some kind of story. They thought he was a drunk because of the war. He was a drunk who had to be forgiven. The off-duty ones sometimes bought him a beer. And they thought he was also a drunk because of me. They told me that when I asked them round here once. I wanted protection, and they said, But you're driving the poor devil crazy.*

He stood up from the bed to help the pain. He wanted to get the gin. He wanted to bring the bottle through. He wanted to look for the cigarettes. There were still three in the pack, but it hurt to walk. And if he went in there, he might see that it had moved again.

He stood by the wardrobe and he said, *That's just the local station, the* Ordnungspolizei. *We need to speak to the* Kriminalpolizei, *they're a different bunch.* He was saying this, but of course there were no criminals, no crime, it was self-defense.

She said, *But the locals will get involved all the same. They have to, it's their area.*

So, he said, *what are we going to tell them?*

She shook her head. He thought she meant she did not know. But she meant something quite different. It was only two-thirty then, and she already meant something quite different.

Walking his familiar route, he could pretend it had not happened. He was on his way to work, that was all. He would go down into the tunnel, he was looking forward to the tunnel. He had gone out to get the gin. The cigarettes were nowhere. He looked at the shoes. They were further out, he could not doubt it. He could see both socks, and a bare patch of leg with sparse hair. He hurried into the bedroom and told her, but she did not look up. She had folded her arms and she was staring at the wall. He shut the door and poured them both a gin. Drinking it, he thought of the Naafi.

I tell you what, he said. *We'll get the British military police. Or the Americans. I'm attached, you see, it's what I'm meant to do.*

She almost unfolded her arms, then she slotted them back

together. *I'm involved,* she said. *The German police will have to know.*

He was still standing. He said, *I'll tell them it was all me.* A mad offer.

She did not smile or soften her voice. She said, *You're sweet and kind. But he's German, and this apartment is mine, and this was my husband once. They have to tell the German police.*

He was glad the offer was not taken up. He said, *We're getting bogged down. They might think he was a war hero, but they know he was violent, they know he was a drunk, and jealous, and it's our word against his, and if we had wanted to kill him we wouldn't smash his head and report it to the police.*

She said, *If we thought we could get away with it, why not?* And when he did not answer because he had not understood, she said, Totschlag, *that's what they'll say. Manslaughter.*

He was approaching the sentries. It was Jake and Howie on the gate. They were friendly and made a joke about his swollen ear. He still had to show his pass. It was just as good as it had been the day before. Not everything had changed, it wasn't all bad. He went on through, past the sentry box, along the path, his usual route. He met no one on his way to his room.

Pinned to his door was a note from Glass. *Meet me in the canteen 1300 hours.* The room was as he had left it—the workbench, soldering irons, ohmmeters, voltmeters, valve testing equipment, rolls of cable, boxes of spare parts, a broken umbrella he was intending to fix with solder. This was all his stuff, this was what he did, this was what he really did, all quite legal and aboveboard. Or above one board and below another, and not legal by every definition. There were some definitions they were at war with, there were certain definitions they were committed to eradicating. *I've got to stop this,* he thought, *I've got to slow down.*

Manslaughter, she said. He had to go and sit on the bed, never mind the pain. It sounded worse than murder. Slaughter. It sounded worse. It sounded about right for what they had next door.

He tried something else. *I tell you what,* he said. *I should go and see a doctor, straightaway.*

She said through a yawn, *Is it really bad?* One more thing she did not want to think about.

He said, *A doctor should look at my collarbone and my ear.* He did not say his testicles. They were hurting now. And he did not want a doctor looking at them, squeezing them and asking him to cough. He writhed where he sat and he said, *I should go. Don't you see, it's our proof that it was self-defense. I should go while it's really bad, and they could take photos.*

But, he thought, *not of my balls.*

And she said, *Would you tell them it was self-defense too, that hole in his face?*

He sat there and he almost passed out.

He went along the corridor to the water fountain. He wanted the water on his face. He passed by Glass's office and checked. Out—there was another plus. He could wave at boys, or say hello to sentries, but he could not talk to Glass. He took some valves and other odds and ends from his own office and locked it. There was a small job left over from yesterday. It might help him slow down. An excuse to be in the tunnel, to collect what he had to fetch from there.

If you see the doctor, she said, *you have to tell him, and that means the police.*

He said, *But at least we'll have the proof of a fight, a fight. He would have torn me to pieces.*

Oh yes, she said. *The proof of self-defense, but what about the hole?*

Well, he said. *You can tell them why I had to do that.*

But I don't know why, she said. *Tell me, why did you bite him like this?*

He said, *Didn't you see? Didn't you see what he was doing?*

She shook her head, so he told her. And when he finished she said, *I didn't see that. You were too close.*

Well, it's true, he said.

She sipped her gin and asked him, *Did it hurt so bad that you had to bite a hole in his face?*

Of course it did, he said. *You'll have to tell them you saw it. It's important that you say that.*

She said, *But you said we had no need to lie, you said we did nothing wrong, we have nothing to hide from them.*

Did I say that? he said. *I mean, we have done nothing wrong, but we have to make them believe it, we have to get our story right.*

Ah well, she said. *Ah so, if we are going to lie, if we are going to pretend things, then we must do it right.* And she uncrossed her arms and looked at him.

He walked past the spoil piled to the basement ceiling. They said mushrooms sometimes grew on the dark slopes, but he had never seen one. He didn't want to see one now.

He was standing by the rim of the shaft, and he was feeling better. The sound of the generators, the bright bare lights at the mouth of the tunnel, the dim ones up here, the cables and field lines feeding down, the ventilation, the cooling systems . . . *The systems,* he thought, *we need systems.* He showed his authority and said to the guard that he would be bringing up a couple of things and he would need the lift. "You got it, sir," the man said.

The old vertical iron ladder was gone. These days you got down by way of a set of stairs that spiraled one and a half turns on the wall of the shaft. *They think of everything,* he thought, *the Americans.* They wanted to make things possible, and easy. They wanted to look after you. This pleasant lightweight staircase with the nonslip treads and chain-link banisters, the Coke machines in the corridors, steak and chocolate milk in the canteen. He had seen grown men drinking chocolate milk. The British would have kept the vertical ladder because difficulty was part of a secret operation. Americans thought of "Heartbreak Hotel" and "Tutti Frutti" and playing catch on the rough ground outside, grown men with chocolate-milk mustaches playing ball. They were the innocent. How could you steal secrets from them? He had given MacNamee nothing, he hadn't really tried. There was a plus.

It hurt walking down the stairs. He was glad when he was down. He had found out nothing about Nelson's technique, how to separate the clear text echoes from the encrypted message. They had these secrets *and* they had their chocolate milk. He had found out nothing. He had tried a couple of doors. He had not lied to MacNamee, and he had stolen nothing so he did not need to lie to Glass.

She said again, *If we tell them lies* . . . Then she let it hang, and it was his turn.

He said, *We have to be together, we have to have it clear. They'll take us in separate rooms and look for contradictions.* Then he stopped and said, *But there isn't even a lie we can tell them. What can we say, that he slipped on the bathroom floor?*

I know, she said. *I know,* by which she meant, *You're right, so move on to the inevitable conclusion.* But he did not move. He sat and thought about standing up. He poured more gin. It did not seem to reach him somehow, this lukewarm drink.

In the tunnel there was silky black air sifted by machine, and manmade silence, and competence, ingenuity, discretion everywhere he looked. He had the valves in his hand, he was on a job. He walked between the old railway lines, the lines that had brought the dirt out.

You're drinking too much, she said. *We have to think.*

He emptied the cup so he could put it down on the bed. He could think better when he closed his eyes. It hurt his ear less.

I'll tell you another thing, she said. *Are you listening? Don't go to sleep. They know at the Rathaus, the city hall, that he was claiming a right to this place. They have the correspondence, all the papers.*

He said, *So what? His claim was all nonsense, you told me.*

Es macht nichts, she said. *He had a grievance, and we had a reason to quarrel.*

You mean a motive, he said. *You're saying that would be*

our motive? Do we look like people who solve a housing dispute this way?

Who knows? she said. *It's difficult to find a place here. In Berlin, people have killed each other for less than that.*

All that says, he said, *is that he had a grievance and he came here to fight and it was self-defense.*

When she thought they were getting nowhere she folded her arms again. She said, *At work I heard this English word,* manslaughter, *from the major. He told me. This happened the year before I started work there. One of the mechanics in the workshops, a German civilian, got in a fight in a* Kneipe *with another man and he killed him. He hit him over the head with a beer bottle and it killed him. He was drunk, and angry, but he didn't mean to kill. He was very sorry when he saw what he had done.*

And what happened to him?

He was sent to prison for five years. He's still there now, I think.

It was a normal day in the tunnel. Hardly anyone around, everything in order, the place running smoothly. It was fine, it was how the rest of the world should be. He stopped and looked. Tied to this fire extinguisher was a label showing that the weekly check had been carried out at 1030 hours the day before. Here were the initials of the engineer, his office phone number, the date of the next check. Perfection. Here was a telephone point, and by it a list of numbers: the duty officer, security, the firefighting unit, the recording room, the tap chamber. This cluster of lines, held in bunches like a little girl's hair with a bright new clip, ran from the amplifiers to the recording room. These were the lines to the tap chamber, this piping circulated water to cool the electronics, these were the ventilation ducts, this line carried a separate current to the alarm systems, this was a sensor with a probe out deep into the surrounding soil. He put his hand out and touched them. It all worked, he loved them all.

He opened his eyes. Neither of them had spoken for five minutes. Perhaps twenty minutes had gone by. He opened his eyes and started speaking. *But this wasn't like a fight in a pub*, he said. *He attacked me, he could have killed me.* He stopped and remembered. *He attacked you first, he had you by the throat.* He had forgotten her throat. *Let me look*, he said. *How does it feel?* There were red marks all the way around and right up to her chin. He had forgotten about that.

It hurts when I swallow, she said.

There you are, he said. *You should come with me to the doctor. This is going to be our story, and it's the truth, it's what happened. He would have strangled you.*

Yes, he thought. *I stopped him.*

She said, *It's four o'clock. No doctor will see us now. And even if he did, I tell you.* She stopped, and then she unfolded her arms. *I tell you, I'm thinking all the time about the police, and what they see when they come in here.*

We'll take the blanket off first, he said.

She said, *It doesn't matter about the blanket. I tell you what they see. A mutilated corpse.*

Don't say that, he said.

A smashed-in skull, she said, *and a hole in his face. And what do we have between us? A red ear, a sore throat?*

And my balls, he thought, but he didn't say a thing.

There were a couple of technicians working by the amplifiers. All he had to do was nod at them. Then he stopped at the end of the racks. There was a desk, and there they were, stowed underneath, just as he remembered them. But he could stop on the way back. He had to do his job, it would help him. Not even that. He wanted to do it, he had to hold on. He passed through the pressurized doors, into the tap chamber. There were two men in here as well, people he always said hello to but never got to know. One had the headphones on, the other was writing. They smiled at him. Talking was discouraged in here; you could whisper if it was essential, that was all. The one who was writing pointed to the swollen ear and grimaced.

One of the two recorders, the one not in use, needed a valve replacement. He sat down to the job and took his time unscrewing the cover plates. This was what he would have been doing if nothing had happened. He wanted it to last. He replaced the valve and then he poked around, looking at the connections and the soldered points on the signal activation. When he had the covers back on he continued to sit there, pretending to think.

He must have fallen asleep. He was on his back, the light was on, he was fully dressed and he couldn't remember a thing. Then he remembered. She was shaking his arm and he sat up.

She said, *You can't sleep and leave everything to me.*

It was coming back to him. He said, *Everything I say, you're against it. You tell me.*

She said, *I don't want to tell you. I want you to see it for yourself.*

See what? he said.

For the first time in hours she stood. She put her hand to her throat and said, *They won't believe it about self-defense. No one will. If we tell them, then we go to prison.*

He was looking around for the gin bottle, which wasn't where he left it. She must have moved it, and that was fine with him because now he was feeling sick. He said, *I don't think that's necessarily true*. But he did not mean it; it was true, they were going to prison, German prison.

So, she said. *I have to say it. Someone has to say it, so I'll say it. We don't have to tell them, we don't say a thing. We take him out of here and put him where they don't find him.*

Oh my God, he said.

And if they do find him one day, she said, *and they come and tell me, I'll say, Oh, that's very sad, but he was a drunk and a war hero, he was bound to get into trouble.*

Oh God, he said, and then, *If they see us taking him out of here, then we're finished, it will look like murder. Murder.*

That's true, she said. *We must do it right*. She sat down beside him.

We have to work together, he said.

She nodded, and they held hands and did not speak for a while.

In the end he had to go. He had to leave the cosy chamber. He nodded at the two men and went out through the double doors, and swallowed hard to adjust his ears to the lower pressure. Then he was kneeling by a desk. There were the two empty cases. He decided to bring them both. Each one could hold two of the big Ampex recording machines as well as spares, microphones, reels and cable. They were black with reinforced edging, and had big snap locks and two canvas straps that buckled around for extra safety. He opened one up. There was no lettering, inside or out, no Army codes or manufacturer's name. There was a wide canvas strap handle. He picked them up and started along the tunnel. He had trouble squeezing them by the people by the amplifier racks, but one of the men took a case and carried it along to the far end for him. Then he was on his own, bumping along the tunnel to the main shaft.

He could have carried them up the stairs one at a time, but the fellow at the top saw him there and swung the derrick out and started the electric winch. He put the cases on the pallet, and they were up before he was. He went back past the earth mounds, up to ground level, out through some awkward double doors and along the side of the road to the sentry. He had to open up his cases for Howie—just a formality—then he was off along the open road, off on his holidays.

It was deep enough to be a nuisance, his new luggage. It banged his legs and forced his arms out and made his shoulders ache. And this was empty luggage. There was no sign of the carrot-top kid. In the village he had trouble reading the bus timetable; the figures drifted upward diagonally. He read them as they moved. He had forty minutes to wait, so he set the cases against a wall and sat on them.

He was the first one to speak. It was five A.M. He said, *We could drag him down the stairs now, carry him to one of the bomb sites. We could put the bottle in his hand, make it look like something happened with the other drunks.* He said all this, but he knew he did not have the strength, not now.

She said, *There are always people on the stairs. They come in from the night shifts, or they go off early. And some of them are old and never sleep. It's never really quiet here.*

He was nodding all the time she spoke. It was an idea, but it was not the best idea and he was glad they were thinking it through now. At last they were agreeing, at last they were getting somewhere. He closed his eyes. It was going to be all right.

Then the bus driver was shaking him. He was still on the cases, and the driver had guessed he was waiting for his bus. This was the end of the line, after all. He had forgotten nothing, he knew it all the moment he opened his eyes. The driver took one of the cases, and he took the other. Some mothers with small children were already seated, off to the city center, to the department stores. That's where he was going, he had not forgotten a thing. He would tell Maria, he had stayed with it. His arms and legs were weak, he had not got them going yet. He sat at the front, with his luggage on the seat behind. He did not have to look at it all the time.

As they headed north they stopped to pick up more mothers and children and their shopping bags. This was the purposeful, head-down punctuality of rush hour. Now it was cheerful, chatty, festive. He sat with their separate voices behind him, the mothers' bright conversation founded on agreement, ruptured by little laughs and complicit groans, the children's irrelevant squawks, finger-pointing exclamations, lists of German nouns, sudden frets. And him alone at the front, too big, too bad for a mother, remembering the journeys with her from Tottenham to Oxford Street, in the window seat, holding the tickets, the absolute authority of the conductor and the system he stood for, which was true—the stated destination, the fares, the change, the bell ring—and hanging on tight until the great vibrating important bus had stopped.

He got off with everyone else near the Kurfürstendamm.

She said, *Don't go to the* Eisenwarenhandlung, *go to a department store where they won't remember you.*

There was a big new one across the road. He waited with a crowd for a policeman to stop the traffic and wave the people on. It was important not to break the law. The department store was new, everything was new. He consulted a list on a board. He had to go to the basement. He stepped on the escalator. In the land of the defeated, no one need walk downstairs. The place was efficient. In minutes he had what he wanted. The girl who served him gave him the change and the *Bitte schön* without a glance and turned to the man at his side. He took the U-Bahn from Wittenbergplatz and walked to the flat from Kottbusser Tor.

When he knocked on the door she called out, *"Wer ist da?"*

"It's me," he said in English.

When she opened the door, she looked at the cases he was carrying, and then she turned back inside. Their eyes had not met. They did not touch. He followed her in. She had rubber gloves on; all the windows were open. She had cleaned up the bathroom. The place had the atmosphere of a spring clean.

It was still there, under the blanket. He had to step over it. She had cleared the table. A pile of old newspapers was on the floor, and on a chair, folded up, were the six meters of rubberized cloth she had said she would get. It was bright and cold in here. He set the cases down by the bedroom door. He wanted to go in there and lie on the bed.

She said, "I made some coffee."

They drank it standing up. She did not ask about his morning; he did not ask about hers. They had done their jobs. She finished her coffee quickly and began to spread the newspaper on the table two or three sheets thick. He watched her from the side, but when she turned in his direction, he looked away.

"Well?" she said.

It was bright, and then it was brighter still. The sun had come out, and though it did not shine directly into the room, the reflected light of huge cumulus clouds illuminated every corner, every detail—the cup in his hand, an upside-down headline on the table in Gothic script, the cracked black leather of the shoes protruding from under the blanket.

If all this suddenly disappeared, they would have a hard enough time getting back to where they had once been. But what they were about to do now would block their way forever. Therefore—and this seemed simple—therefore, what they were doing was wrong. But they had been through all that, they had talked the night out. She had her back to him and she was looking out the window. She had removed the gloves. Her fingertips were resting on the table. She was waiting for him to speak. He said her name. He was tired, but he tried to say it in the old way they had used, tilted gently upward like a question, whenever they recalled each other to the essentials—love, sex, friendship, the shared life, whatever.

"Maria," he said.

She recognized it and turned. Her look was hopeless. She shrugged, and he knew she was right. It would make it harder. He nodded his acknowledgment and turned away and knelt beside one of the cases and opened it. He took out a linoleum cutting knife, a saw and an axe and set them to one side. Then, leaving the blanket and the last in place, and with Leonard at the head, Maria at the feet, they lifted Otto toward the table.

18 FROM THE VERY BEGINNING, from the moment they laid hands on him, it went wrong. Now that rigor mortis had set in, it was in fact all the easier to lift him. His legs stayed out straight and he did not sag in the middle. He was face down when they picked him up, and like a plank. The transformation caught them unprepared. Leonard fumbled his grip under the shoulders. The head drooped. The last, pulled by its own weight, slid out of the skull and fell onto Leonard's foot.

Over his shout of pain Maria cried, "Don't put him down now. We are almost there."

Worse than the pain of what he thought might be a broken toe was the fact that there was issuing from under the blanket, from Otto's brain or mouth, a cold liquid of some sort, which was soaking into the lower part of Leonard's trousers.

"Oh Christ," he said, "get him up there now, then. I'm going to be sick."

There was just room for the body stretched out diagonally on the table. With the lower part of his trousers clinging to his shins, Leonard limped into the bathroom and hunched over the lavatory bowl. Nothing came. He had had nothing to eat since the *Rippchen mit Erbsenpüree* of the night before. He preferred to think only of its German name. When he looked below his knees, however, and saw a smear of gray matter edged with blood and hair highlighted against the dark wet cloth, he retched. At the same time he struggled to take his trousers off. Maria was watching him from the bathroom door.

"It's on my shoes as well," he said. "And my foot is broken, I'm sure of it." He got his shoes and socks and trousers off and shoved them under the basin. There was nothing to show on his foot but a faint red mark at the base of his big toe.

"I'll rub it for you," she offered.

She followed him into the bedroom. He found some socks in the wardrobe, and trousers rumpled from Otto's occupation. By the bed were his carpet slippers.

Maria said, "Perhaps you should wear one of my aprons." That seemed all wrong. Women made pies and baked bread in aprons.

He said, "I'll be all right now."

They went back into the other room. The blanket was still in place, that was something. On the floor where Otto had been were two big damp patches on the carpet. The windows were wide open and there was nothing to smell. But the light was relentless. It picked out the fluid that had soaked Leonard. It was greenish and was dripping from the table to the floor. They stood around, reluctant to make the next move. Then Maria went to the chair where her purchases were and began to explain them. She took a deep breath at the beginning of each sentence. She was trying to keep things moving.

"This is the cloth, how do you say it, *wasserdicht?*"

"Waterproof."

She was holding up a red tin. "This is the glue, rubber glue, which dries quickly. Here is a brush to spread the glue. I use these dressmaking scissors to cut the pieces." Like a demonstrator in a department store, she cut a large square of cloth as she spoke.

This detailing of her methods helped him. He took his

own things over to the table and set them down. There was no need to explain them.

"Right, then," he said too loudly. "I'll make a start. I'll do a leg."

But he did not move. He stared at the blanket. He could see each separate fiber of the weave, the infinite replication of its simple pattern.

"Take the shoe and sock off first—" was Maria's advice. She had the lid off the tin and was stirring the glue with a teaspoon.

That was practical. He put his hand on Otto's ankle and eased the shoe off by its heel. It came easily. There were no laces. The sock was a disgrace, matted with embedded filth. He peeled it off quickly. The foot was blackened. He was glad he was by an open window. He rolled the blanket up until the legs were exposed from just above the knees. He did not want to start alone.

He said to her, "I want you to hold him steady with both hands here." He indicated the upper leg. She did as he asked. They were together now, side by side. He took up the saw. It was finely toothed, and was sheathed for safety in a fold of cardboard held in place by a rubber band. He got that off and stared into the crook of Otto's knee. The trousers were black cotton and shiny from wear. He held the saw in his right hand, and with his left he held Otto's leg just above the ankle. It was colder than room temperature. It drew the heat from his hand.

"Don't think about it," Maria said. "Just do it." She snatched another breath. "Remember I love you."

It could not be, of course, but it was important that they were together in this. They needed a formal declaration. He would have told her that he loved her too, but his mouth was so dry.

He drew the saw across the crook of Otto's knee. It snagged immediately. It was the cloth, and below that, stringy tendons. He lifted the saw out and, without looking at the teeth, put it in position again and tried to pull it toward him. The same thing happened.

"I can't do this," he cried. "It won't go, it doesn't work!"

"Don't push down so hard," she said. "Do it gently. And do the first few strokes toward you. Afterward you can go backward and forward."

She knew about carpentry. She could have made a better shelf in the bathroom. He did as she suggested. The saw was moving with lubricated ease. Then the teeth snagged again, this time on bone, and then they were engaged. Leonard and Maria had to tighten their grip on the leg to keep it still. The saw made a muffled rasping sound.

"I have to stop!" he shouted, but he did not. He kept going. He should not have been going through bone. The idea was to get into the joint. His idea of it was vague, derived from roast chicken Sunday lunches. He angled the saw this way and that, and went at it hard, knowing that if he stopped he would never resume. Then he was through something, then it was grating bone again. He was trying not to see, but the April light exposed it all. The upper leg was oozing almost black, covering the saw. The handle was slippery. He was through, there was only skin below, and he could not get at it without sawing the table. He took the linoleum knife and tried to scour it with one stroke, but it puckered under the blade. He had to get in there, he had to put his hand into the chasm of the joint, into the cold mess of dark, ragged flesh and saw at the skin with the blade of the knife.

"Oh no!" he shouted. "Oh God!" And he was through. The whole of the lower leg was suddenly an item, a thing in a cylinder of cloth, with a bare foot. Maria was ready for it. She rolled it tight in the square of waterproof cloth she had prepared. Then she glued the ends and sealed them. She tucked the package into one of the cases.

The stump was oozing heavily; the whole table was covered. The newspaper was sodden and disintegrating. Blood was seeping down the table legs and was already all over the paper on the floor. The paper stuck to their feet when they walked over it, exposing the carpet underneath. His arms were a uniform reddish-brown from the fingertips to above the elbow. It was on his face. Where it was drying it itched. There were spots on his glasses. Maria's hands and arms were covered too, and her dress was smeared. It was a quiet time of day, but they called to one another as though they were in a storm.

She said, "I'm going to wash myself."

"There's no point," he said. "Do it at the end." He took up the saw. Where it had been slippery, it was now sticky. This would aid his grip. They took hold of the left leg. She was on his right, this time steadying the lower leg with both hands. It should have been quicker, this one, but it was not. He began well enough, but the saw stuck halfway through, wedged tight within the joint. He had to get both hands on the saw. Maria had to stretch over him and steady the upper leg as well. Even so, as Leonard struggled with the saw, the body jerked from side to side in a mad face-down dance. When the blanket dropped away, Leonard kept his eyes off the skull. It was at the edge of vision. Soon it would have to be dealt with. They were sodden now from the waist down, from where they were pushing up against the table. It no longer mattered. He was through the joint. It was the skin again, and he had to put his hand in with the knife. Would it have been easier, he thought, if the flesh had been warm?

The second parcel was in the case. Two rubber boots side by side. Leonard found the gin. He drank from the bottle and handed it to Maria. She shook her head.

"You're right," she called. "We must keep going."

They did not discuss it, but they knew they would do the arms. They started with the right, the one Leonard had tried to wrench. It was crooked and stiff. They could not pull it out straight. It was difficult finding a way in, or a place to stand to get the saw into the shoulder. Now that the table and the floor, their clothes and arms and faces, were bloodied, it was not that bad being near the skull. The whole of the back of it had collapsed inward. There was only a little brain to be seen, pushed up along the line of the fractures. After red, gray was easy. Maria held the forearm. He started in the armpit, straight into the Army jacket and the shirt underneath. It was a good saw, sharp, not too heavy, just supple enough. Where the blade met the handle there was an inch or two not yet obscured by blood. The maker's crest was there, and the word *Solingen*. He repeated it as he worked. They were not killing anyone here. Otto was dead. Solingen. They were dismantling him. Solingen. Nobody was missing. Solingen, Solingen. Otto is disarmed. Solingen, Solingen.

Between the arms he drank the gin. It was easy, it was sensible. An hour's mess, or five years in prison. The gin bottle was sticky too. The blood was everywhere, and he accepted it. This was what they had to do, this was what they were doing. Solingen. It was a job. After he had given Maria the left arm, he did not pause. He got his hands behind Otto's shirt collar and tugged. The vertebrae at the top of the spine were designed to hold a saw in place. He was through the bone in seconds, through the cord, neatly guiding the flat of the saw against the base of the skull, snagging only briefly on the sinews of the neck, the gristle of the windpipe, and through and through with no need for the linoleum knife. Solingen, Solingen.

Otto's banged-up head clunked to the floor and settled among the crumpled pages of the *Tagesspiegel* and *Der Abend* and offered up his long-nosed profile. He looked much as he had done in the wardrobe—eyes closed, skin unhealthily pale. His lower lip, however, was no longer giving him trouble. What was on the table now was no one at all. It was the field of operations, it was a city far below that Leonard had been ordered to destroy. Solingen. The gin again, the sticky Beefeater, then the big one, the thighs, the big push, and that would be it, home, a hot bath, a debriefing.

Maria was sitting on a wooden chair by the open cases. She took each part of her ex-husband onto her lap and patiently, with an almost maternal care, set about folding it away and sealing it and packing it carefully along with the rest. She was wrapping the head now. She was a good woman, resourceful, kind. If they could do this, they could do anything together. When this job was done, they would start again. They were engaged, they would resume the celebrations.

The saw blade rested snugly along the line of the crease

where the buttocks met the leg. He would not aim to find the joint this time. Straight through the bone, a sturdy piece of two-by-two, and a good saw to cut it with. Trouser, skin, fat, flesh, bone, flesh, fat, skin, trouser. The last two he took with the knife. This one was heavy, dripping at both ends when he took it to her. His carpet slippers were black and heavy. The gin, and the other leg. This was the order of things, the order of battle: everything twice, except the head. The big lump that remained on the table to be wrapped, the cleaning up, the washing and scrubbing of skin, their skin, the disposal of things. They had a system, they could do this again if they really had to.

Maria was gluing the cloth around the second thigh. She said, "Take his jacket off."

That was easy too, what with no arms to mess with. It just lifted off. Everything so far was fitting into one case. The torso would go in the second. She packed the second thigh and closed the lid. She had a dressmaker's tape measure. He took one end and they laid it along the piece on the table. One hundred and two centimeters from gaping neck to stumps. She took the measure and knelt down by the cases.

"It's too big," she said. "It won't go in. You'll have to cut it in half."

Leonard came down, he emerged from a dream. "That can't be right," he said. "Let's measure it again."

It was right. The cases were ninety-seven centimeters long. He snatched the tape and took the measurements alone. There was surely some means of bringing the figures closer.

"We'll squeeze it in. Wrap it up and we'll squeeze it in."

"It won't go. It's a shoulder bone here, and the other end

is thick. You have to cut it in half." It was her husband, and she knew.

Arms and legs, and even the head, were extremities that could be lopped off. But cutting into the rest was not right. He fumbled after a principle, some general notion of decency to support his instinctive certainty. He was so tired. When he closed his eyes he felt himself lifting away. What was needed here were some guidelines, a few basic rules. It simply was not possible, he heard himself telling Glass and a handful of senior officers, to make abstractions and define general principles when you were right in the middle of a job. These things had to be thought through beforehand, leaving the men free to concentrate on the work itself.

Maria had sat down again. Her sodden dress sagged in her lap. "Do it quickly," she said. "Then we can get cleaned up." She had found the pack with the three cigarettes inside. She lit one, took a drag and passed it to him. He did not mind the red smudges all over the paper, he honestly did not care. But when he went to pass it back to her, the cigarette stuck to his fingers.

"You keep it," she said, "and let's start."

Soon he had to change his grip to avoid burning his fingers. The paper came away and the tobacco spilled out. He let it all fall to the floor and stamped on it. He took up the saw and untucked Otto's shirt, exposing the back just above the waistband of the trousers. Right on the spine was a big mole. He felt squeamish about cutting through it and positioned the blade half an inch lower. His saw cut now was the whole width of the back, and again the vertebra kept him on track. He was through the bone easily enough, but an inch or so further in he began to feel that he was not cutting through things so much as pushing them to one side. But he kept on. He was in the cavity that contained all that he did not want to see. He was keeping his head raised so that he did not have to look into the cut. He looked in Maria's direction. She was still sitting there, gray and tired and not wanting to watch. Her eyes were on the open window and the big cumulus clouds that drifted over the courtyard.

There was a glutinous sound that brought him the memory of a jelly dessert eased from its mold. It was moving about in there; something had collapsed and rolled onto something else. He was through to the bottom, and now he faced the old problem. He could not cut through the belly skin without sawing into the wood. It was a good table, too, sturdily constructed of elm. And this time he was not reaching his hand in. Instead he turned the carcass through ninety degrees and pulled it forward by the front half, so that the saw cut was in line with the table's edge. He should have asked for Maria's help. She should have foreseen the difficulty and come to his rescue. He was supporting the top half with both hands. The lower half still rested on the table. How then was he supposed to use the knife to cut through the belly skin? He was too tired to stop, even though he knew he was attempting the impossible. He brought his left knee up to bear the weight and stretched forward for the knife, which was on the table. It might have worked. He could have held the upper body with his knee and his hand, and with his free hand he could have reached under and cut through the skin. But he was too tired to be balancing on one leg. He almost had the knife in his hand when he felt himself toppling. He had to put his left foot down. He tried to get the free hand back in time, but the whole thing fell from his grasp. The top half swung on its hinge of skin toward the floor, exposing the vivid mess of Otto's digestive tract and pulling the bottom half with it. Both tipped to the floor and disgorged onto the carpet.

There was a moment before he left the room when Leonard suddenly had the measure of the distance they had traveled, the trajectory that had delivered them from their successful little engagement party to this, and how all along the way each successive step had seemed logical enough, consistent with the one before, and how no one was to blame. Before he made his run for the bathroom he had an impression of liverish reds, glistening irregular tubing of a boiled-egg bluish-white, and something purple and black, all of it shining and livid at the outrage of violated privacy, of secrets exposed. Despite the open windows, the room filled with the close stench of musty air, which itself was a medium for other smells: of sweet earth, sulfurous crap, and sauerkraut. The insult was, Leonard had time to think as he stepped hurriedly round the upended halves of the torso that were still joined, that all this stuff was also in himself.

As if to prove it, he gripped the edges of the toilet bowl and brought up a mouthful of green bile. He rinsed his mouth at the basin. The contact with clean water was a reminder of another life. No matter that he had not yet finished; he had to be clean—now. He kicked off his slippers, removed his shirt and trousers and added them to the pile under the basin and got into the bath. He crouched down and washed himself under the running taps. Dried blood was not easily removed in icy water. The pumice stone was the most effective, and he scrubbed his skin with no other thought for a long time—half an hour, perhaps twice that.

By the time he had finished, his hands, arms and face were rubbed raw and he was shaking from the cold.

His clean clothes were in the bedroom. He had forgotten everything, it had left him for the period of his ablution, and now he would have to walk back through there in his clean bare feet, past his uncompleted work.

But when he arrived in the living room with a towel around his waist, still dripping, Maria was lifting the largest of the sealed parcels into one of the cases.

She spoke as though he had been there all the time and had just asked a question. "It goes like this now. Lower body, arm, top and bottom leg, and head in this one. And in this one, upper body, arm and top and bottom leg."

By the table was a dustpan and a bucket. The rest was in there. He helped her close the cases up, and then, while she sat on them, he secured the canvas straps as tight as they would go. He lugged the cases over to the wall. Now there was only luggage and a certain degree of residual mess, which could easily be cleaned up. He noticed she had a kettle and saucepans heating on the stove for her wash. He went into the bedroom, planning to dress and then snatch ten minutes' sleep while she was in the bathroom. He wasted time looking for his shoes before he remembered where they were. He lay down and closed his eyes.

Immediately she was there, cleaned up and in her dressing gown, searching the wardrobe for the right clothes.

"Don't go to sleep now," she said. "You'll never wake up in time." She was right, of course.

He sat up, found his glasses and watched her. She always turned her back on him while she was getting dressed, an aspect of her modesty that usually touched him, excited him even. Now it was irritating, when he considered what they had been through together, and how they were engaged. He got off the bed, edged past without touching her and went into the bathroom. He picked his shoes up from under the pile of bloody clothes. It really was not difficult at all to wipe them clean with a washcloth. He put them on and threw the cloth down with the rest of the stuff. Then he began to clean up the living room. Maria had collected several large paper bags. He was stuffing the newspaper pages into them when she came in from the bedroom and joined him. They rolled the carpet up and put it by the door. It would have to be thrown out later. To scrub the table and floor they needed the bucket. Maria emptied it into the largest of her saucepans, turning her head away as she did so.

Leonard fetched a scrub brush and was sprinkling scouring powder on the table when she said, "It's stupid, both doing this. Why don't you take the cases now. I'll finish here."

It was not only that she knew she would make a better job of the table and the floor than he would. She wanted him out, she wanted to be alone. And to him the prospect of leaving this place, setting off by himself, even with heavy luggage, was attractive. It felt like freedom. He wanted to be away from her just as much as she wanted him to go. It was as bleak and simple as that. For now they could not touch each other, they could not even exchange glances. Even the most conventional gestures—taking her hand, for example— repelled him. Everything between them, every detail, every transaction, chafed and irritated, like grit in the eye. He saw the tools. The axe was there, unused. He tried to recall why he had thought he would need it. The imagination was even more brutal than life.

He said, "Don't forget to do the knife and the saw and all the teeth."

"I won't."

He put his coat on while she opened the front door. He stood between the cases, braced himself, lifted, then made a quick straight run with them out onto the landing. He put them down and turned. She stood in the doorway, one hand on the door, ready to close it. If he had felt the fraction of an impulse, he would have gone over to her, kissed her cheek, touched her arm or hand. But what hung in the air between them was disgust, and it was not possible to pretend.

"I'll be back" was all he could manage, and that seemed an extravagant promise.

"Yes," she said, and closed the door.

19

FOR TWO MINUTES he stood between the cases at the head of the communal stairs. Once he began on the next stage, there would be no time for reflection. But he had few thoughts now. Beyond the spinning tiredness, he was aware of his pleasure in going. If he was disposing of Otto, in a sense he was disposing of Maria too. And she of him. There was bound to be sorrow in all this, but it could not reach him now. He was leaving. He picked up his bags and started down. By bumping the cases on the steps, he was able to manage both at once. He paused for breath on each landing. A man just in from work nodded as he passed on his way up. Two boys pushed past him while he was resting. There was nothing strange about him. Berlin was full of people with heavy luggage.

As he descended and the distance from Maria's flat increased and he was more completely alone, all his pains returned. The pain in his shoulder was settling to a deep muscular throb. His ear no longer required him to touch it for it to hurt. The act of walking downstairs carrying perhaps more than 150 pounds was causing further damage in his groin. And now, Otto's parting blow: an electric pain flashing outward from the base of his big toe to his ankle. Down he went, and they all hurt more. At the bottom he took the cases one at a time through the door into the courtyard, and then he took a longer rest. He felt raw, as though he had just been boiled, or a layer of skin had been peeled from him. The solidity of things oppressed him. The rasp of a small stone underfoot made his stomach swoop. Grime on the wall round the stairwell light switch, and then the mass of the wall itself, the pointlessness of all those bricks, afflicted him, bore down on him like an illness. Was he hungry? The thought of taking selected parts of the solid world and passing them through a hole in his head and squeezing them through his guts was an abomination. He was pink and raw and dry. He was leaning against the courtyard wall, watching kids playing football. Wherever the ball bounced and wherever shoes skidded in tight turns was a friction that pained him, rubbed his un-lubricated senses sore. His lids chafed his eyes when he closed them.

On level ground, and in the open air, the courtyard was where he could rehearse the carrying of the cases. No one ever really had cases as heavy as these. He picked them up and lurched forward. He went ten yards before he had to set them down. He could not afford to stagger. He had to move like any other traveler. He could not permit himself to wince or examine his hands too frequently. He had to go further than ten yards. He set himself a minimum of twenty-five steps.

He was across the courtyard in three stages, and now he was on the pavement. There were only a few passersby. If anyone offered help he would have to refuse, he would have to be prepared to be rude. He would have to look as though he did not need help, then no one would offer it. He started on his twenty-five paces. Counting was a way of coping with the agony of the weight. It was an effort not to count out loud. He set the cases down and made a show of looking at his watch. A quarter to six. There was no rush-hour traffic on Adalbertstrasse. He had to make it to the next corner. He waited long enough for there to have been a complete change of people around him, then he took the weight and rushed forward. He had made it to twenty-five on all the previous occasions, but this time he was not going to reach twenty. His steps were shorter and quicker. There was a softening in his wrists. His fingers straightened helplessly, and the cases dropped to the pavement. One fell on its side.

He was righting it, blocking the way, when a lady with her dog stepped around him and made a disapproving clucking noise. Perhaps she was speaking for the whole street. The dog, a game-looking mongrel, was interested in the case that Leonard had pulled upright. It sniffed along the length of the case, wagging its tail, and then came round the other side, avid all of a sudden and muzzling hard against the fabric. It was on a leash, but the woman was one of those owners who do not like to cross their pets. She stood patiently, with the leash slack in her hand, waiting for the animal to lose interest. She was less than two feet away, but she did not look at Leonard. She spoke only to the dog, whose sniffing was now frenetic. It knew.

"Komm schon, mein kleiner Liebling. Ist doch nur ein Koffer." It's only a suitcase.

Leonard also indulged the dog. He needed an excuse not to pick up the cases. But now it was growling and whining by turns. It was attempting to close its jaws round a corner of the case.

"Gnädige Frau," Leonard said, "please control your dog."

But rather than pull on the leash, the woman merely increased the torrent of endearments. "Little silly one, who do you think you are? This luggage belongs to the gentleman, not to you. Come on now, little sausage . . ."

A becalmed and abstracted version of himself was speculating that if one had something to dispose of, one could do worse than consider a hungry dog. One would need a pack.

The dog had found a purchase. It had its teeth into the corner of the case. It was biting, growling and wagging its tail.

At last the woman spoke to Leonard. "You must have food in there. Wurst, perhaps!" There was a touch of accusation in this. She thought he was a smuggler bringing cheap food over from the East.

"It's an expensive case," he said. "If your dog damages it, you, *gnädige Frau,* will be responsible." He looked around, as if to summon a policeman.

The woman was affronted. She gave the leash a savage jerk and moved on. Her dog yelped and came to heel, and then seemed to regret its compliance. As its owner walked away, the dog was straining to get back. Through the fogs of species memory it recognized a chance of a lifetime, to devour a human with impunity and avenge the wolf ancestors for ten thousand years of subjugation. A minute later it was still looking back and giving token tugs on its leash. The woman sailed on, refusing any compromise.

There were teethmarks and saliva on the case, but the fabric was not torn. Leonard positioned himself between his burdens and lifted. He walked fifteen steps and had to stop. The woman's disapproval lingered, it was infecting the glances of other passersby. What could he possibly have in those cases that could be so heavy? Why didn't he have a friend to help him? It must be illegal, it could only be contraband. Why did he look so haggard, that man with the heavy cases? Why hadn't he shaved? It was only a matter of time now before a green *Polizist* caught sight of him. They were always on the lookout for trouble. That was the kind of city it was. They had limitless powers, these German police. He would not be able to refuse them if they wanted him to open up his luggage. He could not afford to be seen standing around. He settled for frantic effort, for little dashes of ten or twelve steps. He attempted to transform the trembling rictus of effort into the smile of a respectable traveler fresh from the railway station, who needed neither surveillance nor help. In between, he took the briefest possible rests. Whenever he stopped he glanced around him, for the benefit of the passing traffic, as if lost, or looking for the right house.

By the Kottbusser Tor U-Bahn he set the cases down on the curb and sat on them. He wanted to give attention to the pain in his foot. He needed to get his shoe off. But the cases sagged unpleasantly under his weight, and he stood up immediately. If he could get ten, even five minutes' sleep, he thought, he could manage the luggage with less fuss.

He was close to the *Eckladen* where they sometimes shopped for their daily needs. The owner, who was bringing in his vegetable and fruit racks, saw Leonard and waved.

"Holidays?"

Leonard nodded and at the same time said, "No, no, not yet," and then in his confusion added in English. "It's business, really," a statement he instantly wished to retract. How would he be, answering routine questions from a curious *Polizist?*

He stood by his cases watching the traffic. He was seeing objects drifting on the periphery of vision: an English letter box, a stag with high antlers, a table lamp. When he turned to them, they dissolved. His dreams were starting without him. He had to turn his head to dispel each phantom. There was nothing sinister. Bananas rotated end over end; a tin of biscuits with a thatched cottage on the lid opened by itself. How was he to concentrate when he had to keep turning aside to keep these things at bay? Did he dare leave them where they were?

There was a plan formulated, so long ago that he doubted whether it could still be valid. But there was no other; he had to stay with this one. And yet a kind soft thought was pulling at him. It was getting dark, the cars already had their headlights on, the shops were closing up, people were heading home. Above him a streetlight, screwed wonkily to a crumbling wall, came on with a crackle. Some kids went by, pushing a pram. The taxi he had been looking for was pulling up by the curb. He had not even hailed it. The driver had seen his cases. Even in the dusk he had guessed at their improbable weight. He got out and opened the trunk.

It was an old diesel Mercedes. Leonard thought he would be able to swing one of the cases in before the driver touched it. But it turned out that they heaved it in together.

"Books," Leonard explained. The driver shrugged. It was not his business. They shoved the other case onto the backseat. Leonard got into the front and asked for the Zoo station. The heater was on; the seat was huge and shiny. The soft thought was tugging again. He only had to speak the words and he would be there.

But he did not even remember the taxi pulling away. When he woke, it had stopped and the cases were already on the sidewalk, side by side, and his own door was open. The driver must have shaken him. In his confusion, Leonard overtipped. The man touched the peak of his cap and strolled over to stand with the other drivers who collected by the station rank. Leonard had his back to them and knew they were watching him. It was for their benefit that he made the effort to carry the cases smoothly across the ten yards of pavement to the high double doors that opened onto the station concourse.

As soon as he was inside he set them down. He felt safer. Only a few feet away a dozen British soldiers were lining up with their own regulation suitcases. All the shops and restaurants were open, and there was residual rush-hour bustle for the Stadtbahn trains upstairs. Beyond a lingerie shop and a bookstall was a sign pointing the way to the luggage lockers. Everywhere was the cigar-and-strong-coffee smell of German well-being. The floor was smooth and he could drag the cases across it. He passed fruit stalls, a restaurant, a souvenir shop. It was all so cheerful, it was all such a success! He was a legitimate traveler at last, utterly inconspicuous, a traveler moreover who would not have to drag his luggage upstairs to the trains.

The place to check luggage was a little way down one of the tunnels that led off the main concourse. There was a circular area with newly installed lockers set around the walls facing a counter where two men in uniform stood ready to receive bags and stow them on the racks behind them. Two or three people were waiting to collect or deposit luggage when Leonard arrived. He dragged his cases as far as possible from the counter and found two vacant lockers at floor level. He moved deliberately, lining up the cases, straightening to search his pockets for the change he had brought with him. There was no hurry. He had a fistful of ten pfennig coins. He opened a locker and pushed a case with his knee. Nothing happened. He pocketed the change and pushed harder. He glanced over his shoulder. There was no one at the counter now. The two men there were talking and looking in his direction. He bent down to find the obstruction. The space was an inch or so too narrow. He made a halfhearted attempt to squeeze the case, and then he gave up. If he had not been so tired, he might now have done the right thing. As he stood up he saw that one of the luggage officials, a man with a graying beard, was waving him over. It was logical: if your luggage did not fit in the lockers, you took it to the counter. But he had not prepared for this, it was not in the plan. Was it the right thing? Would they want to know why his cases were so heavy? What powers did their uniforms grant them? Would they remember his face?

The bearded man was resting his knuckles on the tin-plate counter, waiting for Leonard. It was not right that an employee who was really no more than a porter should be dressed like an admiral. It was important not to be intimidated. Leonard made a show of looking at his watch and picked up his cases. He tried to walk away briskly. He took the only route that would not take him closer to the counter. He was waiting for a shout, for the sound of running. He was in a narrowing corridor at the end of which was a set of double doors. He made it all the way without stopping. He went through the doors backward and found himself in a quiet side street. He put the cases against a wall and sat down on the pavement.

He had no clear intentions. He needed to rest his sore foot. If the admiral had come after him, he would gladly have given himself up. What was clear, now that he was sitting down, was that he ought to be making a plan. His thoughts were oozing thickly. They were the secretion of an organ that was not under his control. He could judge the product, but he could not initiate it. He could make another attempt to squeeze the cases into the luggage lockers. He could surrender them to the admiral. He could leave them here, on the street. Just walk away from them. Did they really need the whole week's grace that the luggage lockers allowed? It was now that the pleasant soft thought returned. He could go home. He could lock the door, take a bath, be safe among his own things, sleep for hours in his own bed, and then, once refreshed, make a new plan and implement it—shaved, invigorated, with a clean set of clothes, beyond suspicion.

He thought about home. The rooms as big as meadows, the excellent plumbing, the solitude. He fantasized and dozed, and at last stood up. The quickest way to a taxi was back through the station, past the admiral. But he set off to walk around the outside. His groin was hurting more than his foot. A layer of skin was coming off his hands. It took twenty minutes to get around. He took long pauses, unwatched. He found his taxi in the rank, another big old Mercedes, and this time made no attempt to help lift the cases in, nor did he offer any explanations. It was surely a sign of guilt to be apologizing for their weight.

He left one case on the pavement outside No. 26, and carried the other with both hands all the way to the lift shaft. When he went back outside, the case was still there, which surprised him no less than if it had gone. How was he to know any longer what constituted a surprise? The lift bore the weight easily. He opened his front door and set the cases down just inside the hallway. From where he stood he could see that the lights were on in the living room, and there was music playing. He went toward it. He pushed the living room door open and walked into a party. There were drinks, peanuts in bowls, full ashtrays, crumpled cushions and the AFN on the wireless. All the guests had gone. He turned the wireless off, and the silence was abrupt. He sat in the nearest chair. He had been left behind. The friends, the old Leonard and his fiancée in her rustling white skirt, they had all gone, and the cases were too heavy, the lockers too small, the admiral hostile, and his hands, ear, shoulder, testicles and foot throbbed in unison.

He went to the bathroom and drank from the tap for a long time. Then he was in the bedroom, lying on his back under the covers, staring at the ceiling. With the hall light on and the bedroom door half open, it was as dark as he wanted it. When he closed his eyes a sickening fatigue smothered him. He had to save himself as though from drowning by struggling to see the ceiling again. His eyes were not heavy. As long as they were open he could stay awake. He was trying not to think. He was hurting everywhere. There was no one to look after him. He kept his thoughts empty by concentrating on his breathing. Perhaps an hour passed this way, in a light trance, almost a doze.

Then the phone rang and he was on his way to it before he had come to fully. He crossed the hallway, glancing to his left to see the cases there by the door, and entered the living room without turning on the light. The phone was on the window ledge. He snatched it up, expecting Maria, or possibly Glass. It was a man whose soft-spoken introductory phrase eluded him. Something about a paper pay packet. Then the voice said, "I'm phoning about the arrangements for May the tenth, sir."

It was a wrong number, but Leonard did not want to send the voice away. It was pleasantly accented, and sounded competent and gentle. He said, "Ah yes."

"I've been told to phone and see what it was you wanted, sir."

It was the sir, the unforced, manly respect, that Leonard warmed to. Whoever this man was, he might be able to help. He sounded the sort who might carry the cases and not ask questions. It was important to keep him talking. Leonard said, "Er, what do you suggest?"

The voice said, "Well, sir, I could start from some way off, right out of the building, when everyone is sitting down, and approach slowly. You get the picture, sir. They're all talking and drinking, and then one or two with good ears hear me faintly, and then they all hear me, coming closer all the time. Then I come right into the room."

"I see," Leonard said. He thought he might take this man into his confidence. It was a matter of waiting for an opening.

"And if you're happy to leave the tunes to me, sir. . . . Some reels, some laments. When they've had a few drinks— if you'll excuse me, sir—there's nothing quite like a lament."

"That's true," Leonard said, seeing his chance. "I sometimes get very sad."

"I beg your pardon, sir?"

If the kind voice would only ask why. Leonard said, "Things get on top of me sometimes."

The voice hesitated, and then it said, "Berlin's a long way from home, sir, for us all." There was another pause, and then, "CSM Steele said you'd need me for an hour, sir. Is that correct?"

It was in this way that the Scots Greys piper, Piper Mc-Taggart, was identified. Leonard concluded the business as rapidly as possible. He left the phone off the hook and returned to bed. He turned the hall light out on the way. The conversation had revived him. The edge of his tiredness was dulled, and it was easier to sleep.

He woke some hours later, completely refreshed. From the silence he guessed it to be between two and three o'clock. He sat up. He felt better, he realized, because he had woken with a simple solution. He had let the matter overwhelm him when in fact all that was required was clear thinking and purposeful action. He could get to work while it was all fresh in his mind. Then he could sleep again and wake to a resolved situation.

He stepped out of the bedroom into the hall. He had never known it so quiet. He did not bother with the light. There was just enough of a moon to give a colorless light, although he was not sure quite how moonlight was penetrating here. He went to the kitchen and found a sharp knife. He went back in the hall and knelt by the cases and unfastened the straps on both. Then he opened one of them. The parts were neatly in place, just as Maria had packed them. He lifted out a piece and cut away the waterproof material and laid an arm gently down on the carpet. There was no unpleasant smell; he was not too late. He pushed the wrapping well away to one side, and then he set about freeing a leg, a thigh, and the chest. There was surprisingly little blood, and besides, the carpet was red. He set the pieces down on the hall carpet in their correct positions. The human shape was resuming. He opened the second case and unwrapped the lower body and the limbs. It was there before him, a headless body lying on its back. He had the head in his hands now. He turned it and saw through the material the outline of the nose and the imprecise features of a face.

It was while he was using the point of the knife to prize

away the glued seam that he saw something that caught his attention. He was holding the heavy head down on the floor, but he could no longer move the knife. It was not the prospect of seeing Otto's face. Nor was it the completed figure lying on the carpet next to him. What he had seen was the bedroom wall and his bed. He had forced his eyes open a fraction and seen the shape of his own body under the blankets. For two seconds he had heard the traffic in the street outside, still late-night traffic, and he had seen his own immovable body. Then his eyes shut and he was back here, with the knife in his hand, picking away again at the fabric.

It worried him to know that what seemed so real was a dream. It meant that anything could happen. There were no rules. He was putting Otto back together, undoing the day's work. He was peeling away a layer of rubberized cloth, and here was the side of the head, with the top of an ear visible. He ought to stop himself, he thought, he ought to wake before Otto came to life. With an effort he opened his eyes again. He saw a part of his hand and the impression of his feet under the blanket. If he could move just one part of himself, or make a sound, the tiniest of sounds, he could bring himself back. But the body he occupied was inert. He was trying to move his toe. He could hear a motorbike in the street outside. If someone would come into the room and touch him. He was trying to shout. He could not part his lips or fill his lungs. His eyes were weighing down, and he was in the hall once more.

Why was the material sticking to the side of Otto's face? It was the bite, of course; the blood from Otto's cheek had congealed on the cloth. That was only one reason why Otto was going to punish him. He pulled the cloth and it came away with a rasping sound. The rest was easy. It fell away and the bare head was in his hands. The eyes with the drunk's red rims were watching him, waiting. It was simply a matter of lifting the head onto the torn neck; then it could begin again. He should have been kept divided up, but now it was too late. Even before the head was properly in place, the hands were reaching for the knife. Otto was sitting up. He could see the empty cases, and the knife was in his hand. Leonard knelt in front of him and tipped back his head to offer up his throat. Otto would do the job swiftly. He would have to pack the cases himself. He would carry Leonard to the Zoo station. Otto was a Berliner, he was an old drinking friend of the admiral. Here was the bedroom wall again, the blanket, the edge of the sheet, the pillow. His body was lead. Otto would never carry him alone. Piper McTaggart would help. Leonard tried halfheartedly for a scream. It was better that it should happen. He heard the air pass between his teeth. He tried to bend his leg. His eyes were closing again and he was going to die. His head moved, it turned an inch or so to one side. His cheek touched the pillow, and the touch unlocked all touch and he felt the weight of the blanket on his foot. His eyes were open and he could move his hand. He could shout. He was sitting up and reaching for the light switch.

Even with the light on, the dream was still there, waiting for him to return. He slapped his face and stood. His legs were weak; his eyes still wanted to close. He went into the bathroom and splashed water over his face. When he came out he turned on the hall light. The unopened cases were by the door.

He could not trust himself to sleep. For the rest of the

night he sat in bed with his knees drawn up and the overhead light on and smoked a pack of cigarettes. At three-thirty he went to the kitchen and made a pot of coffee. Toward five o'clock he shaved. The water stung the broken skin on his hands. He dressed and went back to the kitchen to drink more coffee. His plan was simple and good. He would lug the cases to the U-Bahn and ride out to the end of the line. He would find a lonely spot, put the cases down and walk away.

He had gone through his tiredness to a new clarity. He drank his coffee and smoked and passed the time polishing his shoes and putting adhesive strips on his hands. He whistled and hummed "Heartbreak Hotel." For the moment it was enough to be free of his dream. At seven o'clock he straightened his tie, brushed his hair again and put on his jacket. Before opening the front door he lifted the cases experimentally. It was more than weight. There was a pull, an elemental, purposeful earthward pull. Otto wanted to be buried, he thought. But not yet.

He carried the cases one at a time to the lift shaft. When the lift came, he blocked the door with one case while he shoved the other in with his knee. He pressed E for *Etage* but he traveled only one floor down before coming to a halt. The door slid open to admit Blake. He was wearing a blue blazer with silver buttons and he carried an attaché case. The lift compartment filled with the scent of his cologne. The descent continued.

Blake nodded coolly. "Pleasant party. Thank you."

"We were glad you could come," Leonard said.

The lift stopped and the doors opened. Blake was looking at the cases. "Aren't they Ministry of Defense bags?" Leonard picked one up, but Blake beat him to the other and lifted it out into the lobby. "Good Lord. What have you got in here? It's certainly not a tape recorder."

The question was not rhetorical. They were standing by the open lift and Blake seemed to think he was owed an answer. Leonard fumbled. He had been going to say they were tape recorders.

Blake said, "You're taking them out to Altglienicke. It's all right, you can talk to me. I know Bill Harvey. I'm cleared for Gold."

"It's decoding equipment," Leonard said. And then, because he had an image of Blake coming out to the warehouse to look at it, he added, "It's on loan from Washington. We're using it in the tunnel, then it goes back tomorrow."

Blake was looking at his watch. "Well, I hope you've got secure transport laid on. I've got to dash." And he was off across the lobby without another word, and out to where his car was parked in the street.

Leonard waited for him to drive away before he set about dragging the cases outside. The hardest part of his day, the journey to the Neu-Westend U-Bahn station at the far end of the street, was about to begin, and the encounter with Blake had used up his reserves. He had the cases out on the pavement now. His eyes were stinging in the daylight, and the old pains were starting up. There was a commotion across the road, which he thought it better to ignore. It was a car with a particularly noisy engine, and there was a voice. Then the car engine was cut and he heard the voice alone.

"Hey! Leonard. Godammit, Leonard!"

Glass was climbing out of his Beetle and was striding

across Platanenallee toward him. His beard shone glossy black with early morning energy.

"Where the hell have you been? I was trying to reach you all day yesterday. I need to talk about—" Then he saw the cases. "Wait a minute. Those are ours. Leonard, what in God's name have you got in there?"

"Equipment," Leonard said.

Glass already had his hand around one of the straps. "What the hell are you doing with it here?"

"I've been working on it. All night, in fact."

Glass grappled the case to his chest. He was preparing to cross the road with it. A car was coming and he had to wait. He shouted over his shoulder, "We've been through all this, Marnham. You know the rules. This is madness. What do you think you're doing?"

He did not wait for an answer. He bounded across the road, put the case down and opened the Beetle's hood. There was just room inside. Leonard had no choice but to follow with the other case. Glass helped him heave it into the back. They climbed into their seats, and Glass slammed his door hard. The unsilenced engine started with a roar.

As they juddered forward Glass shouted again, "Godammit, Leonard! How can you do this to me? I won't feel safe until this stuff is back where it belongs!"

20

ALL THE WAY to the warehouse Leonard wanted to think about the sentries, who would be obliged to search the cases, while Glass, having exhausted his indignation, wanted to talk about the anniversary celebration. There was very little time. Glass had found a clever route, and they were through Schöneberg within ten minutes and round the edge of the Tempelhof airfield.

"I left a note on your door yesterday," Glass said. "You weren't answering your phone, and then it was busy all night."

Leonard was staring into the hole in the floor at his feet. The asphalt blur was mesmeric. His cases were about to be opened. He was so tired he could welcome that. A process would begin—arrest, interviews and the rest—and he would abandon himself to it. He would offer no explanations until he had had a decent sleep. That would be his one condition.

He said, "I took it off the hook. I was working."

They were in fourth gear and traveling well under twenty miles an hour. The speedometer needle was shaking.

Glass said, "I need to speak to you. I'll be straight with you, Leonard. I'm not happy."

Leonard saw a clean white cell, a single bed with cotton sheets, and silence, and a man outside the door to guard him.

He said, "Oh?"

"On several counts," Glass said. "One, you had more than a hundred and twenty dollars to spend on entertainment for our evening. I gather you've blown it all on one act. One hour."

Perhaps it would be one of the friendly ones on the gate, Jake, or Lee or Howie. They would lift one of the pieces out.

Sir, this isn't electronic equipment, this is a human arm.
Someone might be sick. Glass, perhaps, who was moving to
his second point.

"Two. This one-hundred-and-twenty-dollar hour is going
to be one lonely dude playing the bagpipes. Leonard, bagpipes is not everyone's idea of a good time. It's not *anyone's,*
for Chrissakes. Do you mean we're going to have to sit there
for one hour and listen to this howling shit?"

Sometimes a white line flashed across the hole. Leonard
mumbled into it, "We could dance."

In a theatrical gesture, Glass clamped his hand over his
eyes. Leonard did not look up from his hole. The Beetle held
its course.

"Third. There are going to be some intelligence brass
there, Leonard, including some of your own guys. D'you
know what they're going to say?"

"When everyone's had a few drinks," Leonard said,
"there's nothing quite like a lament."

"Lament is right. They're gonna say, Hmm, American
food, German wines and *Scottish* entertainment. Is it Scotland in Gold? Do we have a special relationship with Scotland? Did Scotland join NATO?"

"There was a singing dog," Leonard muttered without
lifting his head. "But there again, it was English."

Glass had not heard. "Leonard, you've screwed up, and I
want you to fix it this morning, while there's still time. We'll
drop this equipment off, then I'm going to drive you up to
the Scots Greys barracks in Spandau. You're going to talk to
the sergeant, cancel the piper and get our money back.
Okay?"

They were being overtaken by a convoy of trucks, so Glass did not notice that his passenger was giggling.

The antenna cluster on the warehouse roof was visible. Glass was slowing down further. "These guys are going to need to see what we've got here. They can look, but they don't need to know what it is, okay?"

The giggling fit had passed. "Oh God," Leonard said.

They stopped. Glass was winding down his window as the sentry came toward them. It was not a face they recognized.

"This one's new," Glass said. "And his friend. That means it's going to take longer."

The face that filled the window was pink and large; the eyes were eager. "Good morning, sir."

"Morning, soldier." Glass handed both passes to him.

The sentry straightened and spent a minute examining them. Glass said without lowering his voice, "These guys are trained to be keen. They have to do six months' duty before they ease off some."

It was true. Howie might have recognized them and waved them through.

The eighteen-year-old face was in the window again. The passes were handed back. "Sir, I need to look in the trunk, and I have to see inside that bag."

Glass got out of the car and opened the front. He heaved the case onto the road and knelt by it. From where he sat, Leonard watched Glass unbuckling the straps. He had ten seconds or so left. He could, after all, just run off down the road. It could hardly make matters worse. He got out of the car. The second sentry, who looked even younger than the first, had come up behind Glass and was touching him on the shoulder.

"Sir, we'd like to see it in the guard room."

Glass was making a great show of arguing with no one. In security matters, his enthusiastic compliance was intended to set an example. One of the straps was already undone. Ignoring it, he hugged the whole case to his chest and staggered with it to the hut by the side of the road. The first soldier had opened Glass's door, and now he stood back politely to allow Leonard to drag the other case out. The two sentries followed him as he carried the case with two hands to the hut.

There was a small wooden table with a telephone on it. Glass put the telephone on the floor and with a squeezed-out grunt lifted his case onto the table. There was barely room for four of them in the hut. Leonard knew Glass well enough to recognize that all the straining and heaving had made him bad-tempered. He stood back, breathing noisily through his nose and stroking his beard. He had carried the case over; now it was up to the sentries to open it. And if they failed in their procedures, they could be sure of being reported.

Leonard set his case by the table. He had it in mind to wait outside while the examination took place. After his dream, he did not want to see any more, and there was a good chance one of the young sentries was going to throw up in the confined space. Perhaps all three of them would. He stood in the doorway, however. It was hard not to watch. His life was about to change, and he felt no particular emotion. He had done his best, and he knew he was not an especially bad person. The first soldier had set his rifle down and was unbuckling the other strap. Leonard watched on, as though from a great distance. The world that had never much cared for Otto Eckdorf was about to explode with concern at his death. The soldier raised the lid and they all looked in at the covered pieces. Everything was packed in tight, but it did not much look like electronics. Even Glass could not conceal his curiosity. The smell of glue and rubber was rich, like pipe smoke. From nowhere, Leonard had an idea, and he acted without premeditation. He pushed his way to the table just as the sentry was reaching out to take hold of one of the pieces.

Leonard held the young man's wrist while he spoke. "If this search is going to proceed, then there's something I have to say to Mr. Glass in private. There are serious security implications, and I won't need more than a minute."

The soldier withdrew his hand and turned to Glass. Leonard closed the case.

Glass said, "Is that okay, boys? One minute?"

"That's fine," one of them said.

Glass followed Leonard out of the hut. They stood by the red-and-white-striped barrier.

"I'm sorry, Bob," Leonard said. "I didn't know they were going to go right into the packing."

"They're new, that's all. And you shouldn't have taken the stuff out of here."

Leonard relaxed against the barrier. He had nothing to lose. "There were reasons for that. But listen. I'm going to have to break with procedure to protect a more important matter. I have to tell you now that I have level four clearance here."

Glass seemed to come to attention. "Level *four*?"

"It's largely technical," Leonard said, and reached for his wallet. "I'm level four, and those chaps are messing about with highly sensitive material. I want you to phone MacNamee at the Olympic Stadium. This is his card. Get him to call the duty officer here. I want this search called off.

What's in those cases is beyond classification. Tell MacNamee that—he'll know what I'm talking about."

Glass asked no questions. He turned and walked quickly back to the hut. Leonard heard him tell the sentries to close and secure the case. One of them must have queried the order, for Glass shouted, "Jump to it, soldier! This is a lot bigger than you!"

While Glass was on the phone, Leonard wandered off along the roadside. It was turning into a fine spring morning. There were yellow and white flowers growing in the ditch. There were no plants he could identify. Five minutes later Glass came out of the hut, followed by the soldiers carrying the cases. Leonard and Glass stood back while the soldiers loaded the luggage into the car. Then they raised the barrier and stood at attention as the car went through.

Glass said, "The duty officer gave those poor guys hell. And MacNamee gave the duty officer hell. That's quite a secret you're carrying around."

"It really is," Leonard said.

Glass parked the car and switched the engine off. The duty officer and two soldiers were waiting for them by the double doors. Before they got out Glass put his hand on Leonard's shoulder and said, "You've come quite a way since your cardboard-burning days."

They got out. Leonard said over the Beetle's roof, "It's an honor to be involved."

The soldiers took the cases. The duty officer wanted to know where they were to be taken, and Leonard suggested the tunnel. He wanted to go down there and be soothed. But it was not quite the same, making the descent with Glass and the duty officer at his side, and the two soldiers coming up behind. Once they were down the main shaft, the bags were loaded onto a little wooden truck, which the soldiers pushed. They passed the barbed-wire coils that marked the beginning of the Russian sector. A few minutes later they all squeezed past the amplifiers, and Leonard showed the place under the desk where the cases were to be stowed.

Glass said, "I'll be damned. I've passed those bags a hundred times and never thought of looking inside."

"Don't start now," Leonard said.

The duty officer put a wire seal on both cases. "To be opened," he said, "on your authority alone."

They went up to the canteen for coffee. Leonard's level four revelation had conferred a kind of promotion. When Glass mentioned going out to Spandau to find the Scots Greys sergeant, it was the easiest thing in the world for Leonard to put his hand to his forehead.

"I can't face it. I've been up two nights in a row. Tomorrow, perhaps."

And Glass said, "Don't worry. I'll do it myself."

He offered Leonard a ride home. But Leonard was not certain where he wanted to be. He had new problems now. He wanted to be where he could think about them. So Glass dropped him off on the way into town, at the Grenzallee station at the end of the U-Bahn line.

For several minutes after Glass had left, Leonard strolled around the ticket hall, exulting in his freedom. He had been carrying those cases for months, for years. He sat down on a bench. They weren't here now, but he had not disposed of them yet. He sat and stared at the welts on his hands. The temperature in the tunnel was eighty degrees, perhaps more under the desk by the amplifiers. In two days or less the cases would be stinking. It might be possible to get them out with some kind of elaborate level four story, but even now MacNamee would be on his way to the warehouse from the stadium, bursting to know just what equipment Leonard had managed to get his hands on. It was a mess. He had set out to leave the cases in the public anonymity of a railway station with international connections, and he had ended up leaving them in a confined and private space where they were entirely identified with him. It was a terrible mess. He sat trying to think his way through the problem, but all that came was what a mess it was.

The bench he was on faced the ticket office. He let his head drop. He was wearing a good suit and a tie and his shoes were shiny. No one could take him for a tramp. He drew his feet up and slept for two hours. Though his sleep was deep, he was aware of the footsteps of passengers echoing in the hall, and it was comforting somehow to be safely asleep among these strangers.

He woke in a panic. It was ten past noon. MacNamee would be at the warehouse looking for him. If the government scientist was impatient or careless, he might even try to use his authority to have the seals broken on the cases. Leonard stood up. He had only an hour or two in which to act. He needed to talk to someone. It pained him to think of Maria. He could not bear to go near her flat. The bench slats had cut into his buttocks, and his suit was creased. He wandered toward the ticket office. It was a characteristic of his tiredness that he did not make plans. Instead he found himself beginning to follow them through, as though under orders. He bought a ticket to Alexanderplatz, in the Russian sector. There was a train waiting to leave, and one came in immediately at Hermannplatz, where he had to change. This ease confirmed him in his intention. He was being drawn to it— to a huge, an appalling solution. He had a ten-minute walk from Alexanderplatz along Königstrasse. At one point he had to stop and ask the way.

The place was larger than he had imagined it. He had been expecting something narrow and intimate, with high-backed booths for whispering in. But the Café Prag was vast, with a remote and grubby ceiling and scores of small round tables. He chose a conspicuous place and ordered a coffee. Glass had once told him that you only had to wait until one of the *Hundert Mark Jungen* came across. The place was filling up for lunch. There were plenty of serious-looking types at the tables. They could just as easily have been local office workers as spies from half-a-dozen nations.

He passed the time drawing a map in pencil on a paper napkin. Fifteen minutes went by, and nothing happened. It was, Leonard decided, one of those Berlin stories. The Café Prag was said to be a stock exchange of unofficial information. In fact it was a large, dull East Berlin café where the coffee was weak and lukewarm. He was on his third cup and feeling sick. He had not eaten in two days. He was searching his pockets for East marks when a young man, face ablaze with freckles, sat down opposite him.

"Vous êtes français." It was a statement of fact.

"No," Leonard said, "English."

The man was about Leonard's age. He had his hand up for a waiter. He seemed to feel no need to explain or apologize for his error. It was simply an opening line. He ordered two coffees and extended a speckled hand across the table. "Hans."

Leonard shook it and said, "Henry." It was his father's name and felt less like a lie.

Hans took out a pack of Camels, offered one and was rather self-conscious, Leonard thought, with his Zippo. Hans's English was faultless. "I haven't seen you here before."

"I haven't been here before."

The coffee that did not quite taste of coffee arrived, and when the waiter had left them Hans said, "So, you like it here in Berlin?"

"Yes, I do," Leonard said. He had not imagined there would have to be small talk, but it was probably the custom. He wanted to get things right, so he asked politely, "Did you grow up here?"

Hans replied with an account of a childhood in Kassel. When he was fifteen his mother had married a Berliner. It was hard to concentrate on the story. The pointless details made him feel hot, and now Hans was asking him about his life in London. After Leonard had given a brief sketch of his childhood there, he concluded by saying that he found Berlin far more interesting. Immediately he regretted his words.

Hans said, "But surely this can't be so. London is a world capital. Berlin is finished. Its greatness is all in the past."

"Perhaps you're right," Leonard said. "Perhaps I just like to be abroad." That too was a mistake, for now they were talking about the pleasures of foreign travel. Hans asked Leonard which other countries he had been in, and Leonard was too tired to offer less than the truth. He had been to Wales and West Berlin.

Hans was exhorting him to be more adventurous. "You are English, you have the opportunities." Then there followed a list of places, headed by the United States, that Hans intended to visit. Leonard looked at his watch. It was ten past one. He was not certain what that meant. People would be looking for him. He was not certain what it was he was going to tell them.

As soon as Leonard looked at his watch, Hans brought his list to a close and glanced around the room. Then he said, "Henry, I think you came looking for something. You wanted to buy something, is that right?"

"No," Leonard said. "I want to give something to the right person."

"You have something to sell?"

"It doesn't matter. I'm happy to give it away."

Hans offered Leonard another cigarette. "Listen, my friend. I'll give you some advice. If what you have is free, people will think it's worthless. If it's good, then you must make people pay."

"Fine," Leonard said. "If someone wants to give me money, that's fine."

"I could take what you have and sell it myself," Hans said. "All the profit would be mine. But I like you. Perhaps I'll visit you in London one day, if you give me your address. So I'll take a commission. Fifty percent."

"Anything," Leonard said.

"So then. What is it you have?"

Leonard lowered his voice. "What I have is of interest to the Soviet military."

"That's good, Henry," Hans said at normal volume. "I have a friend here today who knows someone in the High Command."

Leonard produced his map. "On the east side of the

Schönefelder Chaussee, just north of this cemetery here in Altglienicke, their telephone lines are being tapped. They run along a ditch here. I've marked the spot where they should look."

Hans took the map. "How can they tap these lines? It's not possible."

Leonard could not help his pride. "There's a tunnel. I've marked it with a thick line. It runs from what looks like a radar station in the American sector."

Hans was shaking his head. "It would be too far. It's not possible. No one will believe this. I wouldn't get twenty-five marks."

Leonard was close to laughter. "It's a huge project. They don't have to believe it. They just need to go and look."

Hans took the map and stood up. He shrugged and said, "I'll talk to my friend."

Leonard watched him cross to the far side of the room and speak to a man who was obscured by a pillar. Then both went out through a set of swing doors to where the lavatories and telephone were. A couple of minutes later Hans came back, looking livelier.

"My friend says it looks interesting, at least. He's trying to reach his contact now."

Hans went back across the room. Leonard waited until he was out of sight, then he left the café. He was fifty yards down the street when he heard a shout. A man with a white tablecloth tucked around his waist was sprinting toward him waving a slip of paper. He owed for five coffees. He was just paying up and apologizing when Hans came running up. His freckles were garish in daylight.

The waiter went away and Hans said, "You were going to

give me your address. And look—my friend paid two hundred marks."

Leonard walked on, and Hans kept by his side. Leonard said, "You keep the money, and I'll keep my address."

Hans linked his arm through Leonard's. "This isn't what we agreed."

The touch gave Leonard a thrill of horror. He shook his arm free.

"Don't you like me, Henry?" Hans said.

"No, I don't," Leonard said. "Bugger off." He increased his pace. When he glanced over his shoulder, Hans was walking back toward the café.

At Alexanderplatz Leonard fell into another dither. He needed to sit down and rest his foot, but before he did that, he had to decide where to go. He ought to see Maria, and he knew he still could not face her. He wanted to go home, but MacNamee might be waiting for him. If the seals had been broken on the cases, the military police would be there. In the end he bought a ticket to Neu-Westend. He could make up his mind on the train.

He got off at the zoo, having decided to go into the park and find somewhere to sleep. It was a sunny day, but once he had walked for twenty minutes and found a quiet stretch on the banks of the canal, he found the wind a little too brisk to permit him to relax. For half an hour he lay shivering on the newly cut grass. He walked all the way back through the gardens to the station and took the U-Bahn home. Sleep was now his only priority. If the MPs were there, he would only be confronting the inevitable. If it was MacNamee, he would think of a story when it was necessary.

He glided along the pavement from Neu-Westend to

Platanenallee. Tiredness dissociated him from the action of his legs. He was being walked home. There was no one waiting for him. Inside the apartment two notes had been put through the door. One, from Maria, said, "Where are you? What's happening?" The other, from MacNamee said, "Phone me" and gave three numbers. Leonard went straight to the bedroom and pulled the curtains. He took all his clothes off. He did not bother with pajamas. In less than a minute he was asleep at last.

In less than an hour he was awake with an urgent need to urinate. The phone was ringing, too. He hesitated in the hallway, not knowing which to attend to first. He went to the phone and knew as he picked it up that he had made the wrong decision. He would not be able to concentrate. It was Glass, sounding distant and very upset. In the background there was a commotion of some sort. He was like a man having a bad dream.

"Leonard, Leonard, is that you?"

Shivery and naked in his sunless living room, Leonard crossed his legs and said, "Yes, it's me."

"Leonard? Are you there?"

"Bob, it's me. I'm here."

"Thank God. Listen. Are you listening carefully? I want you to tell me what's in those cases. I need you to tell me right now."

Leonard felt his legs going weak. He sat down on the carpet among the debris of the engagement party. He said, "Have they been opened?"

"Come on, Leonard. Just tell me."

"Bob, for a start, it's classified, and anyway, this is not a secure line."

"Don't give me that shit, Marnham. All hell is breaking loose here. What's in those bags?"

"What's happening there? What's all that noise?"

Glass was shouting to be heard. "Christ! Haven't you been told? They found us. They broke into the tap chamber. Our people just made it out. No one had time to close the steel doors. They're all over the tunnel, it's all theirs, right up to the sector boundary. We're clearing stuff out of the warehouse just to be safe. I'm seeing Harvey in an hour and I have to give him a damage report. I need to know what was in those cases. Leonard?"

But Leonard could not speak. His throat was constricted by a joyous gratitude. The speed and simplicity of it all. And now the great Russian silence could descend. He would get dressed now and go and tell Maria that everything was fine.

Glass was shouting his name. Leonard said, "Sorry, Bob. I was stunned by the news."

"The cases, Leonard. The cases!"

"Right. It was the body of a man I hacked into pieces."

"You asshole. I don't have much time."

Leonard was trying to keep the lightness out of his voice. "Actually, you don't have much to worry about. It was decoding equipment that I was building myself. It was only half completed, and it turns out the ideas were out of date."

"So what was the big deal this morning?"

"All decoding projects are level four," Leonard said. "But listen, Bob, when did all this happen?"

Glass was talking to someone else. He broke off. "What was that?"

"When did they break in?"

Glass did not hesitate. "Twelve fifty-eight."

"No, Bob. That can't be right."

"Listen, if you want to know more, just tune into Deutschlandsender. They're talking about nothing else."

Leonard felt a spreading coldness in his stomach. "They can't go public with it."

"That's what we thought. They'd lose face. But the commandant of the Soviet Berlin garrison is out of town. The second-in-command, a guy called Kotsyuba, must be nuts. He's milking it for propaganda. They're going to come out of this looking stupid, but that's what they're doing."

Leonard was thinking of the joke he had just made. He said, "It can't be true."

Again someone was trying to talk to Glass. He spoke hurriedly. "They're holding a press briefing tomorrow. They're going to show the press corps around the tunnel on Saturday. They're talking about opening it up to the public. A tourist attraction, a monument to American treachery. Leonard, they're going to use every last damn thing they can find."

He rang off, and Leonard hurried to the bathroom.

21 JOHN MACNAMEE INSISTED on meeting Leonard at Kempinski's and wanted to sit outside. It was barely ten o'clock in the morning and all the other customers were inside. It was the same bright, cold weather. Each time an enormous white cumulus cloud drifted in front of the sun, the air became icy.

Leonard had been feeling the cold lately. He always seemed to be shivering. The morning after Glass's phone call he woke with shaking hands. It was no mere tremble, it was a palsied shake, and it took him minutes to button his shirt. It was a delayed muscular spasm, he decided, brought on by carrying the cases. When he went out for his first meal in over two days at a *Schnellimbiss* on Reichskanzlerplatz, he dropped his sausage on the pavement. Someone's dog was there to eat it, mustard and all.

At Kempinski's he was in a sun trap, but he kept his coat on and clenched his teeth to stop them chattering. He could not trust himself to hold a coffee cup, so he ordered a beer, and that too was icy. MacNamee looked comfortable enough wearing a tweed jacket over a thin cotton shirt. When his coffee came he stuffed his pipe and lit it. Leonard was downwind, and the smell and its associations made him feel sick. He went to the lavatory as a pretext for changing seats. When he came back he sat on the other side of the table, but now he was in the shade. He pulled his coat around him and sat on his hands. MacNamee passed the untouched beer across to him. There was condensation on the glass, through which two droplets of water were carving an erratically parallel path.

"Right then," MacNamee said. "What about it?"

Leonard could feel his hands shaking under his buttocks. He said, "When I couldn't get anything from the Americans, I began to have one or two ideas of my own. I started to build something in my spare time. I really thought I could see my way through to separating out the clear text echo from the encoded message. I worked at home for safety. But it didn't come out right. The ideas turned out to be old hat anyway. I brought the stuff in, intending to dismantle it in my room, where I keep all the parts. I never imagined I'd be searched so thoroughly. But there were two new boys on the gate. It wouldn't have mattered, but Glass was right there with me. I couldn't afford to let him see the kind of thing I had. It's hardly in my job description. I'm sorry if it got your hopes up."

MacNamee tapped his stumpy brown teeth with the stem of his pipe. "I was rather excited for an hour or two. I thought you'd got your hands on a version of Nelson's thing from somewhere. But not to worry—I think they're almost there at Dollis Hill."

Now that he had been believed, Leonard wanted to go. He had to get warm, and he had to look at the midday papers.

But MacNamee wanted to reflect. He had ordered another coffee and a sticky tart. "I like to think of the pluses. We knew it wouldn't go on forever, and we had almost a year's run at it. It will take London and Washington years to process everything they've got."

Leonard took his hand out to reach for his beer, changed his mind and put it away.

"From the point of view of the special relationship and all that, the other good thing is that we've worked successfully with the Americans on a major project. They've been slow to trust us since Burgess and Maclean. Now that's all changed for the better."

Eventually Leonard made an excuse and stood. MacNamee remained seated. He was refilling his pipe as he squinted up at Leonard, into the sun. "You look like you need a rest. I suppose you know you're being recalled. The MTO will be in touch."

They shook hands. Leonard disguised his palsy by being vigorous. MacNamee did not seem to notice. His last words to Leonard were "You've done well, despite everything. I've put in a good word for you at Dollis Hill."

Leonard said, "Thank you, sir," and hurried away up the Kurfürstendamm to buy the newspapers.

He scanned them in the U-Bahn to Kottbusser Tor. Two days later, and the East Berlin press was still saturated with the story. Both the *Tagesspiegel* and the *Berliner Zeitung* carried double-page spreads of photographs. One showed the amplifiers and the edge of the desk under which the cases stood. For some reason, the telephone in the tap chamber still worked. Reporters called into the receiver and got no reply. The lights and ventilation were still functioning, too. There were detailed accounts of what it was like to walk the tunnel from the Schönefelder Chaussee end to the sandbagged barrier marking the beginning of the American sector. Beyond the sandbags was "darkness broken only by the glow of two cigarettes. But the observers do not react to our call. Perhaps their consciences are too bad." Elsewhere Leonard read that "the whole of Berlin is incensed by the wheeling and dealing of certain American officers. Berlin will only be at peace when these agents cease their provocations." One headline said STRANGE DISTURBANCES ON THE LINE. The story underneath told how Soviet intelligence had become aware of noises interrupting regular cable traffic. The order was given to begin digging up certain stretches of the line. The article gave no reason why Schönefelder Chaussee was chosen. When soldiers broke into the tap chamber, "conditions were such as to indicate that the spies had left in great haste, abandoning their equipment." The fluorescent light bulbs bore the name of Osram, England, "clearly an attempt to mislead. But screwdrivers and adjustable wrenches give the game away: all are marked 'Made in USA.' " At the bottom of the page, in bold type: "A spokesman for the American forces in Berlin said in response to inquiries last night, 'I don't know anything about it!' "

He skimmed through all the stories. The delay in announcing the discovery of the cases was tiring him. Perhaps the idea was to isolate the story to give it all the more impact later. It could be that investigations were already under way. If it hadn't been for his foolish remark to Glass, the Russian claim that they had found a dismembered body in two suitcases could be easily dismissed. If the East German authorities quietly handed the matter over to the West Berlin *Kriminalpolizei,* they had only to ask the Americans and the cases would be traced to Leonard.

Even if the Americans refused to cooperate, it would not take the police long to identify Otto. There was probably forensic evidence in every tissue of his body to indicate that he was a drunk. Soon it would be noted that he had failed to turn up at his lodgings, that he had not collected his *Sozialhilfe,* that he was no longer in place at his favorite *Kneipe,* where the off-duty police bought him drinks. Surely the first thing the police did when they found a body was to look at their missing-persons list. There were countless and intricate bureaucratic links between Otto and Maria and Leonard: the dissolved marriage, the housing claim, the official engagement. But surely that would also have been so if Leonard had managed to leave the cases at the Zoo station. What was it they were thinking of? It was a struggle to think it through. They would have been questioned, but their stories would have been consistent, the apartment would have been meticulously cleaned. There might have been suspicion, but there would have been no proof.

And what was the essence of his crime? To have killed Otto? But that was self-defense. Otto had broken into the bedroom, he had attacked. Not to have reported the death? But that was only sensible, given that no one would have believed them. To have cut up the body? But it was already dead then, so what difference could it make? To have concealed the body? A perfectly logical step. To have deceived Glass, the sentries, the duty officer and MacNamee? But only to protect them from unpleasant facts that did not concern them. To have betrayed the tunnel? A sad necessity, given everything else that had gone before. Besides, Glass, MacNamee and everyone else were saying that it had always been bound to happen. It could not have gone on forever. They had had almost a year's run at it.

He was innocent, that he knew. Why then should his hands shake? Was it fear of being caught and punished? But he wanted them to come, and quickly. He wanted to stop thinking the same thoughts over, he wanted to speak to someone official and have his words written down, typed up for his signature. He wanted to set out the events, and make known to those whose job it was to have truths officially established how one thing had led to another, and how, despite appearances, he was no monster, he was not a deranged chopper-up of citizens, and that it was not insanity that had caused him to haul his victim around Berlin in two suitcases. Time and again he set out the facts for his imagined witnesses, his prosecutors. If they were men dedicated to the truth, they would come to see it his way, even if laws and conventions constrained them to punish him. He recounted his version, it was all he ever did. Every conscious minute he was explaining, refining, clarifying, barely aware that nothing was actually taking place, or that he had been through it all ten minutes before. *Yes, gentlemen, I plead guilty to the charge as described, I killed, dismembered, lied and betrayed. But when you understand the real conditions, the circumstances that brought me to this, you will see that I am no different from you, that I am not evil, and that all along I acted only for what I took to be the best.* By the hour the language of his defense was being heightened. Without thinking, he drew on the courtroom dramas of forgotten films. At times he spoke at length in a small bare room in a police station to a half-dozen reflective senior officers. At others he addressed, from the witness box, a hushed court.

Outside Kottbusser Tor station he stuffed the newspapers into a litter bin and headed down Adalbertstrasse. And what of Maria? She was part of his plea. He had brought into being a barrister, an authoritative presence, who would invoke the hopes and love of this young couple who had turned their backs on the violent pasts of their respective countries and were planning a life together. In whom lay our hopes of a future Europe free of strife. This was Glass speaking now. And now MacNamee was before the court to testify, as far as was compatible with security, to the important work Leonard had undertaken in the name of freedom, and how he had set out single-handedly and in his spare time to devise equipment that would further that aim.

Leonard walked faster. There were moments, minutes on end, of lucidity, when the repetitions and convolutions of his fantasies sickened him. There were no truths waiting to be discovered. There was only what could be imperfectly established by officials who had many other things to do and who would be only too pleased to be able to fit a crime to its perpetrator, process the matter and move on. Hardly had he set in train that thought, itself a repetition, than he was drawn to some fresh mitigating memory. For it was true, surely, that Otto had seized Maria by the windpipe. *I had to fight him even though I hate violence. I knew he had to be stopped.*

He was crossing the courtyard of No. 84. His first visit back. He started up the stairs. His hands were shaking badly again. It was difficult to hold on to the banister. On the fourth landing he stopped. The truth was that he still did not wish to see Maria. He did not know what to tell her. He could not pretend to her that the cases were safely out of the way. He could not tell where he had put them. That would mean telling her about the tunnel. But he had told the Russians, after all. He could tell anyone after that, surely. He thought what he had already thought: he was in no condition to make decisions; therefore he should keep silent. But he had to tell her something, and he would tell her that the cases were at the station. He tried gripping the banister tighter. But neither was he in a state to pretend anything. He went on up.

He had his own key, but he knocked and waited. He could

smell cigarettes inside. He was about to knock again when the door was opened by Glass, who stepped out onto the landing and steered Leonard by the elbow to the top of the stairs.

He murmured hurriedly, "Before you come in—we have to establish whether they found us by accident or whether we have a security breach on our hands. Among other things, we're talking to all non-U.S. wives and girlfriends. Don't take offense. It's routine."

They went in. Maria came toward Leonard and they kissed on the lips, dryly. His right knee was trembling, so he sat down in the nearest chair. At his elbow on the table was a full ashtray.

Glass said, "You looked tired, Leonard."

He included them both in his answer. "I've been working round the clock." And then to Glass alone, "Doing things for MacNamee."

Glass took his jacket off the back of a chair and put it on.

Maria said, "I'll see you to the door."

Glass gave Leonard a solemn mock salute as he went. Leonard heard him talking to Maria at the front door.

When she came back she said, "Are you ill?"

He held his hands still in his lap. "I feel strange, don't you?"

She nodded. There were shadows under her eyes, and her skin and hair had a greasy look. He was glad he did not feel attracted to her.

She said, "I think it's going to be all right."

This feminine certainty irritated him. "Oh yes," he said. "The cases are in the lockers at the Bahnhof Zoo."

She was looking at him closely, and he could not meet her stare. She started to speak and changed her mind.

He said, "What did Glass want?"

"It was like last time, but worse. A lot of questions about the people I know, where I've been during the last two weeks."

Now he was looking at her. "You didn't talk about anything else?"

"No," she said, but she looked away.

Naturally he was not jealous, because he did not feel anything for her. And he could not bear one more emotion. All the same, he went through the motions. It was something to talk about. "He stayed a long time." He was referring to the ashtray.

"Yes." She sat down and sighed.

"And he took off his jacket?"

She nodded.

"And all he did was ask questions?"

In a few days he would be leaving Berlin, probably without her, and he was talking like this.

She reached across the table and took his hand from his lap. He did not want her to feel it shaking, so he did not let her hold it for long.

She said, "Leonard, I just think it's going to be all right."

It was as if she thought she could soothe him by her very tone of voice. His own was mocking. "Of course it is. It's days before they unlock the lockers, before they come around here—which they will, you know. Have you got rid of the saw and the knife and the carpet and all the clothes with blood on them and the shoes and the newspaper? Do we know that no one saw you? Or saw me leave here with two big bags, or saw me at the station? Is this place so scrubbed out that there's nothing a trained sniffer dog wouldn't find?" He was ranting, he knew, but he could not stop his jaw. "Do we know that the neighbors didn't hear anything of the fight? Are we going to talk about our stories and make them agree to every last little point, or are we going to tell each other that it's all going to be all right?"

"I did everything here. You don't have to worry. The stories are simple. We say it as it happened, but without Otto. We came back here after dinner, we went to bed, you went to work the next morning, I took a day off and went shopping, you came back at lunchtime, and in the evening you went to Platanenallee."

It was a description of a past that should have been theirs. The happy couple after their engagement. The normality of it was a mockery, and they fell silent. Then Leonard came back to Glass.

"Was this the first time he's been here?"

She nodded.

"He was in a hurry to leave."

She said, "Don't speak to me like this. You need to calm down." She gave him a cigarette and took one for herself.

Presently he said, "I'm being recalled to England."

She drew breath and said, "What do you want to do?"

He did not know what he wanted. He kept thinking about Glass. In the end he said, "Perhaps some time apart would be a good thing, give us a chance to get our thoughts straight."

He did not like the ease with which she was agreeing with him. "I could come to London in a month. That's the earliest I could leave my job."

He did not know whether she meant it, or whether it mattered. As long as he was sitting here next to an ashtray full of Glass's stubs he would not be able to think.

"Look," he said. "I'm terribly tired. You are too." He stood up and put his hands in his pockets.

She stood too. There was something she wanted to tell him, but she was holding back. She seemed older; her face was giving warning of how she would look one day.

They made no effort to prolong their kiss. Then he was on his way to the door. "I'll be in touch as soon as I know my flight." She saw him to the door, and he did not look back as he started down the stairs.

During the next three days Leonard spent most of his time at the warehouse. The place was being stripped down. All day and night Army trucks arrived to take away furniture, paperwork and equipment. Out in back the incinerator was stoked up, and three soldiers were posted around it to make sure that unburned papers did not blow away. The canteen was taken apart, and a van came at midday to serve sandwiches and coffee. There were a dozen people working in the recording room, rolling up cable and packing up tape recorders six to a wooden crate. All the sensitive documents had been moved within hours of the break-in. Most of the time the work was done in silence. It was as if they were all checking out of an unpleasant hotel; they wanted the experience behind them as quickly as possible. Leonard worked in his own room, alone. The equipment had to be inventoried and packed. Every valve had to be accounted for.

Despite this activity and all his other worries, the tunnel was not on his conscience. If it was right to spy on the

Americans for MacNamee's interests, it was fine to sell the tunnel for his own. But that was not what he really meant. He had been fond of the place, he had loved it, he had been proud of it. But now it was hard to feel anything at all. After Otto, the Café Prag was nothing. He went down to the basement to take one last look. There were armed guards at the top and bottom of the shaft. Also down there, standing with his hands on his hips, was Bill Harvey, the station chief and head of the operation. A U.S. Army officer with a clipboard was listening to him. Harvey seemed to be bursting out of his suit. He was making a point of letting all around him see the holster he wore under his jacket.

As for Glass, during all this time he did not appear at the warehouse once. That was strange, but Leonard had no time to think about it. His preoccupation remained his arrest. When was he going to be taken away? Why were they waiting so long? Did they want to tie up their case? Or could it be that the Soviet authorities had decided that a dismembered body would only complicate their propaganda victory? Perhaps—and this seemed most plausible—the West Berlin police were waiting for him to present his passport at the airport. He lived with two futures. In one he flew home and began to forget. In the other, he stayed here and began to serve his time. He still could not sleep.

He sent Maria a card telling her the details of his flight on Saturday afternoon. She wrote back by return of post and said that she would be at Tempelhof to say goodbye. She signed herself "Love, Maria," and the *love* was underlined twice.

On Saturday morning he took a long bath, and when he was dressed he packed his cases. While he was waiting to hand over the apartment to the transport officer, he strode from room to room, the way he had done in the old days. He had made very little impact here, apart from a small stain on the living room carpet. He stood by the telephone a while. It bothered him now that he had not heard from Glass, who must surely know that he was leaving. Something was going on. He could not bring himself to dial his number. He was still standing there when his doorbell rang. It was Lofting, with two soldiers. The lieutenant appeared unnaturally happy.

"My chaps are doing the handover and the inventory," he explained as they all came in. "So I thought I'd take the chance of coming out to say goodbye. I've also found a staff car to take you to the airfield. It's waiting downstairs."

The two men sat in the living room while the soldiers counted the cups and saucers in the kitchen.

"You see," Lofting said, "you yourself have been handed back to us by the Americans. You're in my care now."

"That's nice," Leonard said.

"Jolly good party last week. Do you know, I'm seeing rather a lot of that girl Charlotte. She's a marvelous dancer. So I have to thank you both for that. She wants me to meet her parents next Sunday."

"Congratulations," Leonard said. "She's a nice girl."

The soldiers came through with forms for Leonard to sign. He stood to do it.

Lofting too got to his feet. "And what about Maria?"

"She has to work out her notice, then she'll be joining me." It sounded quite plausible as he said it.

The inventory and the handover were completed, and it

was time to go. The four men were in the hallway. Lofting pointed to Leonard's suitcases, which were standing by the front door. "I say, would you like my chaps to carry those down for you?"

"Yes," Leonard said. "I'd like that very much."

22

THE DRIVER OF THE STAFF CAR, a Humber, who turned out to be driving to Tempelhof to meet someone off a plane, seemed to feel no obligation to help Leonard with his luggage. It felt comparatively light as he bumped his way into the terminal building. But to be encumbered like this again had its effect. By the time he joined the long queue for the London flight, he was feeling demented. Could he risk putting the bags on the scales? Already there were people behind him. Could he leave the queue without arousing suspicion? The people around him were a strange assortment. There was a down-at-heel family in front—grandparents, a young couple and two small children. They had enormous cardboard suitcases and cloth bundles tied with string. They were refugees, obviously. The West Berlin authorities could not risk sending them out by rail. Perhaps it was a fear of flying that silenced the whole family, or an awareness of the tall man behind them, sliding his cases forward with his foot. Behind him was a group of French businessmen talking loudly, and behind them were two British Army officers standing erect and beaming quiet disapproval at the French. What all these passengers had in common was their innocence. He was innocent too, but it would take some explaining. Over by a newspaper stand was a military policeman with his hands behind his back and his chin up. *Polizisten* were standing by the entrance to passport control. Who was going to pull him out of the queue?

When he felt a hand on his shoulder, he started and turned too quickly. It was Maria. She was wearing clothes he had never seen before. This was her new summer outfit, a floral print skirt with a wide belt and a white blouse with puffy sleeves and a deep V neck. She wore an imitation pearl necklace he had not known she had. She looked like she was sleeping well. She had a new perfume, too. She put her hand in his as they kissed. It was cool and smooth. He sensed something light and simple returning to him, or at least the idea was there. Soon he might be able to feel for her again. Once he was away from her he would begin to miss her, and separate her from a memory of that apron, the patient wrapping and application of glue along the edges.

"You look very well," he said.

"I'm feeling better. Have you been able to sleep?"

Her question was indiscreet. There were people close behind them. He pushed his cases forward into the gap that had appeared behind the refugees.

He said no and squeezed her hand. They could be an engaged couple, surely. He said, "I like that blouse. Is it new?"

She stepped back for him. There was even a new clip in her hair, blue and yellow this time, more childish than ever. "I wanted to give myself a treat. What do you think of the skirt?" She made a little turn for him. She was pleased and excited. The Frenchmen were watching her. Someone right at the back gave a wolf whistle.

When she stepped in closer he said, "You look beautiful." He knew it was true. If he kept on saying it, if only to himself, he would really know it.

"All these people," she was saying. "If Bob Glass were here, he could do something and get you to the front."

He chose to ignore this. She was wearing the engagement ring. If they could simply hold to the form of things, the rest would follow. It would all come back. As long as no one was coming for them. They held hands as they shuffled toward the check-in counter.

She said, "Have you told your parents yet?"

"About what?"

"Our engagement, of course."

He had meant to. He had intended to write to them the day after the party.

"I'll tell them when I'm home."

Before he did, he would have to believe it again himself. He would have to get back to that moment when they were climbing the stairs to her place after their supper, or to the time when her words reached him like silver drops falling in slow motion, before he had discerned their sense.

He said, "Did you give your notice?"

She laughed, and she seemed to hesitate. "Yes, and the major was not at all pleased. 'Who's going to boil my egg now? Who can I trust with cutting the soldiers?' "

They laughed. They were being merry because they were about to part, which was what engaged couples did.

"Do you know," she said, "he tried to talk me out of it."

"What did you say?"

She wiggled her ring finger in the air. She said mock naughtily, "I told him I'd think about it."

It took half an hour to get close to the counter. They were almost there and still holding hands. After a silence he said, "I don't know why we haven't heard anything by now."

She said immediately, "It means we never will."

Then there was another silence. The refugee family was checking in its cases and bundles. Maria said, "What do you want to do? Where do you want to be?"

"I don't know," he said in a movie sort of voice. "It's your place or mine."

She laughed loudly. There was something quite wild in her manner. The British European Airlines official looked up. Maria was being so free in her movements, almost wanton. Perhaps it was joy. The Frenchmen had long since stopped talking to each other. Leonard did not know if that was because they were all watching her. He was thinking he really did love her as he lifted the bags onto the scales. Nothing at all—barely thirty-five pounds together. When his tickets had been checked, they went to the cafeteria. There was a queue here too, and it did not seem worth joining it. There were only ten minutes left.

They sat at a Formica table cluttered with dirty teacups and plates smeared with yellow cake that had been used as ashtrays. She pulled her chair nearer to him and linked her arm with his and leaned her head on his shoulder.

"You won't forget that I love you," she said. "We did what we had to and we are going to be all right now."

Whenever she told him that everything was going to be all right he felt uneasy. It was like asking for trouble. Nevertheless, he said, "I love you too."

They were announcing the flight.

She walked with him to the newsstand, where he bought a *Daily Express,* flown in that day. They stopped by the barrier.

"I'll come to London," she said. "We can talk about everything there. Here there's too much . . ."

He knew what she meant. They kissed, though hardly the way they used to. He kissed her lovely forehead. He was going to go. She took his hand and held on with both of hers.

"Oh God, Leonard!" she cried. "If only I could tell you. It's all right. It really is."

That again. There were three military policemen on the gate who looked away when he kissed her for the last time.

"I'll go up on the roof and wave," she said, and hurried off.

The passengers had fifty yards of pavement to cross. As soon as he was clear of the terminal building he looked around. She was up on the flat roof, leaning on the parapet at the front of the observation deck. When she saw him she made a merry little dance and blew him a kiss. The Frenchmen looked enviously at him as they passed. He waved at her and walked on until he arrived at the foot of the aircraft steps, where he stopped and turned. He had his right hand half raised to wave. There was a man at her side, a man with a beard. It was Glass. He had his hand on Maria's shoulder. Or was it his arm around her shoulder? They both waved, like parents to a departing child. Maria blew him a kiss, she dared to blow him the same kiss. Glass was saying something to her, and she laughed and they waved again.

Leonard let his hand drop and hurried up the steps into the plane. He had a window seat on the terminal side. He fussed with his seatbelt, trying not to look out. It was irresistible. They seemed to know just which little round window was his. They were looking right at him and continuing to wave their insulting goodbye. He looked away. He took his paper and snapped it open and pretended to read. He felt such shame. He longed for the plane to move. She should have told him just now, she should have confronted him, but she had wanted to avoid a scene. It was a humiliation. He blushed with it and pretended to read. Then he did read. It was the story of "Buster" Crabbe, a naval frogman who had been spying on a Russian battleship moored in Portsmouth harbor. Crabbe's headless body had been retrieved by fishermen. Khrushchev had made an angry statement; something was expected that afternoon in the House of Commons. The propellers were spinning to a blur. The ground crew was hurrying away. As the plane edged forward, Leonard took one last look. They were standing close together. Perhaps she could not really see his face, because she raised one hand as if to wave and let it fall.

And then he could see her no longer.

23 IN JUNE 1987 Leonard Marnham, the owner of a small company supplying components to the hearing-aid industry, returned to Berlin. It took him no more than the taxi ride from Tegel airport to the hotel to become accustomed to the absence of ruins. There were more people, it was greener, there were no trams. Then these sharp differences faded and it was a European city like any other a businessman might visit. Its dominant feature was traffic.

Even as he was paying the driver, he knew he had made a mistake in choosing to stay on the Kurfürstendamm. He had taken a certain pleasure in being knowing and specific with his secretary. The Hotel am Zoo had been the only place he could name. There was now a transparent structure sloping against the facade. Inside a glass lift slid across the surface of a mural. He unpacked his bag, swallowed his heart pill with a glass of water and went out for a stroll.

In fact it was not quite possible to stroll, the crowd was so dense. He got his bearings from the Gedächtniskirche and the hideous new structure at its side. He passed Burger King, Spielcenter, Videoclips, Das Steak-Restaurant, Unisex Jeans. The store windows were filled with clothes of babyish pastel pinks, blues and yellows. He became caught up in a surge of Scandinavian children wearing McDonald's cardboard visors, pressing forward to buy giant silver balloons from a street vendor. It was hot and the traffic roar was continuous. Disco music and the smell of burning fat were everywhere.

He went down a side street, thinking to walk around in front of the Zoo station and the entrance to the gardens, but soon he was lost. There was a confluence of major roads he did not remember. He decided to sit down outside one of the big cafés. He passed three, and every last bright plastic chair was taken. The crowds moved aimlessly up and down, squeezing by each other wherever the pavement space was taken up by café tables. There was a crowd of French teenagers all wearing pink T-shirts with FUCK YOU! printed front and back. He was amazed to find himself lost. When he looked around for someone to ask, he could find no one who did not look like a foreigner. Eventually he approached a young couple on a corner buying a pancake with a crème de menthe filling. They were Dutch, and friendly enough, but they had never heard of the Hotel am Zoo, nor were they entirely certain of the Kurfürstendamm.

He found his hotel by accident and sat in his room for half an hour sipping an orange juice from the minibar. He was trying to resist irritable reminiscence. *In my day.* If he was going to take a walk down Adalbertstrasse, he preferred to remain calm. He took from his briefcase the airmail letter he had been rereading on the plane and put it in his pocket. He was not yet sure what he wanted from all this. He was eyeing the bed. The experience on the Ku'damm had drained him. He could happily have slept the afternoon away. But he forced himself up and out once more.

In the lobby he hesitated as he handed in his key. He wanted to try out his German on the receptionist, a young chap in a black suit who looked like a student of some sort. The Wall had gone up five years after Leonard had left Berlin. He wanted to have a look while he was here. Where should he go? What was the best place? He was conscious of making elementary errors. But his understanding was good. The young man showed him on a map. Potsdamerplatz was best. There was a good viewing platform and postcard and souvenir shops.

Leonard was about to thank him and cross the lobby, but the young man said, "You should go soon."

"Why's that?"

"A little while ago the students were demonstrating in East Berlin. Do you know what they were shouting? The name of the Soviet leader. And the police hit them and chased them with water cannon."

"I read about that," Leonard said.

The receptionist was in his stride. This seemed to be a pet theme. He was in his mid-twenties, Leonard decided.

"Who would have thought that the name of the Soviet general secretary would be a provocation in East Berlin? It's amazing!"

"I suppose so," Leonard said.

"A couple of weeks ago he came here, to Berlin. You probably read about that, too. Before he came everyone was saying, 'He'll tell them to take down the Wall.' Well, I knew he wouldn't, and he didn't. But next time, or the time after—five years, ten years. It's all changing."

There was an admonitory grunt from the inner office. The young man smiled and shrugged. Leonard thanked him and walked out into the street.

He took the U-Bahn to Kottbusser Tor. As he emerged onto the pavement he struggled into a hot gritty headwind, which brought with it scraps of litter. Waiting for him was a skinny girl in a leather jacket and tight stretch pants patterned with moons and stars. As he walked by her she murmured, *"Haste mal 'ne Mark?"* She had a pretty but wasted face. Ten yards past her he had to stop. Was it possible he had got off too soon, or too late? But there was the street sign. Ahead of him a monstrous apartment complex straddled the way into Adalbertstrasse. On the concrete pillars at its base were spray-painted graffiti. At his feet were empty beer cans, fast-food wrappers, sheets of newspapers. A group of teenagers, punks he supposed, were lying by the curb, propped on their elbows. They all had the same bright orange Mohican haircuts. Their relative baldness made their ears and Adam's apples protrude unhappily. Their heads were bluish-white. One of the boys was inhaling from a plastic bag. They grinned at Leonard as he stepped around them.

Once he had walked under the apartments, the street was half familiar. All the gaps had been filled in. The shops—a grocery, a café, a travel agency—all had Turkish names now. Turkish men stood around on the corner of Oranienstrasse. The amiable vacancy of southern Europe looked unconvincing here. The buildings that had survived the bombing still bore the marks of gunfire. The machine gunning of No. 84 was still there above the ground-floor windows. The big front door had been repainted blue many years ago. In the courtyard, the first thing he noticed was the dustbins. They were huge and mounted on rubber wheels.

Turkish children, girls with their younger brothers and sisters, were playing in the yard. They stopped running when they saw him and watched in silence as he crossed to the rear doorway. They did not respond to his smile. This pale, large, elderly man, dressed inappropriately for the heat in a dark suit, did not belong here. A woman called down what sounded like a harsh command, but no one stirred. Perhaps they thought he had something to do with the government. It had been his plan to walk up to the top landing and, if it seemed the right thing, to knock on the door. But the stair-well was darker and narrower than he remembered and the air was close, saturated with unfamiliar cooking smells. He stepped back and looked over his shoulder. The children con-tinued to stare. A bigger girl picked up her younger sister. He looked from one set of brown eyes to another, then he walked back past them and into the street. Being here did not bring him any closer to his Berlin days. All that was apparent was how far off they seemed.

He went back to Kottbusser Tor, gave the girl a ten-mark note as he passed and took a train to Hermannplatz, where he changed for Rudow. These days it was possible to go right through Grenzallee, all the way by U-Bahn. When he arrived he found a six-lane road cutting across what he sensed was his direction. Looking back toward the center of the city, he saw clusters of high-rise buildings. He waited at the pedes-trian lights and crossed. Ahead of him were low apartment buildings, a pink stone cycling path, neat rows of streetlights, and parked cars lining the curb. How else could it be, what could he really have expected? The same flat farmland? He passed the little lake, a rural memory preserved by barbed-wire fencing.

He had to look at his street plan to find the turn. Every-thing was so neat and crowded. The road he needed was called Lettbergerstrasse, and its shoulders had been newly planted with sycamore trees. On his left were new apart-ments, barely two or three years old by the look of them. On his right, replacing the refugee shacks, were the eccentric one-storey holiday homes of Berlin apartment dwellers, with their intensely cultivated gardens. Families were eating out in the deep shade of ornamental trees; a green Ping-Pong table stood on an immaculate lawn. He passed an empty hammock slung between apple trees. Barbecue smoke rose from the shrubbery. The sprinklers were on, soaking stretches of pavement. Each tiny plot of land was a proud and orderly fantasy, a celebration of domestic success. Even though scores of families were packed together, a contented, inward silence drifted upward with the heat of the afternoon.

The road narrowed into something like the track he remembered. There was a riding school, expensive suburban houses, and then he was walking toward a new high green gate. Beyond it, a hundred feet of rough ground; then, still encircled by its double perimeter fence, the remains of the warehouse. For a moment he stayed where he was. He could see that all the buildings had been leveled. The white sentry box stood tipped at an angle by the inner gate, which was wide open. On the green gate immediately in front of him a sign proclaimed that the land belonged to an agricultural company and warned parents to keep their children away. To one side was a thick wooden cross commemorating the attempts of two young men to climb the Wall in 1962 and 1963, *"von Grenzsoldaten erschossen."* On the far side of the warehouse, a hundred yards beyond its outer fence, was the pale concrete curtain, blocking the view to Schönefelder Chaussee. He thought how strange it was that he should come here to get his first sight of the Wall.

The gate was too high for a man of his age to climb. By

trespassing along someone's drive he was able to get over a low wall. He passed through the outer fence and stopped by the second. The barrier, of course, was gone, but its post was still there, standing clear of the weeds. He peeped into the lopsided sentry hut. It was filled with planks. The old electrical fittings were still in place, high on its inner wall, and so was the shredded end of a telephone line. He walked on into the compound. All that remained of the buildings were crumbling concrete floors where weeds were breaking through. The rubble had been bulldozed into piles at one end of the compound to form a high screen facing the Wall—one last titillation for the Vopos.

The main building was different. He walked over and stood a long time by its remains. On three sides, beyond the fences and the rough ground, the holiday homes pressed in. On the fourth was the Wall. Radio music was playing in a garden somewhere; the German taste for military rhythms lingered in its pop music. There was a weekend laziness in the air.

What remained in front of him was a huge hole, a walled trench, a hundred feet long and thirty feet wide and perhaps seven feet deep. He was staring into the old basement, now open to the skies. The great heaps of tunnel workings were all there, thick with weeds. The basement floor must have been another five feet down, under the earth, but the pathway between the heaps was clear enough. The main shaft at the eastern end was lost under rubble. It was so much smaller than he remembered. As he clambered down, he noticed that he was being watched through binoculars by two border guards in their tower. He walked the path between the piles.

There was a lark twittering high above him, and in the heat it was beginning to irritate him. The ramp for the forklifts was here. The shaft started there. He picked up a piece of cable. It was the old three-core, with its thick, unyielding copper wire. He poked at some earth and stones with the toe of his shoe. What was he expecting to find? Evidence of his own existence?

He climbed out of the basement. He was still being observed from the tower. Brushing away some dirt from the brick ledge, he sat down, with his feet dangling into the basement. This place meant far more to him than Adalbertstrasse. He had already decided not to bother with Platanenallee. It was here in this ruin that he felt the full weight of time. It was here that old matters could be unearthed. He took the airmail letter from his pocket. The envelope with its crossed-out addresses was fascination enough, a biography whose chapters were a succession of endings. It was from Cedar Rapids, Iowa, and had left the United States ten weeks before. The sender was thirty years out of date. It had been sent to him initially in care of his parents, to their terraced house in Tottenham, where he had grown up and where they had lived until his father's death on Christmas Day, 1957. From there it had been forwarded to the nursing home where his mother had spent her last years. Then it had been sent on to the big house in Seven Oaks where his own children had grown up and where he had lived with his wife until five years ago. The present owner had kept the letter for many weeks and then had forwarded it with a batch of circulars and junk mail.

He opened it and read once more.

1706 Sumner Drive
Cedar Rapids, Iowa
March 30, 1987

DEAR LEONARD,

I think there's only the smallest chance in the world this letter will ever reach you. I don't even know that you're alive, though something tells me you are. I'm going to send it to your parents' old address and who knows what will happen to it then. I've written it so many times in my head that I might as well get it down anyway. If it doesn't reach you, it might help me.

When you last saw me at Tempelhof on May 15, 1956, I was a youngish German woman who spoke good English. Now I guess you could say I'm a suburban American lady, a high school teacher staring retirement right in the face, and my good Cedar Rapids neighbors say there isn't a trace of German in my accent, though I think they're only being kind. What's happened to all the years? I know that's what everyone asks. We all have to make our own arrangements with the past. I have three daughters, and the youngest finished college last summer. They all grew up in this house, where we've lived for twenty-four years. I've taught German and French in the local high school for the past sixteen. For the last five I've been president of our Women in Church organization. That's where my years have gone.

And in all this time I've thought about you. A week hasn't passed when I haven't gone back over things, what we might or should have done, and how it could have been different. I was never able to speak about it. I think I was afraid that Bob might guess at the strength of my feelings. Maybe he knew anyhow. I couldn't talk to any of my friends here, even though it's a close sort of place and there are some good people I trust. There would have been too much explaining to do. It was so bizarre and horrific and it would have been hard to make anyone understand. I used to think I might tell my eldest when she was grown up. But that time, our time, Berlin, is so far away. I don't think I could get Laura to really understand, so I've lived with it alone. I wonder if it's been the same for you.

Bob left the service in 1958 and we settled here. He ran a business retailing agricultural machinery and made quite a success of it, enough to keep us all comfortably. I taught school because I was always used to having a job. It's Bob I want to write to you about, or he's one of the things. In all this time I've known that there has been an accusation hanging in the air, a silent accusation from you and one that you ought to know is completely unfounded. This is something I've needed so much to get straight. I hope God helps this letter reach you one day.

I now know of course that you were working with Bob on the Berlin tunnel. The day after the Russians found out about it, Bob came around to Adalbertstrasse and said he needed to ask me some questions. It was all part of some security routine. You'll have to remember just exactly what was going on at that time. You'd left with the suitcases two days before and I hadn't heard a word. Nor had I slept. I spent hours scrubbing the flat.

I took our clothes to a public dump. I went right over to my parents' neighborhood in Pankow and sold the tools. I dragged the carpet three blocks to a construction site where they had a big fire and got someone to help me throw it in. I had just finished cleaning out the bathroom when Bob was at the door wanting to come in and ask questions. He could see that something was wrong. I tried to pretend I was ill. He said he wouldn't take long, and because he was being so kind and concerned, I broke down and cried. And then before I knew it, I was telling him the whole story. The need to tell someone was really powerful. I wanted someone to understand that we weren't criminals. I poured it out to him and he sat very quiet. When I told him that you'd gone off to the railroad station with the cases two days before and I hadn't heard a thing, he just sat there shaking his head and saying 'Oh my God' over and over again. Then he said he would see what he could find out, and he left.

He came back the next morning with a newspaper. It was full of stuff about your tunnel. I hadn't heard anything about it. Bob told me then that you were part of the tunnel operation and that you'd actually put the cases down there not long before the Vopos broke in. I don't know what led you to do that. Perhaps you went crazy for a day or two. Who wouldn't? The East Germans had handed the cases over to the West Berlin police. Apparently a murder investigation was already under way. They were only hours from getting your name. According to Bob, he and several others had actually seen you bring the cases in. We would have been in big trouble if Bob hadn't persuaded his superiors that this would be bad publicity for Western intelligence. Bob's people made the police drop the inquiry. I guess in those days it was an occupied city and the Germans had to do what the Americans told them. He got the whole thing covered up and the investigation was dropped.

This is what he told me that morning. He also swore me to secrecy. I was to tell no one, not even you, that I knew what he had done. He didn't want anyone to think he had perverted the course of justice, and he didn't want you to know that I'd been told about your involvement in the tunnel. You remember how scrupulous he was about his job. So all that was happening that morning, and then you turned up right in the middle of it, suspicious and looking really terrible. I wanted to tell you we were safe, but I didn't want to break my promise. I don't know why. It might have saved a lot of sadness if I had.

Then a few days later there was Tempelhof. I knew what you were thinking, and you were so very very wrong. Now I am writing it down I realize just how much I want you to hear me and believe me. I want you to receive this letter. The truth is that Bob was running all over town that day with his security investigation. He wanted to say goodbye to you and he got to the airport late. He bumped into me as I was on my way up to the roof to wave to you. That's all it was. I wrote to you and tried to explain without breaking my promise to Bob. You never answered me properly. I thought of coming to London to find you, but I knew I could not bear it if you turned me away. The months passed and you stopped answering my letters. I told myself that what we had been through together had made it impossible for us to get married. I had a friendship then with Bob, for my part based mostly on gratitude. Slowly that turned to affection. Time played its part too, and I was lonely. Nine months after you left Berlin I began an affair with Bob. I buried my feelings for you as deep as I could. The next year, in July 1957, we were married in New York.

He always spoke very fondly of you. He used to say we would come and look you up in England one day. I don't know if I could ever have faced that. Bob died the year before last of a heart attack while on a fishing trip. His death hit the girls hard, it hit us all very hard and it devastated our youngest, Rosie. He was a wonderful father to the girls. Fatherhood suited him, it softened him. He never lost that wonderful bouncing energy. He was always so playful. When the girls were tiny it was a marvel to watch him. He was so popular here, his funeral was a major event in the town, and I was very proud of him.

I'm telling you this because I want you to know that I'm not sorry I married Bob Glass. I'm not pretending either that we didn't also have some awful times. Ten years ago we were both drinking a lot and there were other things too. But we were coming through that, I think. I'm losing my thread. There are too many things I want to tell you. I sometimes think about that Mr. Blake from downstairs who came to our engagement party. George Blake. I was amazed when he was put up for trial all those years ago, 1960 or '61. Then he escaped from prison, and then Bob found out that one of the secrets he gave away was your tunnel. He was right in on it from the beginning, at the planning stage. The Russians knew all about it before the first shovelful had been dug out. So much wasted effort! Bob used to say that knowing that made him all the happier that he had got out. He said they must have diverted their most important messages away from those telephone lines, and that they left the tunnel in place to protect Blake and waste CIA time and manpower. But why did they break in when they did, right in the middle of our troubles?

It was late afternoon when I began this letter and now it's dark outside. I've stopped a few times to think about Bob, and about Rosie who still can't let him go, and about you and me and all the lost time and the misunderstanding. It's funny to be writing this to a stranger thousands of miles away. I wonder what's happened to your life. When I think of you, I don't only think of the terrible thing with Otto. I think of my kind and gentle Englishman who knew so little about women and who learned so beautifully! We were so easy together, it was such fun. Sometimes it's as if I'm remembering a childhood. I want to ask you, do you remember this, do you remember that? When we biked out to the lakes at weekends to swim, when we bought my engagement ring from that huge Arab (I still have that ring) and when we used to dance at the Resi. How we were the jiving champions and won a prize, the carriage clock that's still up in our attic. When I first saw you with that rose behind your ear and I sent you a message down the tube. When you made that wonderful speech at our party and Jenny—do you remember my friend Jenny—who made off with that radio man whose name I can't recall. And wasn't Bob going to give a speech that evening too? I loved you dearly, and I never got closer to anyone. I don't think it dishonors Bob's memory to say that. In my experience, men and women don't ever really get to understand each other. What we had was really quite special. It's true and I can't let this life go by without saying that, without setting it down. If I remember you rightly you should be frowning by now and saying, she's so sentimental!

Sometimes I've been angry with you. It was wrong of you to retreat with your anger and silence. So English! So male! If you felt betrayed you should have stood your ground and fought for what was yours. You should have accused me, you should have accused Bob. There would have been a fight, and we would have gotten to the bottom of it. But I know really that it was your pride that made you slink away. It was the same pride that kept me from coming to London to make you marry me. I couldn't face the possibility of failure.

It's odd that this familiar creaky old house is unknown to you. It's white clapboard, surrounded by oak trees, with a flagpole in the yard erected by Bob. I'll never leave here now, even though it's way too big. The girls have all their childhood things here. Tomorrow Diane, our middle daughter, is visiting with her baby. She's the first to produce. Laura had a miscarriage last year. Diane's husband is a mathematician. He's very tall, and the way he sometimes pushes his glasses up his nose with his pinky reminds me of you. Do you remember when I swiped your glasses to make you stay? He's also a brilliant tennis player, which doesn't remind me of you at all!

I'm rambling again and it's getting late. What I mean is, these days I get tired early in the evening and I don't feel I should be apologizing for it either. But I feel reluctant to end this one-sided conversation with you, wherever you are and whatever you've become. I don't want to consign this letter to the void. It won't be the first I've written to you that received no reply. I know I'll have to take my chances. If all this seems irrelevant to your life now and you don't want to reply, or if the memories are somehow inconvenient, please at least let your twenty-five-year-old self accept these greetings from an old friend. And if this letter is going nowhere and is never opened and never read, please God, grant us forgiveness for our terrible deed and be a witness to and bless our love as it was.

Yours,

MARIA GLASS

He stood and dusted down his suit and folded the letter away, and then began a slow stroll around the compound. He trampled weeds to get to the place where his own room had been. Now it was a patch of oily sand. He walked on around to look at the twisted pipes and smashed gauges of a basement boiler room. Right under his feet were fragments of pink-and-white tiles he remembered from the shower rooms.

He looked over his shoulder. The border guards in their tower had lost interest in him. The radio music from the weekend-home garden had changed to old-fashioned rock and roll. He still had a taste for it, and he remembered this one, "Whole Lotta Shakin' Goin' On." It had never been a great favorite of his, but she had liked it. He wandered back past the gaping trench toward the inner perimeter fence. Two steel girders had been placed to warn trespassers of a concrete-lined hole filled with black water. It was the old cesspit, whose drainage field the sergeants had tunneled through. So much wasted effort.

He was at the fence now, looking through it across the hummocky wasteland to the Wall. Rising above it were the trees of the cemetery in full leaf. His time and her time, like so much unbuilt-on land. There was a cycling path running along this side of the Wall, right at its base. A group of children were calling to each other as they pedaled by. It was hot. He had forgotten this clammy Berlin heat. He had been right, he had needed to come all this way to understand her letter. Not to Adalbertstrasse, but here, among the ruins. What he had not been able to grasp in his Surrey breakfast room was clear enough here.

He knew what he was going to do. He loosened his tie and pressed a handkerchief to his forehead. He looked behind him. There was a fire hydrant beside the teetering sentry box. How he missed Glass too, the hand on his elbow and "Listen, Leonard!" Glass softened by fatherhood—he would have liked to have seen that. Leonard knew what he was going to do, he knew he was about to leave, but the urgency was not on him yet, and the heat pressed down. The radio was playing jolly German pop music again in strict two-four time.

The volume seemed to be rising. Up in the tower a border guard took a languid peek through his binoculars at the gentleman in a dark suit dawdling by the fence and then turned away to speak to his companion.

Leonard had been holding on to the fence. Now he let his hand drop and made his way back along the side of the big trench, through the perimeter gates, across the weeds to the low white wall. Once he was over, he took off his jacket and folded it over his arm. He walked quickly, and that created a little breeze on his face. His footsteps were marking the pace of his thoughts. If he had been younger, he might have broken into a run along Lettbergerstrasse. He thought he remembered from the old days when he traveled for his company. He would probably need a flight to O'Hare, in Chicago, where he could pick up the local service. He would send no warning, he was prepared to fail. He would emerge from the shade between the oak trees, he would pass by the white flagpole on his way across the sunlit lawn to the front door. Later he would tell her the radio man's name and remind her that Bob Glass did give a speech that night, a fine one too, about building a new Europe. And he would answer her question: they broke into the tunnel when they did because Mr. Blake told his Russian controller that a young Englishman was about to deposit decoding equipment down there for one day only. And she would tell him about the jiving competition, of which he had no memory, and they would bring down the carriage clock from the attic and wind it up and set it going again.

He had to stop on the corner of NeuDecker Weg and stand in the shade of a sycamore. They would return to Berlin together, that was the only way. The heat was intense, and there was still half a mile to the Rudow U-Bahn. He closed his eyes and leaned back against the young trunk. It could take his weight. They would visit the old places and be amused by the changes, and yes, they would go out to Potsdamerplatz one day and climb the wooden platform and take a good long look at the Wall together, before it was all torn down.

Author's Note

THE BERLIN TUNNEL, or Operation Gold, was a joint CIA-MI6 venture that operated for just under a year, until April 1956. William Harvey, the CIA station chief, was in charge. George Blake, who was living at Platanenallee 26 from April 1955 on, probably betrayed the project as early as 1953, when he was secretary to a planning committee. All other characters in this novel are fictional. Most of the events are too, although I am indebted to David C. Martin's account of the tunnel in his excellent book, *Wilderness of Mirrors.* The site as described in Chapter 23 was how I found it in May 1989.

I wish to thank Bernhard Robben, who translated the German and researched extensively in Berlin, and Dr. M. Dunnill, University Lecturer in Pathology, Merton College, Andreas Landshoff, and Timothy Garton-Ash for their helpful comments. I would like to thank in particular my friends Galen Strawson and Craig Raine for their close readings of the typescript and many useful suggestions.

I. M.
Oxford
September 1989

About the Author

IAN MCEWAN received the Somerset Maugham Award for his collection of short stories *First Love, Last Rites*. This was followed by another collection *In Between the Sheets*. His previous novels are *The Child in Time, The Cement Garden,* and *The Comfort of Strangers,* which was nominated for the 1981 Booker Prize. He lives in Oxford, England, with his wife and their four children.